ODYSSEUS
ASCENDANT

ALSO BY EVAN CURRIE

Odyssey One Series

Into the Black
The Heart of Matter
Homeworld
Out of the Black
Warrior King
Odysseus Awakening

Odyssey One: Star Rogue Series

King of Thieves

Warrior's Wings Series

On Silver Wings
Valkyrie Rising
Valkyrie Burning
The Valhalla Call
By Other Means
De Oppresso Liber
Open Arms

The Scourwind Legacy

Heirs of Empire
An Empire Asunder

Other Works

SEAL Team 13
Steam Legion
Thermals

The Atlantis Rising Series

The Knighthood

ODYSSEUS ASCENDANT

odyssey one

(Book 7)

EVAN CURRIE

47NORTH

Text copyright © 2018 by Cleigh Currie

Published by 47North, Seattle

www.apub.com

Amazon, the Amazon logo, and 47North are trademarks of Amazon.com, Inc., or its affiliates.

ISBN-13: 9781503901070
ISBN-10: 1503901076

Cover design by Adam Hall

Printed in the United States of America

ODYSSEUS
ASCENDANT

CHAPTER 1

Forge Facility, Ranquil

▶ Her footsteps echoed off the floor and walls of the arching corridor as she strode through the immense structure that rested inside the corona of the Priminae System's primary star. Normally, the sheer concept of this cosmic engineering marvel would occupy most of her mind, but Admiral Gracen had no time for that now.

Her courier ship had just arrived in system, bypassing the normal meet and greet on Ranquil as it dived directly into the star that hid the Forge and docked with one of the hundreds of orbital stations that made up the shield system preserving the world within from the burning fires of the star.

She had very little idea as to what exactly had happened to the commodore's task force in this last mission, but whatever it was had to be serious. Weston was many things, but an alarmist wasn't one of them, and while he was certainly more than able to be insubordinate for the right reasons, he rarely ever was rude unless wasting time with frivolities was about to get someone killed.

Thus his message—via encrypted Priminae messenger crystal and delivered by hand by the *Odysseus'* first officer—which all but *ordered* her to take time to visit the Forge facility where the *Odysseus* was undergoing repairs and refit, was unusual for the man.

Whatever it was, Weston's reveal had best be good.

Or very, very bad. All things considered, she supposed she was betting on the latter.

That was just how her luck went.

She stepped around a corner and into one of the open sections of the station. The observation windows showed a vista of the roiling stellar plasma that lay beyond the shield as well as the serene world floating below. She only had eyes for the form of the *Odysseus*, berthed opposite her position.

The big ship had taken a beating, and the admiral felt a pang in her chest at the carbon scoring that seemed to eclipse the white ceramic of the hull. Most of the holes had apparently been patched, but according to reports, the ship's certification for deep-space travel was currently in limbo at the request of Commodore Weston.

If she didn't trust the man, she would be on a warpath already.

We can't have our damn flagship being held up in repairs one bit longer than needed. The Odysseus *needs to be making regular returns to Earth's orbit.*

Politics being what they were, the military situation on Earth was touchier than she'd ever seen, and she had served through three major wars that included "the big one," as if that appellation hadn't been used before. Right now, anything that upset the apple cart on Earth was a genuine threat to planetary security.

So trust or not, Weston better have a damn good reason for requesting a hold on the certification.

From what she could see, carbon scoring aside, the battle cruiser appeared to be in decent enough shape. A few combat scars would be an asset in the current climate back on Earth, giving the people a little evidence of the troubles that were still going on beyond the influence of the sun. Barring new information, Gracen wanted that ship back in space and doing its job.

Yesterday.

"Admiral Gracen?"

She turned to see a young Priminae ithan, the local equivalent of a lieutenant by comparative ranks, approaching her. "Yes Ithan?"

"I was sent to show you the way to the meeting concerning the *Odysseus*," the young woman said. "If you'll follow me."

Gracen gestured and then fell in behind the ithan as they started through the corridors. It didn't take her long to recognize that they weren't heading for the shuttle docks.

"Excuse me, why aren't we holding this meeting on the *Odysseus*?" Gracen asked.

"I'm afraid I wasn't cleared for any information regarding the *Odysseus* repairs," the ithan admitted. "The entire section has been under rather extreme security since the arrival of the task group. Admiral Tanner's orders, on request of Commodore Weston."

Gracen fell silent then and followed as the ithan led her through the maze of corridors.

▶▶▶

▶ Eric Stanton Weston stood in the conference room with hands clasped behind his back, eyes on the ship that floated approximately a hundred meters away. He'd requested the farthest slip available, wanting to keep his ship and the being that had apparently taken possession of it as far away as possible from any other similar entities.

He estimated that would ultimately prove to be a losing proposition as long as they kept the ship intact, but he had to at least try. Whether they would finish the core repairs to the *Odysseus* was the most important part of the upcoming meeting with the admiral, a subject he had decidedly mixed feelings on.

The entity, Odysseus, was unlike the others he had encountered.

Central was very much like the Priminae themselves. Far too calm and self-assured for his liking, but with the very real knowledge and experience to back up those assurances. Gaia had been, well, the force of nature she was named after. Or perhaps she pretended to be a force of nature. He really didn't know, nor did he especially care at this point. Neither of the entities he had dealt with before was as young as Odysseus, nor as innocent in appearance or action.

Eric didn't have a clue how to act with a child on his ship, let alone a child *being* his ship in a very real way.

This is going to be a long discussion.

A tone from the door signalled that someone was approaching, and he turned just as it opened to admit the admiral. Eric straightened to attention and saluted automatically as she walked in, eyes on him briefly before she looked past him to the *Odysseus* floating in the distance.

"As you were," Gracen ordered simply, "and let's get this over with, shall we? I doubt I've been called all the way out here on short notice to hear anything good, so break the bad news already."

Eric realized his thoughts were evident on his face, judging by the way the admiral's expression changed before he even began to talk. She sighed deeply, holding up a hand to cut him off even as he took a breath to begin.

"Damn it, Commodore, this is going to be another Weston Special to clean up, isn't it?"

"Ma'am . . ." He tipped his head slightly. "I'm afraid this goes back to my second mission to Ranquil. There was an aspect of that mission that's been downplayed in the reporting. I left out some details about the Priminae System designated as Central."

"You . . ." Gracen paused, head cocking slightly as she seemed uncertain she'd heard him correctly. "You *left out* some details? Commodore, you had best explain yourself right now. That statement could be interpreted as a dereliction."

Eric sighed. "I know. Didn't feel I had a lot of choice at the time and, like most secrets, it snowballed on me faster than I would ever have thought possible. During the invasion I . . . encountered Earth's version of Central."

"Stop."

Gracen's voice snapped sharply as she held up a hand, glaring at him past the outspread fingers. She took a breath, her arm dropping slowly. "Something tells me I need more details than that. What the hell are you talking about?"

"Central isn't a computer system, Admiral," Eric said. "Not in the traditional sense, at least, not any more than you or I are computer systems. I'm not even sure what the hell Central is, and I doubt the Priminae have the slightest clue either. It's an intelligence, certainly, maybe more than that. People would have called it a god, once upon a time, but I wouldn't care to make any real statements to that effect myself. Earth's version is currently calling herself Gaia, so you make what you want of that."

Gracen pulled out a seat on the frictionless runners and slumped into it, a hand coming up to cover her face.

"Commodore, if you need some time off, there *are* easier ways to ask."

He smiled slightly. "I wish it was that simple, but that's the reason why I didn't report this fully after the mission. No evidence, and I didn't really feel like spending quality time with the psych coats."

The admiral grimaced. "Damn."

"Ma'am?"

"Well, you wouldn't have said *that* unless you currently *do* have evidence, I suppose. Which means that you're probably telling the truth . . . which means now I have to figure out how to explain this lunacy to the Alliance leadership." She paused. "Okay, hit me. What the hell do you have?"

"I have another one of those intelligences," Eric answered. "One that's a lot more talkative than the first two, for better and worse. There's no keeping the secret now—too many people have seen it."

"It?"

Eric glanced over his shoulder, out to where the ship was resting.

"Him, maybe?" Eric said thoughtfully with an uncertainty to his tone. "It's calling itself Odysseus."

Gracen's eyes snapped to the ship floating against the backdrop of the roiling plasma, then widened as she began to grasp what he was saying.

"Your *ship* . . . ? But . . . *how*?"

"Wish I knew," Eric admitted. "Whatever it is, however it happened, I couldn't even begin to speculate. What I know is that my crew is now half convinced that the ship is haunted . . . and they're not exactly wrong."

"Setting aside the evidence, which I will be looking at, what can these things do?" Gracen asked.

"Can't really answer that either," Eric said. "I know it's more than I've seen, and what I've seen is bad enough."

Gracen stared evenly at him, not saying a word. She didn't have to. He knew full well what she was asking.

"They're mind readers, or close enough to make little difference. Any mind in their range, they scan automatically," he said. "There's no intent behind it, just autonomic reflex if Central is to be believed. I'm pretty certain they can warp space-time somehow . . . I'd be dead if Gaia hadn't intervened when the *Odyssey* came down over New York. How they do it, even what they do, I really don't know. Central and Gaia are . . . the quiet sort. They apparently did their sowing of wild seeds long enough ago that now they're relatively content to play a more subtle role in their respective worlds."

He glanced over his shoulder to where the *Odysseus* was floating. "Odysseus, however . . . isn't. He's . . . Lord, I don't know what he is, but he's emulating a child, maybe twelve years old. He's excitable, craves adventure, wants to fight, or at least he did. Not sure he liked his first taste of a real battle."

"A child?" Gracen's tone was disbelieving, not that Eric blamed her.

What he was describing, on every conceivable level, was utterly ridiculous.

His ship was, in effect, a preteen.

If it weren't so damn serious he'd be laughing so hard his guts would hurt.

That, or cry.

"Well, I suppose you'd best show me to this . . . evidence of yours," Gracen said after a moment, pushing back and rising from the seat. "Lord, if you're telling the truth, the security breach alone is . . ."

"Why do you think I've never brought my ship inside the magnetic field of Ranquil since that second mission?" Eric asked as he walked around the small conference table and gestured to the door.

"That's all well and good, Commodore," Gracen snapped, "but we still send *people* down, extremely knowledgeable people or those of high rank. Myself included."

"Never figured out how to tell the admiral she couldn't visit the homeworld of our allies," Eric said. "If it's any consolation, they've sent people just as highly placed to us. I suppose that we're even in that regard."

Gracen snorted. "Get me Gaia's contact number and maybe I'll buy that. In the meantime, let's see to *Odysseus*."

Eric nodded. Her reply was really about the best he could expect. Unfortunately, he wasn't done with his report yet.

"There's more I'm afraid."

"Oh God," Gracen said, groaning and pausing midstep. "Some other alien impossibility you want to drop on me, I suppose?"

"No, this is purely a military issue, but it's not a small one."

"I can deal with military issues," Gracen said as they started to walk. "What is it?"

"The Imperials managed to get a partial data dump of a Priminae cruiser," he said. "We have a list of their search terms, but no confirmation on exactly what they were able to escape with."

"I'm assuming that there's something within those terms that concerns you?" Gracen asked as they started down the hall.

"One in particular."

"Hit me," the admiral said, visibly steeling herself as they walked.

"They looked for the data the Priminae had on any 'allies,' as well as the locations of those allies' homeworlds."

Gracen froze in place, face ashen. "Do we have any idea what they escaped with?"

"Not fully. But on the plus side, the Priminae didn't store Earth's location in their ship's database, so we know they didn't get *that*," Eric answered. "I believe that was at your request."

She breathed a little easier. "Yes, it was."

"Unfortunately, the Imperials likely got one thing of import," Eric said. "Apparently, the Priminae mentioned in the database that we only have one world, one system."

Gracen closed her eyes. "Fuck."

CHAPTER 2

Imperial Space, World Kraike

▶ "One system."

Navarch Misrem winced but nodded simply. "Yes, My Lord."

"One system. One world. How is this *possible*?" Lord Jesan Mich rose to his feet, arms thrown up as he stalked forward. "According to your data, they're *barely* infants at that."

"The data seems to be consistent," Misrem said, "though it is possible that we're dealing with some form of subterfuge, of course. However, based on what we've been able to gather from other sources, and our own records in battle . . ." She hesitated before repeating herself. "It seems to be consistent."

"This is absurd," Jesan grumbled. "How certain are we that the initial contacts were with a single ship rather than a string of individual ships?"

"Not very," Misrem admitted with an annoyed frown. "Our best scans of the area were always based on the gravitic power curve of the combatants, and the unknown contact had effectively zero power curve we could detect. That makes identification extremely difficult, especially since we didn't dare put any vessels close enough to get solid visual confirmation."

"I see. I do not like acting without sufficient information. The initial invasion with the tame Drasin was . . . mishandled."

"In my opinion, My Lord, it was a bad idea entirely," Misrem said. "What was the plan? The Drasin *destroy* worlds. We could not have moved in afterward, as there would have been no controlling those planets after the Drasin were through."

"The point was never control, My Lady Misrem," Jesan said softly. "The plan was annihilation."

Misrem blinked, uncertain she entirely believed what she'd heard.

"Pardon?"

"You didn't mishear."

"That's madness," she insisted. "There's no benefit to the Empire in that."

"Yes and no. There is, in fact, a benefit to the Empire, but that wasn't the point of the invasion."

"What was the point, then?"

"Revenge. Some of our people hold long grudges," Jesan answered. "Longer than you or I might want to believe."

Misrem gaped at him for an instant before she managed to get her expression under control.

"Revenge? For something that happened before even *our* recorded history? Who was so abysmally *insane?*"

"That is the question, isn't it?" Jesan said, a rhetorical hint to his tone. "Unfortunately, even I don't know the answer. Whoever initiated that operation did so while covering their tracks quite effectively. Everyone I've been in contact with reacted much the same as you. Going after the Oathers makes sense, but unleashing the Drasin the way we have does not. Certainly not on their homeworld. That is a rich world worth much to the Empire, and if any of the legendary technology the Oathers were supposed to have absconded with still exists, that planet would be the most likely location. Every analyst I've spoken with seemed to have been under the impression that we would offer a chance to surrender after the Drasin annihilated the Oather fleet.

Unfortunately, the people who were holding the reins of those monsters had rather different orders."

"Treason?" Misrem asked.

One word, a simple question, but not so simple in truth.

"No," Jesan answered, his undiluted response surprising her. "The orders were authentic. I even know who issued them, but the Imperial Command structure is a web of confusion the likes of which a fleet navarch like yourself could only have nightmares about."

"So you don't know who originated the intent behind the orders."

"Not at all," Jesan said, then gestured casually, with some disinterest in his expression. "Not that it matters. It's all academic really. No one cares if the Oathers die. Most might prefer it. Wasteful, yes I agree, but the only difference between the majority of the Empire and whoever did authorize that invasion is that most Imperial citizens do not especially care enough to make the Oathers' end happen. Someone did. So be it."

"So be it? Have you seen the size of the mess they've left us to clean up?" Misrem said.

"Yes, well, it would have been better if they'd been *competent* in their actions, I will agree." Jesan sighed. "Still, that's not relevant for the moment. What is relevant is whether we can trust the data you acquired. According to the reports your team had to transmit through jamming, they weren't allowed to escape?"

"None of them got off that ship, My Lord," she responded.

"Good," Jesan said. "Then the data is more likely to be accurate. I believe we can risk acting on it, but I will have to ensure success this time."

"My squadron stands ready, My Lord."

"No Navarch, not this time," Jesan answered. "This time I believe I'll bring up the sector fleet."

Misrem stared for a moment, rather stunned.

"That seems . . . excessive, My Lord."

"I know, but I've had enough of the issues caused by this mess," Jesan answered. "It's time to put an end to them, for good."

▶▶▶

▶ The sector fleet.

Misrem was stunned, honestly, that the lord of the Imperial Sector would authorize something that extreme. Her squadron, with some augmentation, should be enough to handle the size of the enemy forces they had been able to determine existed from the data.

The total number was stunningly small. If she had known just how minuscule the might of the enemy was, she would have pressed the fight to its conclusion at their last encounter. Certainly, she would have lost much of her squadron, but the crippling of the opposing forces would have been worth the tally.

At most she had expected a second squadron to be assigned, not the entire sector fleet.

The Empire only had seven sector fleets, including Home Fleet. Each was more than sufficient to fight a major war. Often sector fleets had been known to handle two or three such wars while putting down a couple of minor uprisings. Based on the data she'd retrieved from the Oather vessel, sending an entire sector fleet wasn't just overkill, it was pure *waste*.

Her squadron consisted of between twenty-four and forty vessels, depending on how much the Empire saw fit to augment her forces for given missions. While she commanded one of the more powerful squadrons in the sector, it was only one of eighteen assigned to the sector fleet's command structure. The fleet itself also had another twenty Dreadnought Class vessels, each massing nearly as much individual firepower as her entire squadron.

She couldn't believe that Lord Jesan was going to uncover his sector for a pacification program like this.

No. He wouldn't recklessly uncover his sector. It's tactically and strategically foolish. Jesan is many things, but a fool isn't among them. What's his plan, then?

The Oathers were annoyingly inoffensive and hardly a threat to the Empire, and Misrem was unable to imagine what about them would cause the sector lord to commit his entire fleet to a mission. Perhaps the others were the cause, then. They were far from the inoffensive nonthreat of the Oathers . . .

Still, that didn't track either.

The enemy just didn't have the numbers to draw out a force like the sector fleet.

She supposed it didn't matter. His orders were now set, but she would be bothered until she worked out his true intent.

▶▶▶

▶ Jesan watched as the door closed behind the withdrawing figure of the navarch, unsurprised to see her intense confusion and thoughtfulness. Misrem had a reputation for tactical excellence and skill in strategic maneuvers. If she had encountered such fierce resistance in both of her forays into the enemy sector, then the matter was serious.

Both times from the species they had only identified as the anomalies.

Now they had a name, though he supposed one name was as good as another.

Humans.

What they called their species. Unsurprisingly, it was likely what they called both Imperials and Oathers as well. They were obviously of the same initial programmed genetic drift that seemed to be a galaxy-wide phenomenon.

Truly bizarre intelligences did exist, he knew. The Empire had annihilated more than a few, species so different that communication was effectively impossible. Ending them was really the only acceptable outcome. The Imperial Standard, however, seemed the most common form in the galaxy . . . and the most successful.

With good reason.

It was the height of foolishness to allow a species one couldn't converse with to have even the *possibility* of space travel. There were far too many ways to commit genocide once you could leave your own world and travel the stars. No sane species would leave another alive as long as the slightest chance existed of such an outcome.

It would be immoral beyond the most perverse depths of depravity to risk your own in such a way. The Empire learned that difficult lesson a long time ago. Kill those who might become the enemy lest they do the same to you first.

These self-named humans, however, were an interesting dilemma. They could communicate, and they were clearly willing to make treaties and alliances. Unfortunately for them they elected to side with the Oathers, but the humans might still have some things worth acquiring before the war was ended.

Obviously, they had new takes on technical advances. The sorts of things that would be of inestimable value within the Empire. Clearly, however, if they could fight off the Drasin, then taking their world would be difficult.

One world, however, could not possibly defend itself against the might of a sector fleet. Even if some of the intelligence returned by the navarch's squadron was fabricated, he intended to be certain that he brought enough force to the confrontation to end this farce once and for all.

Once they had everything they wanted from the Oather and human homeworlds, then he would have the firepower he needed to ensure that this dragon was put back to sleep.

Once, and for all time to follow.

▶▶▶

▶ Captain Aymes glowered as he strode down the corridors of his vessel, frustrated beyond belief by the nonsense he'd been dealing with since orders had come down for mandatory refits of all ships in the region. Considering the massive weapons and armor refit they were undergoing that appeared to be based on the systems they believed the anomalous species used, his forces were seemingly shifting from an exploratory stance to one of full-scale war.

He shouldn't have been surprised.

He'd had access to the intelligence captured from the boarding of the Oather vessel, and the information was rather explosive.

Even forgetting about the actual intelligence they'd gathered— items that could be proven—Aymes was well aware the idea that a single world had caused them as much trouble as it had wouldn't sit well with the upper echelon of the fleet, nor would the nobles receive such news particularly well.

He knew that. He accepted that.

War was his business, after all, and he'd never been found wanting for places to conduct his affairs.

The fact that they were *tearing his damn ship apart* without so much as a little advance warning, *that* was pissing him off.

Aymes schooled his expression into a more neutral mask as he approached the bridge. He knew of two political informants on his command staff, and likely was missing at least one other unless Fleet Intelligence had gotten sloppy, so he saw no reason to give any of them munition to use against him.

Actual political officers wouldn't be so bad. They were already in their assigned spot and not technically in the chain of command. When dealing with one of those, in Aymes' experience, you just worked out where they stood and learned to convey what they expected of an officer. All but the most unhinged and, frankly, stupid ones generally understood that even captains were occasionally prone to emotions.

The stupid ones usually didn't last too long before suffering an accident.

He'd arranged two of those in a row once before Fleet Intelligence sent him someone with a polite request to be more subtle about his machinations in the future. Since the person issuing the request *was* his new political officer at the time, Aymes thought that the message had been amusingly clever. The new man decided not to be too much of a pain about things, however, so Aymes decided that Fleet Intelligence wasn't so bad.

At least they had a sense of humor, dark though it might be.

Unfortunately, when they suborned his *staff*, that was a whole other problem. His staff were in his chain of command, which meant that if he were suddenly removed from command for, oh, treason as an example, everyone below him was possibly positioned for a bump in rank.

Aymes hated having to tread lightly around spies in his chain of command, but some weren't smart enough to work out that a bump in rank gained via subterfuge was as likely to end with them in an interrogation cell as behind a better desk.

Smart spies he could handle, but the stupid ones were dangerous.

His crew, while down to minimum staffing, were working efficiently as Aymes stepped onto the command deck and looked around briefly. He expected no less, but was still gratified to see them in action.

Most of the internal systems were down for refit, which blacked out three-quarters of the displays and stations, and being in a refit slip meant that they were getting basically nothing on any of their external equipment, which blacked out almost all of what remained.

Masking a frustrated sigh, Aymes settled into his station and called up his personal files.

With refits continuing apace, he had to assume that the vessel would be deploying for action just as soon as the work was done. If the system lord intended them to have time to properly work up to a reasonable fitness level, he would have broken up the refits into more manageable chunks.

So Aymes put aside as many of his frustrations as he could and set to work building simulations that would allow his teams to practice with the new equipment.

It was a bad way to conduct a war, frankly, but he had little choice, so he would work with what he was given.

CHAPTER 3

AEV (Allied Earth Vessel) *Odysseus*, Forge Facility, Ranquil

▶ The deck was quiet as the commodore and admiral walked across the expanse, the lights dim, as most of the lines to the reactor were cut and the reactor itself was being held on the edge of stability for safety reasons. Gracen felt a chill that she knew had to be psychosomatic. The idea of intentionally keeping a ship's reactor on the edge of stability bothered her on a deeply instinctual level despite her academic understanding of the process.

Unlike most reactors, when working with a singularity system, the last thing you wanted was an out-of-control stable reactor. Being stable was incredibly bad, because it meant that the singularity had sufficient mass to be self-sustaining and couldn't be shut down. While under way, keeping the system somewhat stable was necessary, if only barely, but the last thing anyone wanted in orbit of a habited world—or, worse in this case, *within* a stellar primary—was a stable singularity.

My ship ate the sun would be a lousy epitaph for a civilization.

"If you're right, Commodore, this is going to turn bad on us much quicker than we feared," Gracen said as she considered what Eric had unveiled concerning the intelligence coup the Empire had likely pulled off.

Eric nodded, his expression grim. "I can't really find a way to put a shine on this one, Admiral. If they did get the intel we think they got, then they know that we've just been pulling the interstellar equivalent of a stone-cold bluff. My read on the Empire says that if they work that out, if they even *think* that's what's been happening, then they'll call us on it."

Gracen grunted in disgust but had to agree.

The Imperials were a confrontational sort. Even the few prisoners Terran and Prim forces had managed to gather showed that, right down to the lowest ranked among the enemy. They challenged on everything, and not just once either. If they thought circumstances might have changed, they challenged again, even though they had to know that the odds weren't in their favor.

She supposed it might have something to do with them being held by the Priminae, who were notoriously soft by most standards, but Gracen didn't really think that was the case. Despite the Priminae being a lot nicer about things than she knew Terran guards were, Gracen couldn't fault the discipline the Priminae brought to the job. They didn't just take crap and smile but followed their protocol every time, no matter the provocation or how many times they'd repeated certain tasks.

No, the Imperial prisoners were just programmed to challenge near constantly, she suspected, and if that was a social aspect of their culture, then there was no question in her mind that Weston was right. If they suspected a bluff, even for a moment, they would call it without any hesitation. Social programming was rather difficult to evaluate, at least without a decent understanding of the society in question. Unfortunately, while Gracen's people had been progressing quite well in understanding just how the Priminae and Imperial genomes varied from solar humans, their cultures were still largely mysterious. Even the Priminae, who were open about theirs, had too much social history to quickly parse and break down.

For the moment, all they knew was that the Imperials were incredibly confrontational and didn't like to back down. Not until they'd been *made* to back down, and even then their submission might not hold for long.

"We'll have to increase patrols," she said finally.

"It'll stress our people," Eric offered. "We don't have enough ships to properly schedule them."

"Can't be helped. I'll write up the orders as soon as I get back."

Eric nodded, agreeing with her despite the issues involved with upping their patrol schedules. As it was, he didn't expect his people to see a home port for quite some time; that was the way of things when you were in the military, more so when there was a real conflict looming.

Months away from home at a given time were bread and butter for a military man, but it could be hard all the same.

He just accepted the orders, however, knowing that his people would suck it up and deal with new realities. They were professionals.

"I'll have to put the *Big E* back on the rotations," Gracen said hesitantly.

"Do it," Eric told her, no hesitation.

"That ship isn't up to modern standards, Eric," she said sternly. "If I'd had my way we'd have scrapped that hull, not given her a legacy name."

Eric sighed, knowing that she had a point. The *Enterprise* had sacrificed herself during the last battle that pushed the Drasin off Earth and out of the solar system, and she'd done so *spectacularly*. There would always be a *Big E* in the fleet after that, but he agreed that they should have waited and given the name to one of the new Heroics coming along, rather than slapping it on a near-finished hull from pre-invasion.

After what Captain Carrow had done, and what the *Enterprise* sacrificed, it deserved better than to be obsolete before it was even commissioned.

Still, he believed that she was underestimating just what that ship could do.

"The Odyssey Class isn't far off the Rogues, Admiral," Eric responded finally. "And the *Big E* packs how many squadrons of the Vorpals now? Four?"

"Five actually, but the enemy has been soaking up ship-to-ship missiles with little effort," Gracen said as they continued to walk. "I don't want to set our pilots up against targets like that. It's suicide."

"Admiral, pilots *want* to fly. Fighter pilots want to fight. If you're in doubt, just ask them. Not only will they all stand up and volunteer, they'll start ripping into every bit of intelligence we have on enemy formations, looking for holes. If nothing else, they'll be able to harass and tear into the enemy Parasite ships and destroyers, freeing up shipboard missiles for the big boys."

Gracen grimaced but didn't feel like she had any other choice. They needed every ship they could get out on patrol, and putting the *Enterprise* on the line would let her keep one more Heroic in Sol as a part of the Home Defense shield. Ideally, she would prefer to put most of that shield out on patrol as well, but that was a politically impossible option.

"I may do just that, Commodore . . ." Gracen's voice trailed off slowly as she spotted a figure sitting in the center of the deck up ahead of them.

It was clearly a child, the proportions all wrong for anything else. Slightly gangly arms and legs, a body that seemed to be lost in the armor the figure wore, and a head just a little too large, proportionally, for an adult.

Though the helmet might be affecting my thoughts there, Gracen admitted to herself as she examined the figure closely.

The armor was ancient, either Greek or Roman, or possibly some melding of the two. She was familiar enough with that historic period to recognize elements of both, but Gracen was also aware that both cultures had developed a vast array of variations between them. The attire was clearly pre–Roman Empire, however, of that she was certain.

The shield that rested on the floor a short distance away was Greek, beyond any shadow of a doubt. A classic hoplite, commonly recognized as the Spartan shield. It looked far too heavy for the boy to carry normally, let alone into battle.

"Admiral," Eric said, distracting her slightly, causing her eyes to flicker over to the man standing beside her in a space-black casual uniform. "Allow me to present Odysseus. Odysseus, this is the Admiral."

Gracen's gaze flicked back, and she started as she saw that in her split second of distraction, the armored figure had somehow managed to silently get to his feet, turn to face them, and throw up a perfect modern salute, which he then followed up with a thump of his fist over his heart.

"Admiral!" the slightly too-high voice said with the intensity she would have expected from a boot-camp graduate.

"Odysseus," she said softly, taking in the boy's face and committing the features to memory.

The eyes, she realized, reminded her of the commodore's more than anything. In a startled moment of recognition, Gracen suddenly saw several features she knew in that face. Features of the commodore, some of his command . . . especially Commander Michaels, unless she was mistaken, and . . . *herself?*

And another item caught her attention.

Why is he wearing glitter-pink eye shadow?

"I like pink," the boy replied, as though she had spoken aloud, his voice solemn.

"Ah . . . I . . . see?" Gracen said, swallowing as she glanced at Eric, who shrugged slightly. "Pleasure to . . . meet you?" she said uncertainly. "Odysseus, is it?"

"Yes ma'am," the boy said firmly. "Odysseus, the warrior king. You named me."

"I suppose I did, yes." She nodded, cocking her head slightly. "Do you like your name?"

That seemed to set the boy back for a moment, his face closing up as he slowly appeared to consider the question deeply. Finally, he looked back at her. "I don't know. Am I supposed to?"

"Some people do, some don't," Eric said. "There's nothing deep in the question, Odysseus, just what it sounded like."

"Oh," the boy said, thinking again for a moment.

Gracen found herself unsure about how to take in the whole situation, which was ethereal and entirely unreal. And yet she couldn't seem to disassociate herself from this being. The boy in front of her was somehow . . . *a starship?*

Worse, to her mind at least, he was one of the most powerful starships in the recorded history of two cultures, one of which had been a spacefaring civilization since before their acknowledged history. And this vessel was one of the most important symbols of human strength in the galaxy.

Yet the ship seemed honestly confused as to whether it liked its name.

There is so much wrong with this, I don't know where to begin.

Gracen had to forcibly keep herself under control, unwilling to start publicly ranting or raving about impossibilities. She would save that for the privacy of her quarters, preferably with a bottle of gin to fuel the moment. For now, she *refused* to be made, or make herself, a spectacle.

"I think . . . ," the boy said, looking up at her through the surprisingly intense eyes that were surrounded by luminous glitter, "I think I like the name. That's good, right?"

Gracen noted that the boy looked to Eric, expression uncertain but more open than he had been.

"Yes, I would say that's good," Eric said with a very slight smile. "Names can have a big impact on our lives . . . or they can have no impact at all."

"Strange." The boy, Odysseus, frowned. "If they're important sometimes, why aren't they always important?"

"People are strange, Odysseus," Gracen answered before she could stop to analyze her own thoughts any more. "Some people let their name define them. Others choose to define their name through their actions. We all approach life in surprisingly different ways, so you can't expect one person to react in the same way as another."

Odysseus seemed genuinely bothered by that. "That seems . . . wrong. Math describes the universe, doesn't it?"

"It seems to," Eric said.

Math was far from Gracen's personal specialty, though she was competent in the concepts she dealt with as part of her position, of course. She also knew that Eric could do interception calculations in his head faster than any computer, though admittedly not as precisely. As a fighter pilot, he had always held this key advantage over the vast majority of his opponents.

Often he would be leaning in the right direction by the time the computer spat out the precise numbers needed to resolve a situation, giving him as much as two or three extra seconds over his opponents. Eternity in a dogfight, the difference between life and death.

The sort of math Odysseus was referring to was well over both their heads, however, and Gracen was aware of that.

"Math is reliable, but people aren't?" Odysseus frowned. "But people are ruled by math, deep down? I don't understand."

Gracen started to respond, but Eric's hand brushed her shoulder. As she glanced over, he nodded behind her and she acceded to the suggestion, drawing away from Odysseus at the commodore's direction.

"Every conversation with him eventually ends up like this," Eric said softly as they walked. "He's learning, and fast, but he experiences the universe from more perspectives than we do. Every set of eyes on the ship are his eyes. The ship's computers seem to be his brain, as much as . . . I don't know. We know when he's accessing the computers, since our security systems can track when he calls up files. But he clearly has a brain of his own too."

"He can see through the ship's scanners, then?" Gracen asked, her own tone matching the commodore's.

"Yes. He thinks in deep math. Only a handful on board can keep up with him in regards to the equations, but he's still developing what we would call intuition. Every now and then I can get ahead of him just because I get a feeling of where the math is going faster than he can. I think it drives him a little nuts when that happens."

Gracen glanced a little sourly at Eric's clear amusement. "Please don't antagonize the warship that can glass the surface of planets."

"Well, good news there," Eric said. "He can't override our hardline safety systems. I wouldn't want to rely on the software systems, but our heavy stuff all requires bridging a *real* circuit to release them for combat."

"Thank God for small favors," Gracen muttered.

She glanced over her shoulder, remembering what the commodore had told her earlier. "Wait, he can read minds?"

"Yes ma'am."

"So why . . . ?"

"Are we being quiet?" Eric asked, and she nodded confirmation. "Odysseus recognizes our desire for privacy, even if he doesn't understand it. If we're quiet, he mostly won't answer questions we don't ask, or comment on our conversation later."

"But he's still . . . ?" She let the question trail off as Eric gave her a knowing look.

"Every thought is automatically scanned, as I understand it," Eric said, "though I shouldn't say 'scanned' exactly. He doesn't process them as external thoughts. Every thought you have, he has at the same time, as though it's his own. Keeping in mind that we're really still trying to figure all this out ourselves"—Eric frowned seriously—"I've spoken with Rame and a few others about trying to better comprehend what's going on. As best we can determine, people within Odysseus' range of influence are like . . . neurons firing in his brain. We're independent, but we're also part of him."

"That is . . . both fascinating and incredibly disturbing," Gracen admitted.

"I can't imagine it's any better for him. From his point of view, he *has* to be thinking what we might call suicidal thoughts quite often."

"What?" Gracen asked sharply.

"How many times have you thought about how to eliminate him since you came on board?" Eric asked pointedly.

Gracen paled, considering that.

If her thoughts were interpreted by Odysseus as his own . . . then . . . ?

She groaned, pinching her nose.

"My brain hurts," she grumbled.

"Understandable." Eric chuckled. "Most people who deal with Odysseus seem to have that reaction."

"Most?" Gracen asked dryly.

"Steph thinks he's a great kid." Eric rolled his eyes. "There's always been something wrong about Steph. I love him, don't get me wrong, but he's nuts."

"I seem to recall more than a few people saying the same of you in your jacket, Commodore. The part about you being nuts, at least."

Eric just gestured casually, not worried about any notations like that in his record. "I was a US Marine. If we weren't nuts, we weren't doing the job right."

Gracen snorted, and then her mind was brought back in line with the current situation.

"Damn it, we don't need this right now," she hissed. "I can't clear you or this ship for missions, Eric."

"I know."

"But we can't lose an *entire Heroic* either. What the hell are we going to do?" She wiped her hand down her face in exasperation. "If I don't clear this ship for duty, I'm going to have to explain this before the Naval Council, and there is no way I'm doing that without a hell of a lot more information and corroborating evidence backing me up. Commodore, you bring me the *worst* migraines."

"Sorry about that, Admiral," Eric said, not sounding apologetic in the least. "We have some time before you have to make that decision, thankfully. Full repairs will take some more time. I'd say we'd be here another couple weeks if the ship weren't on a priority run."

"How long actually, then?" Gracen asked dryly.

"Few more days, but we can be creative with the paperwork."

"Do it," she ordered. "I'll find some way to explain why you're not out in the black. But damn it, Commodore, get this figured out. I don't care how you do it, but we *need* the *Odysseus* in the line."

"Understood, ma'am."

►►►

► "She's gone."

Eric sighed but didn't jump as the voice came from where no one had been standing just an instant earlier. "I know, and what have I told you about sneaking up on people like that?"

"Sorry."

Eric wished he had a better idea of how to deal with kids, but then again he had no idea if Odysseus was actually as young as he seemed. He couldn't help but compare the entity to a child, but he was also aware of how potentially dangerous that line of thinking was.

"She didn't like me," Odysseus told him, the boy's voice a little flat.

"She doesn't know you," Eric corrected. "She didn't like that we can't deploy until we have a better understanding of what happened."

"I will be fully prepared for battle within two days, five hours, and forty-three minutes according to the current schedule," Odysseus responded with just a hint of indignation. "We may deploy at any time. The remaining repairs can be handled while under way."

"There's more here than repairs, and you know it," Eric told the boy sternly, wondering when he'd become babysitter or, so much worse, a daddy.

Odysseus was silent for a long moment before reluctantly conceding the point.

"My presence compromises crew efficiency."

Eric nodded. "Yes it does."

"Perhaps the thoughts are right. I should . . . go away," Odysseus said, his tone suddenly soft.

Eric stamped down on his knee-jerk reactions, though he knew that Odysseus would have *thought* every one of them at the same moment as well. He knew all the arguments, both logical and emotional, that had raged among those exposed to Odysseus on board the ship. He couldn't stop the boy, entity, whatever . . . Eric couldn't stop him from interacting with the crew, and Odysseus seemed much more desirous of interaction than either Central or Gaia.

His existence, while still confusing to most of the crew, was well on its way to becoming a well-known and almost accepted part of shipboard operations.

There was still a lot of misinformation surrounding the entity, of course, which ranged from a ghost haunting the ship to an alien invader. Sometimes, to be honest, Eric didn't know which of the two he leaned toward.

"I think," he said slowly, running the thoughts through his mind carefully, more for his own benefit than that of his companion, "that you could be a great benefit to the efficiency of the crew, in time."

That much was the truth, of course. He'd seen how the boy had managed to play with the ship's functions, making his namesake a veritable powerhouse the likes of which should never have been physically possible.

Still, the boy's aim sort of sucked, of course, and Lord knew the kid didn't have a clue how to operate the ship in combat.

Those were all skills that could be taught, however, and Eric had found himself excited to do just that.

"Perhaps," Odysseus replied after a moment. "I . . . I was excited for battle, you know."

"I do. What do you feel now?"

"I don't know. The fight . . . hurt," Odysseus admitted. "It hurt *bad*. Did I do that to others?"

Moments like that were when Eric rather wished that his mind wasn't an open book to the entity at his side. Lying would be so much easier.

"Yes, maybe not in exactly the same ways, but yes you did," Eric said. "Or, the ship did, at my orders."

"Why?"

"That's a question no human has ever had a good answer for, not on the level you want at least. I can tell you why we did those specific actions, but you already have the answers. You want to know why we do violence at all, and I don't have an answer for that."

"I thought I was the mind reader."

"You are, but you're also asking questions every young soldier asks himself sooner or later."

"What answer do they come to?"

"Everyone comes to their own," Eric said, "but most tend to reach some variation of a single response."

"Which is?"

"We fight for the man standing beside us," Eric answered instantly. "The men and women who stand and fall at our side. Home, nations, ideologies—they all come in a distant second, sometimes even farther down the list. In the moment, all those things bleed away, and when the bullets fly, we fight for the women and men who are right there with us, in the mud and in the blood."

Odysseus was silent for a long time before fading away, apparently either satisfied with the answer or going away to mull it over.

Eric hoped the entity would be satisfied.

▶▶▶

▶ Gracen's mind whirled as she sat quietly in the bolstered seat of the courier vessel as it left the Forge facility.

She could always count on the commodore to bring her a migraine, she reflected as they passed through the solar corona and into the open space of the Ranquil System.

"Admiral," the ship's captain, Commander Nikala, called back to her. "Automated message from Admiral Tanner. He wishes to invite you for a dinner before we return to Earth space."

"Negative, Commander. Please issue my regrets to the admiral, but we won't have time to divert to Ranquil."

"The admiral seems to have anticipated that, ma'am. He's suggesting a meeting on the Priminae flagship, a Heroic Class just cleared from the Forge. They're offering to meet and pace us on our way out of the system."

Gracen considered that for a moment, realizing that Tanner had to know at least part of the story now. The commodore had needed him to help cover up the oddities in the Odysseus' situation.

"Very well, arrange to rendezvous with the Heroic. I'll meet with the admiral for that meal."

"Aye ma'am."

If nothing else, she supposed, the dinner discussion should be fascinating.

CHAPTER 4

AEV *Bellerophon*, Ranquil System

▶ "The commodore's shuttle has landed, Captain."

"Thank you, Lieutenant," Captain Jason Roberts said, standing up. "Commander, you have the bridge."

"Aye Captain," his first officer responded automatically, "I have the bridge."

Jason made his way from the command deck, moving up through the ship's other decks via the lifts to the exterior, where the shuttle bays were located. He was unhurried, knowing that it took some time to move a shuttle inside and then to pressurize the connections to allow people to disembark.

He hoped that the commodore had some answers.

The rumors that had been floating around were getting out of hand, no matter how absurd they were. Jason was well aware that even the least likely of rumors would be able to disrupt shipboard operations if enough people started to believe it might be true.

The idea that the Odyssey was *haunted*—of all the insane and inane things—was, of course, the most ludicrous thing he'd heard in a damn long time, but crews could be superstitious in absurd ways. He still remembered those fools painting "containment circles" in the pulse torpedo containment areas. Eric had taught him that you were better to leave the harmless superstitions be, but stamping on the troublesome ones had to be a priority.

Why hasn't he stamped out this damn ghost rumor?

The lift opened on the flight deck, and he almost immediately saw Commodore Weston's shuttle, secured into place and being offloaded on the other side of the sealed observation deck. He settled in to wait for the commodore to get through the pressure seals.

Only a few moments passed before the sealed hatch opened and the commodore stepped off ahead of the rest of the crew and passengers.

"Commodore," Roberts said, standing straight as he greeted his CO. "Welcome aboard the *Bellerophon.*"

"Glad to be aboard, Captain," Eric Weston said firmly before smiling. "I understand the *Bell* is shipshape again?"

"All repairs complete. We're ready to go, sir."

"Good, good." Eric glanced around briefly. He nodded to the exit. "Walk with me, Captain. We need to talk."

Roberts nodded automatically, but the phrasing set alarm bells ringing.

What the hell is going on?

The commodore led him out but not to the lift, instead turning and heading along the inner ring that linked the shuttle and flight decks. It wasn't quite the most private place on the ship, but it was close.

"This is going to be one hell of a conversation, isn't it, sir?" Roberts asked stiffly.

"More than you're going to know for a while, Captain," Eric said with a tired smile. "Captain . . . Jason, you're going to be leading the squadron for a while."

"Sir?" Roberts looked over at him sharply. "Did the admiral . . . ?"

He'd known that the admiral had visited, but it never occurred to him that Weston was in any significant trouble over the confrontation with the Imperials.

"No Captain, I've not been relieved." Eric chuckled, clearly guessing where his colleague's mind had gone.

"Then what's going on, sir?"

"The *Odysseus* is going to be undergoing an extensive recertification," Eric explained. "I can't tell you why, just that it's related to the reason for the ship suddenly overcharging on us during the fight."

Roberts hesitated, thinking about that.

"Is there any risk that our ships will do the same?" he asked, thinking about the *Bell* and the *Bo* in particular.

"Can't say for sure. We haven't figured out what caused it on the *Odysseus* yet," Eric admitted. "Not what initiated it, anyway. Still, seems highly unlikely that you'll see anything of this nature happen on your own ship."

"Pardon me if I'm a little relieved at that, sir."

Eric laughed as they walked. "Completely understandable."

"What will our mission be in the meantime?"

"That's going to be the rub, Captain," Eric told him seriously. "Officially we're just stepping up our patrol schedule, commensurate with an increased ability to project force now that Earth's Forge is about to come online."

That, Roberts knew, was a bald-faced lie.

Certainly, Earth's new shipyard was officially online, but it would be some time before the first hulls were ready for crews to take over from the yard rats. Additionally, with the *Odysseus* off the roster, they were actually short a hull and lacking in projection capability.

"We're expecting more incursions, then," Roberts said, not questioning the decision.

"We're expecting more than an incursion, Captain. We're expecting a full-on invasion force next."

Roberts looked at him intently, eyes glittering with deep curiosity. He had known that the enemy managed to escape with intel, but he was under the impression that no one was really sure what they got.

"How certain are we of this?"

"Enough that the admiral is pulling the *Big E* from Home Fleet and sending her out here," Eric said.

Roberts whistled softly.

While in many ways a brand-new ship, the *Enterprise* was effectively Odyssey Class, though modified somewhat to lose the old Island command and control of the original design that mimicked Blue Navy carriers to some degree. She was obsolete as far as starships went, even though she only had a few years on her hull, literally the definition of too valuable to scrap, not useful enough to sail.

"Sir, we can't fight the *Enterprise* the way we currently have our squadron configured. She'll be cut to shreds by Imperial lasers."

Eric nodded. "I know. I'm going to work up new doctrine for her, but we're also getting her a full complement of Vorpals and every drone they can fit on her. I'll find a way to fight her."

Eric knew that Roberts was too disciplined to tell his CO, "Better you than me," but his expression didn't leave much to interpretation.

"Yes sir."

"I'll worry about that, so what you need to do is take the squadron out to the edge of Priminae-controlled territory. We have a decent idea where Imperial space begins, so focus your patrol along the likely approaches they should take."

"Yes. Orders if the enemy does make a move?"

Eric hesitated. "Harass and fall back. Do not risk your command unnecessarily. Get as much intelligence as possible. If you can bleed them out, then go ahead, but we'd rather have you and the squadron intact than otherwise. I don't expect that they'll risk another exploratory probe. We've bloodied their noses twice now. Unless they're complete idiots, they're either going to back off or bring their A game."

Roberts agreed. Frankly, he'd have gone for overwhelming force a lot earlier, but then he did have the advantage of knowing the state of Earth and Priminae defenses.

"I'm assuming that you don't believe they'll back off?" Roberts asked, though he honestly already knew the answer.

"The Imperials aren't the sort to back off," Eric said. "For whatever reason, they *opened* their campaign with genocide, Captain. You don't do that if you have any intentions of backing off."

There was truth there.

"Agreed." Roberts sighed. "Do you want me to leave you a couple of the Rogues?"

"No, take the full squadron. You'll be down one Heroic as it is. Not going to ask you to run any lighter than you must."

"Thank you, sir. I'll get the squadron winding up," Roberts said, then hesitated as he checked around them to see if anyone was in sight. They were alone. "Sir, off the record . . . what's going on?"

Eric sighed.

He'd gone through the grinder with Roberts, more than once. The man was solid as a rock, even if some of his subordinates were known to joke that he had the personality of one too. Eric didn't like keeping things from the man, but how did you explain something like Odysseus?

"Captain, if I told . . . you wouldn't believe me. That's not just me blowing smoke, I swear. The situation is possibly the strangest thing I've ever seen in my life, and you know how strange my life has been."

Roberts chuckled. "Coming from anyone else, I might laugh in their face. It's that classified?"

"It will be, assuming we ever figure out how to explain it to Command. For now it's just *that weird.*"

"You know you need to step on those damn rumors, sir. If the enlisted get it in their heads that the *Odysseus* is a ghost ship, you'll never be able to run up an effective crew again."

"Easier said than done, especially when there's a little truth to the rumors," Eric admitted.

"Sir?"

"I'll explain it to you sometime," Eric said, "preferably when you have time to come aboard for a visit and see the issue yourself. For now, just look after my squadron, alright?"

"Yes sir."

"Good. Let's get something to eat before you ship out," Eric said, shifting his tone to a more jocular one.

"I think I can scrounge something up, Commodore."

▶▶▶

PS *Desay*

▶ Admiral Gracen stepped through the air seal and into the open compartment beyond, where a man was waiting for her. She smiled as she recognized Rael Tanner. The Priminae's high admiral was a man of slight stature but carried with him an intangible aura that marked him as being in charge more than his pristine white uniform ever could.

"Admiral," he greeted her, smiling widely, "welcome aboard the *Desay*."

Gracen was glad to see Rael again. "It's a pleasure to be here, Admiral. She's a lovely ship. I believe we scanned some differences as you approached?"

"Indeed you did, Admiral," Tanner said cheerfully. "We have begun adapting more of your concepts to our vessels, as well as utilizing some old and new concepts of our own. The *Desay* is our new, what was it called . . . flagship?"

"That's right," Gracen said. "And please, call me Amanda."

"Only if you call me Rael, Amanda," he countered.

"Of course, Rael."

"Excellent. Now, our meal will be prepared shortly, but . . ." He became more serious. "I believe we have more weighty discussions to manage first."

"I believe we do."

"I have prepared a secure room," Tanner said, gesturing to the lift.

"Before we retire there," Gracen asked, "might I impose on you for the use of your long-range transmission systems?"

"Of course."

The admiral snapped a finger and a reader was dropped into her hand by an aide, which she handed over to Tanner. "The coordinates and message are within."

"They will be sent immediately." Tanner accepted the reader, only to hand it off quickly to one of his own aides with a nod. "Now, then?"

Gracen nodded and gestured casually to her aides, telling them to wait for her, before she and the admiral entered the lift. It was a short trip to the conference room the admiral had sealed off, neither of them speaking until the door was sealed and they were alone.

"Your Captain Weston has a habit of destroying expectations," Tanner said dryly as he walked over to one of the chairs and slumped into the auto-forming furniture, letting the seat twist and wrap itself around him.

Gracen sat down much more carefully, a little twitchy as the chair beneath her shifted and twisted to provide proper support.

"I wish I could protest him belonging to me, but it seems that, for my sins, I have been afflicted with the commodore."

"Ah yes, commodore, apologies," Tanner said. "We do not have a similar rank."

"We've occasionally lost it ourselves, over the years." Gracen smiled weakly. "Currently, Eric is one of the very few commodores in the Earth's Black Navy. Some nations refer to the rank as a rear or vice-admiral position."

"Ah, yes, I suppose that might be closer to our use," Tanner said. "He has shown you Odysseus?"

"You mean the young boy in ancient battle armor and . . ." Gracen's expression twisted slightly. "Glitter-pink eye shadow?"

"Indeed," Tanner said, apparently missing Gracen's expression. "I find myself uncertain what to think of it all. In fact, I must confess, I did not entirely believe the commodore, not until I returned to my office on Ranquil."

Gracen stiffened. "Central?"

"Precisely," Tanner said, his expression darkening markedly as he remembered. "The moment I sealed my door, he appeared. Central was most fascinated by the existence of Odysseus. He seemed to wish that I ask the commodore to bring his ship close to Ranquil."

"That's not likely to happen."

"I expected much the same," Tanner admitted with a wry smile. "The conversation with Central, however, was very interesting."

"I wonder why he bothered. If he could just read your mind, why show himself?"

"Ah . . ." Tanner relaxed slightly. "I believe you have not quite grasped the nature of the mental link, if you will. As I understand it, these beings do not read minds so much as experience thoughts. They cannot, for example, delve into your memories unless you are actively experiencing those memories."

"So he showed up to prod your brain so you'd think about what he wanted to know."

Tanner spread his arms, fingers splayed out widely, in an expression Gracen recognized as being close to a shrug for the Priminae.

"In effect," Tanner admitted, "though one might also describe it as being close to a conversation about something that interests us. I sense no animosity there, more . . . an almost apathy, at worst?"

"I'm not certain that's any better," Gracen responded.

"Perhaps not, but who am I to judge the minds of immortals?"

"I'll judge them," Gracen growled. "It's my job. If they're a threat to my people, that puts them in my sights."

"I will not argue with that, except perhaps to say that I do not believe that they can be a threat to our people. If the cap . . . sorry, commodore, is correct about them, then they really are nothing, or at least would be far lessened, without us."

"Maybe, but that doesn't mean they need specific groups or individuals," Gracen countered.

"This is true," Tanner conceded. "What will you do?"

That was a question Gracen had been asking herself over and over since she'd left the *Odysseus*, but it was also a question she had no real answer for.

"I suppose I'll do my job," she said finally. "What that is remains to be seen."

"As will I, and as will we all," Tanner said. "This is perhaps the most momentous discovery in the history of my people, and I find that I cannot but wish that it had come at a better time."

The understatement of the century, Gracen thought.

They were facing an existential threat. The Empire was clearly a power that could potentially annihilate every living thing in both Priminae and human star systems. Whether they had the power to do so was still somewhat debatable, but after the Drasin incident there was no question that they had the desire and the will.

The last thing either group needed right now was the added confusion that this news could cause.

Damn near godlike beings right in our midst? The trouble this could stir up with fundamentalist groups alone could be enough to derail every step we've taken to prepare our defenses.

"It's going to be interesting times," she said finally.

Tanner smiled. "I believe that you are correct."

Gracen looked at him, feeling a hint of something almost like pity entering her expression.

"Admiral, let me tell you about an ancient curse from Earth's history," she said softly.

▶▶▶

AEV *Odysseus*

▶ Steph shivered slightly as he bent over a console, working on coding tactical responses to common situations the ship might face in combat.

"Hey, Diss," he said, not looking up.

"How do you do that?" The young voice had a petulant tone. "No one else can sense me, not even the captain."

"Commodore, Diss," Steph corrected him, continuing his work as the boy in armor walked around into his line of sight. "And I'd be surprised if he couldn't, you know. Raze's positional awareness is damn near legendary."

"He's the captain," Odysseus said firmly. "One ship. One captain. There's no commodore in that statement."

The boy seemed to think more about what Steph had said before going on.

"And maybe you're right. He seems surprised when I appear, sometimes, but not always," the boy said, sounding a little more petulant.

"He has a lot more on his mind than physical fight or flight," Steph explained, "and yes, I suppose he is the captain, but his rank is commodore. You have to learn when's the right time to use each."

"I do?"

"You're the ship, which makes you crew too. So yes, you do."

Odysseus frowned, almost pouting.

"So when do I call him commodore?"

"Well, whenever there are outsiders present, for sure. Anyone who isn't one of us doesn't get to think of him as the captain. He's commodore to them. Captain is for crew only. Also, you should call him by his rank in any official recorded sessions, though I don't expect you'll need to worry about that for a while."

"So when can I call him captain, then?"

"If he gives you an order in a fight," Steph said, "it's perfectly fine to say 'Yes Captain' or 'Aye Captain.' Some prefer to call him 'Skipper' then, which also works in the moment. Commodore is fine too, though mostly that'll be for new crewmembers who don't know him well."

"Protocol is weird," Odysseus muttered, annoyed. "The books don't say anything about that."

"Some do, you're just reading the official stuff too closely." Steph finished coding the new routine and straightened up to stretch a little. "Just remember that there's book protocol and actual protocol. The book is strict, and you'll never be judged wrong if you fall back to the book, but actual protocol lets people feel more like part of a team, and that's important too."

The boy nodded seriously, then shifted his focus to the work Steph had just completed.

"You could tighten that code by almost ten percent," the boy suggested. "Just adjust these numbers here by . . ."

Steph held up a hand, cutting him off. "I know. Though I think I could only get about eight percent, so your numbers are better than mine, but you're missing the adaptive section, Diss. If I lock the ship into a purely efficient course in the scenario this is based on, then I'll lose the ability to adapt to likely surprises the enemy might drop on us."

The boy squinted slightly. "*Likely* surprises? Those exist?"

"Everything exists," Steph said, laughing, "or it seems to, the way my life is going these days. A likely surprise is something that we can reasonably predict the enemy might try, but not be certain of. The Empire, for example, likes to use their own ships as potential suicide weapons. They don't do it as their first reaction, but if we push them too hard at any point, they might just decide to kamikaze us."

"Oh, I see."

"A pilot doesn't just think about perfect maneuvers, Diss," Steph explained patiently, opening up another file to continue his work. "We have to consider everything that can go wrong with what we're trying, and plan options for as many of those scenarios as possible. Actually flying the ship is only a small part of the job. Predicting the future is the hardest part."

"There are too many variables to predict the future," Odysseus said grumpily. "The math is incomplete."

Steph smiled, not quite laughing at the boy.

Being introduced to Odysseus had been an interesting experience for him, given that he'd been on the bridge when the boy made his grand entrance. Steph was too busy to react the way he might normally have. He'd also been unarmed, which would have made his normal response rather difficult as well. So he'd allowed the Marines to handle security while he kept most of his attention on flying the ship.

That had also afforded him the chance to observe and listen.

He'd been more surprised at how *unsurprised* Raze had seemed by it all. Though the boss had been, without *any* doubt, horrified, he hadn't seemed surprised.

There was a story in that, one that Steph wanted to hear more about. So far, unfortunately, they'd been too busy with repairs and everything else for him to corner the commodore someplace where he could be informal enough to wrestle the truth out of him.

The boy who called himself Odysseus, though, was something very different.

Others shied away from the boy, but Steph didn't see what the problem was. Sure, the mind-reading trick was a little creepy, but he'd flown with *way* creepier dudes in the past and considered them closer than family. Creepy was a human condition, and not a bad one in his mind.

One thing he'd learned that drove the boy crazy, though, was when the math was incomplete. Working with holes in his equations truly seemed to frustrate Odysseus, which was a really bad thing to be frustrated by in Steph's opinion.

The universe was nothing *but* incomplete equations.

"You don't need every variable to predict the future," Steph said aloud. "You just need the big ones. Getting close is good enough, and the closer you can get the better your reaction time will be when the moment comes and you have to deal with the variables you couldn't identify. Don't let your obsession with perfection become the enemy of being good enough."

Odysseus hummed slightly, not looking happy with the suggestion, before fading away.

Steph just shook his head and went back to work.

▶▶▶

▶ Odysseus was confused by his confusion.

Since awakening, he hadn't been able to answer any of the haunting questions that swirled in his mind. He didn't know what he was, and no one else did either. He thought hundreds of thoughts at the same time, many of them about his own existence, but none of them answered any of his questions.

Much of what he knew came from the computers that had been installed in . . . him?

He thought he was the ship, but he had no proof of that.

Proof seemed to matter to most of the people, he had realized very early on, and Odysseus had dedicated his time to finding proof of everything. To completing the equation.

Now, though, one of the people he . . . liked? Did he like anything?

Odysseus put that aside for a future examination.

One of the people whom he paid more attention to was telling him that proof wasn't everything, and that confused and bothered him intensely. Why was "close enough" an acceptable response to anything?

None of it made any sense to him. It felt like the rules weren't staying the same, and that was just *wrong*.

The rules were supposed to be locked in, references that anyone could look to in order to see where they stood. From protocol to basic laws of the universe, rules were supposed to be standards he could trust and use to determine his place in the universe.

Close enough?

It didn't seem right to settle for close enough.

CHAPTER 5

AEV *Autolycus,* Deep Space

▶ Morgan Passer, captain of the *Auto,* drifted idly in the microgravity environment of the ship's officers' lounge. He watched a movie playing on the large screen across from him, his uniform jacket floating beside him as he rubbed at his shoulder through a sweat-soaked T-shirt.

"Captain, reactor will be back up in five," Daiyu Li announced as she swung into the room. "Doohan's got the maintenance complete, just sealing up now."

"Good." Morgan reached up and grabbed a handle in the bulkhead above him. "It's getting hot in here."

The *Autolycus* was a Rogue Class starship, one of the first off the line after the invasion. Unlike Heroics, the smaller Rogues didn't pack the power of a singularity core. The older fusion reactors had to be maintained regularly, and that meant all nonessential power systems needed to be shut down during the process.

Light-duty items like display screens could run off batteries with no issue, but heat exchangers were a major system that needed the reactor to run. Contrary to most expectations, cold wasn't the biggest risk a starship faced in the vacuum of space. Vacuum was an excellent insulator, and starships were designed to protect against temperature extremes. Without heat exchanges to actively regulate the interior climate, a ship without power built up heat in a hurry.

Eventually, the vessel would have radiated it all away, of course, and the *Auto* would go cold. That event would have been years away, however, and the crew would have all baked to death long before it came to pass.

Morgan flipped his jacket back on and casually buttoned it up, glancing over in Li's direction. "Are we ready to move when power comes back?"

"Yes Captain," she answered instantly. "All ship systems are prepared—everything registers green."

"Excellent, Commander," he said, satisfied as he kicked himself off the bulkhead toward the door.

Li shifted aside as he floated past out into the corridor beyond, then followed in his wake.

The two pulled themselves into the command deck a few seconds later, just as power returned and the hum of life came back to the ship around them.

Morgan sighed in pleasure as the first hints of a cooling breeze touched his face, still warm but infinitely better than the still air they'd been enduring. He was far from the only one so affected.

The main computer array booted after finally taking over from the secondary systems that had been maintaining the ship, and all the big displays came slowly back to life around them as the pair buckled into the stations.

The vessel was sitting in a star system, the only living thing that existed in the hellish place, orbiting around a red giant primary at a safe distance. The *King of Thieves* had been brought out this far as part of Operation Prometheus and the ongoing mission to scout and investigate stellar anomalies for anything of value, or danger, to Earth and her allies.

This particular mission had been a bust. The anomalous stellar scans they got from the closest star had been caused by what appeared to be a collision between the celestial body and a stable black hole. The result had torn the star system to shreds, turning anything of interest into little more than rubble waiting to be swallowed by the monster that now sat at the center of the mess.

"Alright, power up the main drives," Morgan ordered. "Li, you can tell the geeks to grab whatever scans they can on our way out. We've been here long enough."

"Aye aye, Skipper," the young lieutenant at navigation answered as the commander tapped a few commands into her console.

"Done, Captain. I expect they'll be scanning right up until we transition out."

Morgan chuckled. "I don't doubt it. Let them have their fun, I suppose. This whole run has been a bust anyway. Ten stars, nothing but natural phenomena."

"We cannot . . . what is the phrase . . . win the lotto every time?" Li asked.

"Close enough," Morgan said. "And no, you can't. And while I can't help but wish for new things to help Earth, I'll settle for not finding any more threats." He laughed. "At least we've not given the chief any more reason to play with antimatter."

Li shivered, and he didn't blame her. He still did as well whenever the thought of the dreaded event came on him unexpectedly. No man should intentionally expose his own damn ship to antimatter, and he still experienced the occasional night terror over his vessel being in such dire straits.

"No doubt the chief is saddened by that," Li said, a smile playing at her lips as she collected herself. "He seems to enjoy his reputation."

"Only man in the fleet to be banned from setting foot on the *Odysseus*, by Eric Weston himself no less," Morgan said as the *Auto* rumbled to life around them, her drives heating up.

"Would that we could do the same," Li responded, almost wistfully, earning another laugh from Morgan.

He knew that their conversation had been overheard, of course, since they hadn't been trying to mask it in the least. Ribbing the chief was tradition now on the *Auto*, and probably would continue with whoever took over the job when Doohan retired. Some traditions inevitably survived the men who founded them.

"Drives are lit, Captain," the helm officer announced. "All systems are go."

"Alright." Morgan leaned into the straps holding him to the seat. "Let's be moving, then. Give me a course to our next star of interest."

"Aye Skipper. Course is already plotted, loaded, and locked."

"Well, kick the tires, Lieutenant."

"Roger, Skipper. Lighting the fires." The lieutenant responded just before the *Auto* rumbled deeply and they were all forced down into their seats as the ship began to smoothly accelerate upwell of the local star.

When the interior acceleration reached one gravity, the pressure evened off. Counter-mass systems powered up to keep it there as Morgan and the others unsnapped their restraint straps and stood up at the stations to stretch out their limbs. Gravity was a luxury on a Rogue, only present when they were burning for a new destination, and the crew had learned to take advantage when possible.

They hadn't gone deep into the system once they recognized it was of no value, so the *Auto* only had a short climb to the transition point. After a few hours of burn, they were back to free fall while the last-second calculations were made for the jump.

"Skipper!"

Morgan twisted in the straps he was once more locked into, looking over to the signals station. "What is it, Ensign?"

"Tachyon pulse. Coded, sir, it's one of ours," she answered.

"To my station," Morgan ordered. "Hold on transition."

"Aye Skipper. Holding on transition," the helmsman answered automatically.

Morgan got the signal on his station and ran it through the decoding software, frowning as he read through it.

"Well," he said as he hummed in consideration, "isn't that something?"

"What is it, Captain?" Li asked, leaning over in his direction.

Morgan flicked the message to her station, not bothering to answer. She'd get more out of reading it for herself. He instead looked up to see most of the command crew staring at him.

"New transition coordinates," he ordered, "and a new mission. Signal general quarters and start running preparation drills as soon as we arrive. Looks like we're scouting for more dangerous game from now on, people."

▶▶▶

▶ Across a small yet oddly significant swath of the galaxy, a series of lone ships received similar calls and responded in kind. The Rogues shut down their current operations, closing up shop wherever they were, and immediately began climbing out of whatever system they were in.

Operation Prometheus was shutting down. The fires they'd stolen from the gods were blazing well now in human hands, and it was time for them to turn their focus on more mortal targets.

▶▶▶

AEV *Autolycus*

▶ The rendezvous system was unnamed by both Terran and Priminae sources.

There was a reason for that, of course. It was a dead system, no planets to speak of beyond a hot Jupiter orbiting the primary star every four days. The gas giant was so close that the sun's gravity was sucking methane and hydrogen out of the atmosphere, lighting a ribbon of flame between the two that was stretched to breaking by the rapid orbit of the giant world.

Nothing other than sterile rock existed in the entire system, making it of no interest to anyone beyond a few of the more esoteric stellar physicists on board who were even then eagerly turning the scanners of the ship downwell in hopes of finding something that completely escaped Captain Passer's imagination.

No doubt it would be important to someone, sometime, so he let them have at it as long as there was no need for the scanners to be used more practically.

"Transition signature . . . Hold on, Skipper." The signals ensign frowned. "Multiple inbound transitions!"

"On-screen." Morgan was calm. He had a better idea of what was going on than the ensign did.

"Closest signals will be live in . . . thirty seconds."

Morgan waited patiently for the light from the newly arrived ships to make its way to the *Auto*'s scanners. When the first did show, the situation was as he expected.

"That's the *Jesse James*, Skipper," the ensign said a moment later. "And the *Song Jiang* just pulsed . . . They're all Rogues."

"It's old home week," Morgan said. "Prometheus just got a new job."

▶ ▶ ▶

AEV *Boudicca*

▶ Captain Sandra Hyatt looked over the command deck of the *Boudicca* as it and the *Bellerophon* emerged from the solar corona of the Ranquil primary.

The pair of Heroics had worked together under the command of the *Odysseus* since they had sailed out of dry docks. In all that time they'd seen a fair few fights, and a lot of light-years, and now the pair would be sailing without the third sister of the trio.

Hyatt didn't really know what to make of the issues the *Odysseus* was having. The idea that a starship could be haunted in this day and age struck her as simply ludicrous. But something was obviously going on. She'd seen the state of the *Odysseus* and read the initial reports, and there was no way the ship still needed weeks or months of repairs.

Whatever was going on, however, clearly both the commodore and admiral had signed off on the orders, and that was all she needed at the moment. For now, the *Bell* and the *Bo* had their marching orders.

Hyatt contented herself with looking over the state of her command deck and took comfort and pleasure in its smooth-running operations.

Lieutenant Commander Samuels was in the "pit," the sunken section that housed the helm controls, moving almost languidly as she guided the *Boudicca* through the coronal mass of the star and into open space. She made maneuvering the big ship look like child's play despite the relative proximity of the *Bellerophon* and their Rogue escorts.

Like most of the pilots currently commanding the helm and navigation departments on Heroic Class ships, Samuels was a former member of the elite squadron known as the Archangels, something that had made Hyatt cringe more than a few times in their previous missions when the young woman opted to maneuver the massive ship like a twin-reactor air superiority fighter in a dogfight. They'd come through every scrap more or less intact so far, which made up for a lot she supposed.

"Signal from the *Bell*, ma'am," Hyatt's first officer, Commander Cedric Simmons, told her as he approached from the left side. "Course updates. We're to immediately make for the heliopause, orders from the admiral and commodore to follow just prior to transition."

Hyatt nodded absently. "Send the updates to Samuels."

The short, dark-haired man nodded as well, turning back to his task as she wondered just what it was all about. She could make a few educated guesses, of course. The last furball they'd had with the Imperials made it clear that this new war was heating up.

The Empire clearly had no interest in a cold war.

With the limited intelligence she had access to, which was nearly everything Earth knew as far as she was aware, Hyatt had little doubt that they were again on the wrong side of a power differential. Whatever tricks the admiral and commodore had pulled out against the Drasin were unlikely to be enough against a stellar empire the size of what they seemed to be looking at now.

Normally, the move now would be to talk. Even capitulate if that was what it took to buy time.

Unfortunately, the Empire had no interest in talking or, apparently, fighting a war of maneuver. Their idea of a reconnaissance probe was to barrel on headlong into enemy territory and just start destroying things until they could turn up something of value.

The fact that it worked for them just made Hyatt grit her teeth all the more.

That sheer lack of tactical acumen should never be rewarded, she thought fiercely.

Unfortunately, it seemed that the Empire was happy to spend lives until they achieved their goals, and that was a sound enough though wholly callous tactic if you had the lives to spend. Earth could never pull that sort of crap, she was well aware. Such a strategy would work well in the short term—that had been proven multiple times in history—but the current world governments were too open and exposed by the press to survive that kind of idiocy in the long term.

Even a relative press blackout on the actions of Black Navy operations, largely imposed by a simple lack of ability to get reporters anywhere near fleet operations, wouldn't impede news from reaching the masses. In fact the blackout might actually enhance the effect, since the press would likely start speculating as losses began to filter back through the upper echelons of military circles.

Sooner or later the numbers would leak and public relations would degrade in short order.

Running a war the way the Empire seemed to would be political suicide on Earth, which was likely for the best in her opinion, though there were times she could wish otherwise. In a drawn-out war, public fatigue would come into play and begin to reduce support that was desperately needed if the Earth wanted to mount and maintain a credible defense.

We need more time.

Time, however, was one thing that it seemed they no longer had.

▶▶▶

AEV *Bellerophon*

▶ "All ships on course, formation solid, sir."

Jason Roberts nodded curtly, handing off a digital pad to his assistant. "Thank you, Commander Little. Proceed on course. Inform me when Ranquil control issues our transit paths."

"Aye Skipper," Ray Little said from the pit, where he was casually directing the ship while keeping an eye on the surrounding vessels.

They had most of their usual line of battle, minus the *Odysseus*, along with a few Priminae tugs that were peeling off now that they'd transited out of the stellar corona. With those in the clear, he was looking at empty black between the convoy and the heliopause.

"Smooth sailing," he said softly, not really speaking to anyone as he made a few micro adjustments to the navigational vectors to adjust for slight variance in the position of the system's larger planets from their records.

Roberts turned away from the helm and walked back to his command station, tapping out a command without sitting down.

His orders were on the captain's display, and he couldn't help but glance them over again as he thought about what was to come.

He was privy to the details of what the Imperial Recon team had likely managed to get off the Priminae ship, and could read between the lines easily enough. The commodore and the admiral clearly felt that something big and bad was coming down the line and likely to hit them right in the teeth if they weren't ready.

Well, that was fine. He was all in favor of being ready.

The situation with the *Odysseus*, however, was preying on his mind. Unlike most of the squadron, Roberts had been allowed over to see just what the fuss was over. He was still trying to wrap his head around it.

Everything they'd seen over the years had seemed insane in the moment, of course, so perhaps this was just one of those things that would inevitably become part of his daily lexicon, but for now Roberts had real, serious issues with getting his head around the revelations the commodore had brought to him.

Odysseus itself, or himself perhaps, was one thing; having seen the . . . entity with his own eyes, he could reluctantly accept what seemed to be reality there. That the ship had somehow become incarnated as a young boy with a fetish for antiquated armor and pink eye shadow . . .

Okay, frankly, if he were to admit it to himself, and *only* to himself, Roberts had to admit that the pink makeup bothered him more than the idea of the ship having an incarnate soul. He would *not* say that out loud, especially not to anyone outside the service, as it might be viewed (*might, hell*) as being prejudiced against certain groups of people.

However, it wasn't that—it really wasn't. Or he hoped it wasn't at least. Sometimes it was hard to tell what even your own thoughts were.

The color simply insulted his sense of professionalism.

Particularly the glitter.

He was a little scared what precedent Eric would set for the Navy going forward this time, of course, but he doubted that they were going to wind up with a whole fleet of sentient starships, so, if nothing else, any impact would likely be limited to the *Odysseus.*

What the hell is it with that man, anyway? Roberts wondered.

Apparently, if there was anything weird in the galaxy, Eric Weston would trip over it, fall into it, and then pick it up and take it home for adoption.

Better him than me.

▶▶▶

▶ The two big Heroics and their eight escort Rogues began the long slog of a climb out of the gravity well of Ranquil Prime, accelerating steadily as their powerful reactors spun up to full strength and they began warping space for the open black.

The formation was carefully observed by nearly every scanner in the system. Even allies were wont to keep an eye on any source of *that* much sheer destruction sailing through their territory. With no untoward happenings, however, nearly a day later the group of ships made the heliopause and the official safe distance from which they could transition out.

With their orders set, the *Bell,* the *Bo,* and their escorts vanished in a flash of tachyons.

Behind them they left an uneasy peace, fragile and waiting for the hammer blow that seemed certain to come.

CHAPTER 6

Imperial Space, World Kraike

▶ Jesan Mich walked with a careful and practiced cadence, his capped boot heels echoing sharply off the bonded stone floor beneath him. He was approaching the Imperial seat of power in the sector, which was firmly in the front of his mind with every step he took. None of the direct Imperial family would be present, of course, but in his experience that meant it was even more important to watch his step.

The extended cousins who were entrusted with duties in outer sectors were often quite touchy about the positions they held for reasons he was cognizant of, since he was one of those distant cousins himself in some ways. Granted, his position was earned more by merit than theirs, but blood played true just the same, and Jesan was too aware that if he'd been born a little closer to the Imperial throne, he would likely be in command of the Home Fleet and not an outer sector fleet.

Being appointed to a perimeter sector should, in theory, have been a statement of trust in their position and the quality of their work. In practice the move was often perceived as a sign of a general lack of competence. Getting the idiot cousin as far away from real power as possible and all that.

He was one of the few who understood that wasn't the case as a general rule, since perimeter sectors had to run much more autonomously than the core worlds. He had worked his way up the fleet ranks the hard way, putting down spots of violence all over the Empire at least as often in the core as the rim worlds.

Rim lords and ladies, however, could get extremely touchy with people like himself coming into their fiefdom with an Imperial note of authority and throwing their weight around.

He paused in the entry arc, silently waiting to be announced as all eyes in the large vaulted room turned to see who was standing there. In his lord's finest, Jesan waited perhaps a few seconds longer than he should have before he rotated his head just slightly to pin the nearest acolyte with a glare to melt steel.

The man paled and immediately stiffened to attention and hit the announcing chime.

A few moments after the room fell entirely silent, the acolyte spoke up. He didn't use an amplifier for his voice; one wasn't needed. The room was designed to channel and amplify sound from specific places such that everyone in the room could hear anything said from those points with perfect clarity.

"Announcing Her Imperial Majesty's representative, Lord Jesan Mich."

The announcement was soft, steady, not yelled in any way, but everyone in the massive room heard it all the same. Jesan stepped formally into the chambers of the local seat of government and bowed precisely ten degrees forward from the hip as he looked to where the sector governor was watching him.

Jesan was well aware that the governor wasn't going to like what he was about to do.

"You may approach, Lord Mich," the governor said, gesturing him forward with a tired sort of look.

You think you know what's coming, but I'm sorry to say you have no idea, Jesan thought grimly as he walked up to the podium for presenters and appeals to the governor.

He wasn't there to appeal.

Jesan handed off his Imperial note and attached orders to a runner, who passed them along to the governor.

"Very well, Lord Mich," the governor said, looking the two documents over. "These all appear to be in order. What actions are you here to inform us of?"

Jesan fixed his gaze on the governor, not looking around to any of the other faces turned in his direction. "I believe, Governor, that you would prefer if this were made a private matter."

"We do not have time for this," the governor growled. "Some of us have work to accomplish. Present your position or leave."

You asked for it, Jesan thought, considering the man a fool. It would have lost him only a few moments to quietly ascertain what Jesan wanted, and the results of not doing so were wildly unpredictable, since he had no idea what was coming. Still, it wasn't Jesan's problem anymore. He'd made the appropriate gesture.

"Very well, Governor," Jesan said crisply. "I am here to inform you that I am deploying the sector fleet to a forward action."

The governor snapped his head back as though Jesan had somehow managed to reach out and slap him. Murmurs of shock rapidly built around him, but he ignored them as he kept his focus on the governor.

"I don't believe I heard that correctly," the governor said, leaning forward with a dark look on his face.

"I am very much afraid you did, Governor. Events in Oather space have conspired to require my full attention, and that of the fleet as well."

Exclamations of protest erupted all around him, but none of those voices mattered. Jesan didn't care what local officials thought; they were important only in their small local spheres. None of them had any hint of authority that could impinge on him. They were no threat.

The governor, however, was another matter. In practice his own authority was equal to that of the governor. Jesan was, in many respects, a governor himself, only a mobile one. His primary area of authority was over fleet jurisdiction, which, in theory, put him slightly above local governors. But since he rarely had the luxury of building long-term support in a given area, that was offset somewhat by the local governors' network of influence.

"That," the governor said softly, silencing the talk, as his location was one of the acoustic sweet spots that brought his voice to every ear in the room, "would seem to be, at best, precipitous, Lord Mich. At worst I would say it is a panicked overreaction."

Jesan tensed, but forced himself not to react to the jab.

"I would say that it is moving to eliminate a potential problem with alacrity," he said instead, smiling thinly. "The Oathers have recently altered their tactics and capabilities in surprising ways, and this inclines me to end this situation immediately."

"That's fine, Lord Mich, but the *whole* sector fleet? That seems somewhat extreme."

"The more force that can be brought to bear on the issue, the quicker we can resolve it and move on to more important business," Jesan said calmly.

The governor frowned but said nothing.

"But our worlds will be left without protection!"

Jesan barely glanced aside to see who had shouted that, then refocused on the governor without acknowledging the loudmouth.

The governor sighed. "While he spoke out of place, the Honorable Nierey has a point, My Lord."

"Every world has its own guard fleet," Jesan said simply. "If those are unable to temporarily secure your worlds, then I must question whether you have been properly investing as per your agreement with Her Majesty's family."

The governor flushed, but surprisingly didn't look away from Jesan's gaze.

"I assure you, My Lord," he said tersely, "my Guard Fleet is to the full requirements of the law, and beyond."

Jesan inclined his head and opted not to question the governor about the fleets of other worlds. He rather knew what that answer would be and, while it might be satisfying to put the screws to some of the "honorable" gentlemen in the room with him, it would be counterproductive at the very least.

"I have no doubts, Governor."

The governor's lips twisted. He certainly recognized the position his administrator's mouth had put him in; however, it was too late to change what had been said. He sighed and finally tipped his head to Jesan.

"We stand informed of the fleet deployment," he stated. "I will forward your decision to the core worlds with the next dispatches."

"Of course, Governor." Jesan once more bowed the precise ten degrees required by protocol. "I will take my leave, then, the sooner to return the fleet to your jurisdiction."

"As you say."

Jesan retreated from the room, victory under his cloak, but now the real job would begin. He had barely exited the hall when he grabbed his ship communicator and called his adjutant.

"Ferin, has the fleet finished preparations?" he asked as he walked.

"Very nearly, My Lord."

"How long until we can deploy?" Jesan demanded, increasing his pace.

"Within the day, if it is urgent," Ferin said. "Is it?"

"Not such that I want to increase chances of any losses, but yes," Jesan said. "I would be clear of the Oather sector and on to my normal duties as quickly as possible."

"I will ensure that the fleet understands that, My Lord. I believe we will be able to deploy the fleet by tomorrow."

"Excellent. See to it," Jesan ordered, closing the connection before any response could be uttered.

The time for talking was over.

Thank the Makers.

▶▶▶

▶ "Navarch?"

Misrem looked up from her work as the adjutant stood in the doorway. "Yes?"

"Orders from the fleet lord," the adjutant told her. "The fleet is to deploy within the day."

The navarch sighed, nodding tiredly. "Understood. Thank you. Dispatch the news to my sub-commanders, Adjutant."

"As you will it, Navarch," the man said before vanishing back out the door.

Misrem stared at the open door for a time, thinking about what the orders meant. She'd been expecting them for some time, of course. Jesan had given her more than enough warning of his plans. Her squadron was well ready to deploy and could be under way within the hour if that was what the orders stated.

This would be their third encroachment into the anomaly's territory, and this time it would not be a follow-up investigation or a probe with intent.

They saw our tails twice. Misrem wondered if that would make the enemy overconfident or not.

She wasn't sure just what they knew of the Empire, whether they had any idea of the size of the Imperial Fleet. It was possible they actually believed that her squadron was a significant section of the Imperial order of battle.

That seemed unbelievable, however. Based on what her people had retrieved from the Oather ship, it seemed like her squadron *would* represent a very sizeable portion of the enemy's order of battle, so it was not impossible that they might make such a mistake.

She didn't know, couldn't imagine really, what it would be like to see an Imperial sector fleet bearing down on you if you thought a single squadron was impressive.

She smirked, imagining looking into her enemies' eyes upon their fatal discovery.

▶ ▶ ▶

▶ The *Piar Cohn* was a fury of activity as the import of the orders sunk in to everyone, but Aymes simply sat confidently in the center of the hurricane and looked bored.

Internally he was anything *but*, but he refused to show that to the crew around him.

The fleet lord's orders were expected, of course, but they still shook everyone to the core. This would be the first major fleet action in . . . well . . . a long time. He'd have to check the records, but it certainly hadn't happened in this sector in living memory, at the very least.

Unfortunately, it won't be much of an action, assuming the intelligence is correct.

That was the real assumption, of course, but even if it was significantly off, Aymes couldn't imagine that the full sector fleet would experience any serious losses. The fleet lord wasn't doing this just to end a minor border conflict. No, the lord was making a point.

To whom, exactly, Aymes had no clue, but someone had clearly attracted the lord's attention, and he could only presume that someone was about to be full of regret.

For Aymes and his *Piar Cohn*, it just meant that this mission would be ending and they'd be on to another shortly enough.

He had some sympathy for the Oathers, more than many of his fellows, but not enough to muster any true care for what was about to fall upon their heads. He did have some level of curiosity about the anomalous species and the changes they'd wrought.

So many things seemed to have spiraled out of control, all beginning with the first time we scanned that seemingly insignificant vessel.

Aymes would take some enjoyment in reading about their technology once the reports began making the rounds of the fleet commanders in a few years. With a little luck, his ship might recover some interesting pieces of the tech before the fighting was over and give him a first-person look before some official from the core worlds of the Empire claimed it all for the empress.

New technology was rare in the Empire, as very few causes had been found to justify devoting many resources for research. No enemy had given the Empire a real fight in longer than he'd been alive, considerably longer in fact. By and large, the powers that be had no perceived reason to waste time improving what there was no need to improve.

Not until recently, that was.

The heavy new armor that had been retrofitted to his ship and many of the other ships of the fleet showed that the Empire was not totally hidebound in its ways.

There was something hopeful there, he supposed, though that might just be wishful thinking.

▶▶▶

▶ The Imperial sector fleet buzzed with action from the least of its ships to the fleet lord's own itself, every vessel a flurry of activity as the final preparations for deployment were made. Stores had to be transhipped, first from the planet to the logistics vessels, and then in turn to each of the combat vessels. Fuel matter was dragged in from the outer belts of the system as well as positioned strategically for them to finish securing their cores on their way out of the system.

Dozens of light cruisers moved to the vanguard as the heavy cruisers provided the core of the formation being built around the Lord's Own Dreadnought at the center. Destroyers filled out the remaining slots.

Working through the local planet's night, the fleet was assembled and ready to move by the time the lord's shuttle arrived and docked with the Lord's Own Dreadnought shortly after local sunrise.

▶▶▶

Lord's Own Dreadnought, *Empress Liann*

▶ Lord Jesan Mich casually looked over the preparations with a practiced look of mild disinterest.

He found that crews generally tended to get nervous if the fleet lord showed too much interest in their actions, so he did the best he could to allay those reactions, as they tended to cause mistakes. He was generally pleased with the progress that had been made.

He moved on, turning his focus from the actions of his own crew to the reports coming in from the other vessels in the local squadrons of the sector fleet.

So far all was well.

They would have to rendezvous with the remaining squadrons, reforming the fleet before they moved on into Priminae territory, but that would be relatively simple.

Dealing with fleet officers always was, especially compared to Imperial politicians, at least in his experience. He didn't have authority to execute Imperial politicians, for one thing, which always tended to keep people's heads pointed in the right direction.

Jesan finally settled into his own station, surrounded by the reports from every ship in the fleet, though with only the squadron commander's ships presented prominently in his displays. He wiped them all away with a gesture, instead bringing up the reports from Captain Aymes and Navarch Misrem.

Those detailed reports had brought this situation more fully to his attention. There was so much in the Oather sector that had caught his eye once the fleet elements stationed there started actually sending real reports back too. Initially, during the Drasin part of the campaign, reports had been sparse and vague. Only after the entire operation descended into chaos and other fleet elements were assigned did anything resembling useful reports make it back to his station.

Someone had been hiding a lot about that operation from the start. *One more problem to deal with after this is all over.*

On the surface of the reports, of course, the anomalous species was utterly fascinating. Any group that could field a stealth vessel as clearly powerful as that ship had been was simply *not* to be underestimated, no matter what anyone else believed. That was, in part, why he was ending this game now rather than give them any more time to prepare their forces for fighting Imperial incursions.

One world. Amazing.

Of course, the intelligence could be faulty, in which case they would be facing more of a fight than he anticipated. Even in that case, though, he should have more than sufficient force to end the conflict once and for all.

Once the battle was won, he would clean up this mess he'd inherited, bottom to top.

Someone had been inexcusably sloppy in setting the action against the Oathers into play. Once he made certain that there wouldn't be any undue consequences to the Empire, he would have to track the guilty party down and ensure that the culprit never had an opportunity to be so sloppy again.

On Her Majesty's orders.

CHAPTER 7

Forge Facility, Ranquil, AEV *Odysseus*

▶ All systems on the Heroic Class starship were now into the green.

In fact, many systems were performing well in excess of their original specifications. This was partly due to improvements that had been made since the big ship had been built, but also had to do with how rushed the construction had been initially.

All of this was great news, but for Eric Weston it was also a headache he didn't need.

The *Odysseus* was fit for duty, physically. Mentally and socially was another story, and he had no idea how he was going to put any of that into his reports. In the short term they were fudging a lot of the official paperwork, using the time to tweak systems in ways they'd wanted to for a while.

That would only keep things running along for a little while, though, and he was running out of places to tweak.

I'm going to have to take her out, at least for a shakedown cruise. Eric knew that, but he really didn't want to push either his crew or his ship at this point.

The crew were still getting used to the presence of Odysseus, and the young entity was nothing if not curious and inquisitive. He had a bad habit of popping up over people's shoulders, asking questions that they didn't know the answer to, and then looking disappointed when they couldn't respond with anything resembling a true answer. He was driving many of the ship's experts, some of the smartest people in their fields, completely around the bend.

The hell of it was that Eric understood why Odysseus was doing just that. The questions that the crew *knew* the answers to, well, so did Odysseus, by definition. So why would he ever bother asking questions someone could answer?

Unfortunately, that led to frustrations even with the people who were inclined to be tolerant of the entity. For Odysseus, Eric supposed it had to be just as frustrating, if from a different angle.

He knew the boy was aware that he wouldn't be getting an answer when he asked the question. The boy . . . entity . . . no, frankly, Eric had to think of him as a boy. Nothing else made sense in his head.

The boy wasn't looking for answers, from what Eric could tell. He was looking for engagement on the question.

Nudging people with queries was his way of shaping thinking in the direction he wanted it to go, and Eric did understand that, but Odysseus needed to figure out a less intrusive way of handling his business or he would drive people away. Already Eric had received multiple transfer requests that, under normal circumstances, he would have approved immediately. As things stood, however, there was nowhere to transfer staff to, so whether people were happy or not was going to have to be a secondary concern for a while. The *Odysseus* needed to be active.

Eric blew out a long breath.

He got up from his desk, straightening his uniform.

We have a little while before the Enterprise *arrives. It's time for a shakedown tour.*

▶ ▶ ▶

▶ Odysseus watched, or perhaps "experienced" was a better word, every person on board the ship as they went about their work. Dreams from the sleepers on board were his idle moments of drifting thoughts, while hundreds of things went through his mind at any given moment.

Some of his feelings were normal, or they would be for a human at least. He knew that much. However, he experienced things in ways no human ever could, but despite all those experiences beyond the human possibilities, he received no answers whenever he might ask the all-important questions.

Why?

How?

Those two were his favorites, as they generally got people thinking about what they knew of a problem and ways to expand that knowledge. Most people, though, just seemed to default to looking something up if they didn't know enough about it.

Odysseus could do *that* himself.

So he asked more questions.

He thought that was what he was supposed to do, but it soon became clear that approach was having a detrimental effect on how crewmembers were viewing his presence. He had gone from a curiosity to some to an annoyance in surprisingly little time. Those who were afraid of him he generally avoided.

The onboard Marines, surprisingly, had the least issues with him despite the fact that he *knew* he had terrified many of them. For some reason, they seemed to consider that a good thing.

Odysseus was in their heads, and even he couldn't figure out what the hell the Marines were thinking.

Unfortunately, while the Marines didn't mind him in their areas and often tried to answer his questions with patience beyond that of almost any other group on the ship, they simply didn't have the information he needed or the tools to acquire it.

The men and women who did, at least potentially, were the *least* patient with him.

The ship had labs, of course. Too many unknowns existed in the galaxy to fly around blindly without field experts to consult when you encountered new phenomena, but those experts, while infinitely patient with their own work, would almost instantly lose their tempers when he distracted them to the lines of thought that interested *him*.

Odysseus was growing frustrated. There were too many questions he wanted answers to, and not even hints of those answers to be seen.

▶▶▶

▶ Steph lounged on the couch in the officers' ready room, eyes vaguely focused on a movie playing on the screen across from him. If someone had asked him, he couldn't have told them what the movie's title was, who was in it, or what it was about. His mind was in a near fugue state, not blank but not thinking either.

A glimmer of motion in the corner of his eye snapped him out of the zone, and he turned his head just enough to recognize the source. He shifted his legs without speaking, and Milla dropped casually into the place beside him as he rocked upright.

"Tough day?" he asked, noting that she looked tired.

The Priminae officer spread her fingers casually, playing off the question. "We went over all the ship's hardware locks and installed a few new ones as per the capitaine's orders. There was no need for the first part, and the second part was difficult."

"Ah," Steph said, understanding.

He'd had to supervise a similar process in his department, securing the ship's helm and navigation from being overridden by the computer without the explicit permission of the crew. Not exactly something that had been a high priority before, though they did have hardware kill switches, of course.

Concerns over just what the *Odysseus* could do had caused some serious rethinks concerning how the systems were designed. Certainly, it would have been nice to figure out how to intercept the commands that the young intelligence had issued without their knowledge in their last fight. Afterward, of course, it would have been suicide to hit the kill switches, as they'd have been left drifting at high speed right into an enemy formation.

His main problem with the hardware lock solution was that he didn't think it would work. In a fight, seconds mattered, and there was no possible way they'd be able to second-guess the computers in those moments.

So, for the moment at least, Steph was more interested in making sure that Diss knew better than to mess with his board.

"Get everything done?" he asked, leaning back as he glanced at the small, slim woman sitting beside him.

"All new systems were installed and tested, Stephan," Milla said, her accent coming out more than usual from the fatigue, he assumed. She yawned. "But it took all night."

Steph winced.

Milla was in charge of the *Odysseus'* weapons, which were literally everywhere on the ship. He imagined that she must have been running all over the vessel to get hardware circuits installed and tested in every single weapon system. The primaries were all run through the bridge, of course, and had been installed from the start, but it seemed paranoia was the name of the day.

"Okay, come on, time to get you some sleep," he said, noticing that she was almost, though not quite, nodding off right there in the ready room.

He got up, gesturing to her with one hand. "When are you on duty next?"

Milla looked around blearily, noting the time on the closest monitor. "Next shift. Two hours."

"Oh hell no! You've been running ragged since we started the repairs. I'll let your department know you're out for a full shift."

"What? No. I have things left . . . ," Milla protested as Steph reached down and pulled her up to her feet.

"Milla, we've done the refit," he said seriously. "We've just been marking time until the skipper can figure out what to do about Diss."

Milla sighed. "I know, but there's always so much to do."

"Welcome to a warship," Steph said. "There's nothing here that isn't in constant need of babying to keep it running properly, the crew included. We're the toughest, baddest babies in the galaxy. It's a paradox of combat, Milla, but if you let it, a ship like this will eat you alive. And I'm talking about the ones that aren't apparently sentient."

He guided her out of the ready room, waving to the few others who had been watching with some amusement, and headed toward the habitat section.

"I need to go change the roster," Milla protested, moving toward the command deck.

Steph rolled his eyes. "Hey Diss!"

Milla jumped slightly as a small figure in bronze armor appeared, marching alongside them.

"Yes Steph?" the boy asked, a hand casually on the sword he wore.

"Do me a favor, will you? You can access the computer records, right? Mark Milla here as off duty until the next cycle."

Milla looked between Steph and the boy known as Odysseus with wide eyes, blinking rapidly.

Odysseus nodded firmly. "I will see to it."

"Thanks," Steph said as the boy vanished, maintaining lockstep with them even as he faded out. "See? No problem."

"You ask him to do minor tasks?" Milla asked, somewhat incredulous. "Stephan! He is an amazing example of the universe!"

"He is a preteen on a warship," Steph said dryly. "That means he gets to play gopher until he learns the ropes, and probably even after."

"But . . ."

"I was the kid in a military unit once," Steph said as they walked into the habitat section. "I learned more just running errands for people like Raze than I ever did in school. Whatever else he is, Diss is thinking and expressing himself as a child right now, so I'm going to treat him as one. He's curious and he's bored, and that's not a good combination in any normal child."

"Odysseus is not some child, running around the ship with nothing to do, Stephan," Milla blurted, eyes wide. "He is a luminous example of what the universe can produce. He is incredible, a ship made sentient! You cannot treat him like some . . . some errand boy!"

"Oh yeah? Watch me," Steph said, pointing ahead of them. "Your quarters."

Milla ignored his gesture, not looking remotely as tired as she had been. "Do not change the subject, Stephan! This cannot be how you interact with someone so special as Odysseus!"

"How do you interact with him?" Steph asked.

Milla reddened slightly. "I . . . I have not."

"Why not?"

"It would not be so polite to . . . I . . . ," Milla stammered slightly. "He should not be bothered by such trivialities!"

"Why not? He's not doing anything right now, and it's our home as much as his," Steph said. "If he was busy with important work, like you've been, I'd agree. He isn't, however. He's a child, looking to find his way, and he doesn't have all that many options right now. He's as close to warrior born as anyone I've ever seen, and that's where his future lies whether he likes it or not. The *Odysseus* is going back into battle, Milla. This delay is just the admiral and the commodore refusing to see the obvious, and that means Diss is going to be with us in the next fight. Don't you think you should get to know him before that happens?"

Milla stared at him for a moment, her jaw open but no sound coming out. Steph gave her time; then, when no retort was forthcoming, he guided her hand to the door release to her quarters and let the portal pivot open.

"Think about it," he suggested, gesturing to the room, "but try to get some sleep."

She slowly stepped into her room, letting the door close behind her, and he turned and walked away down the corridor. He was almost out of the habitat section when he felt a presence at his side.

"Hey Diss," he said without glancing to the side. "You get the roster changed?"

"Of course," Odysseus answered. "I did it before I left you."

Steph chuckled. "Should have realized that."

"She doesn't think of me the same way you do," Odysseus said, not surprising Steph with the segue in the slightest. "Not many of them do."

"They don't have to," Steph told him. "You're not a kid, Diss. You just choose to act like one right now. But a kid can't be in a hundred places at once, can't change the roster before I finish asking for the favor. A kid doesn't know everything you know, can't do a tenth of what you can. You can find a different balance with every single person here, and you probably should."

"Why?"

Steph chuckled again, amused by the almost childish tone and the very childlike question the entity asked him.

"Because you can," Steph answered simply.

He could see the boy getting ready to ask why again but pause as he realized that Steph had maneuvered the answer such that he had worked out the answer himself, which caused the entity disguised as a boy to scowl at the fighter pilot from under the ancient Greek helmet.

"You do that on purpose," Odysseus practically pouted.

"Yes I do," Steph said. "You can enjoy driving the geeks as crazy as you like, but don't play those games with me. I *will* figure out ways to make you regret it."

"You'll try."

Steph grinned, slapping the boy on his armored shoulder. "Now you're thinking like a combat-ready badass, Diss."

▶▶▶

▶ Milla lay down in the bed that took up the center of her quarters, staring at the ceiling.

She'd been so damn tired only a few minutes ago, and now all she could feel was a growing ire at Steph for treating this opportunity as cavalierly as he was. How that infuriating man could look upon something as *incredible* as the Odysseus entity as a mere child, and then proceed to treat it like some errand boy . . . The reasoning escaped her.

The idea of such a vastly different intellect was one of the earliest dreams she could remember, that somewhere in the depths of the universe there could be other intelligent beings, different life. Her people had never discovered any, not as far back as their records went.

Now, right here, there *was* such a being, and that insufferable man, Stephan, insisted on treating it like a child.

How horribly frustrating.

She twisted in the bed, her mind unwilling to give up the train of thought it was pursuing, made all the more frustrating by the fact that she knew Odysseus was following her every thought.

She tried to force her mind to think about anything else, closing her eyes, finally managing to relax enough so that her fatigue took over and she drifted off.

▶▶▶

▶ Miram Heath raised her eyebrows as she read the brief she'd just received from the commodore, then looked up at him. "Are you certain about this, sir?"

"Hanging around here is just letting people stew and dig themselves in deeper," Eric said. "The longer we let that happen, the more people will let negative thoughts take over. I want everyone working, thinking about working, or sleeping. No more of this sitting around, dwelling on ghosts, and whatever else they've been doing."

Commander Heath nodded. "Understood, sir. I'll issue the orders. We'll be under way as soon as the Forge authorizes out transit through the corona."

"Good, see to it."

Miram saluted quickly and departed, leaving Eric standing in what was normally the squadron command station. He supposed he should shift to the ship's command deck shortly, but he was too used to issuing orders from where he was.

The Enterprise *will be here soon enough anyway I suppose.*

Damned if he wasn't getting used to the whole squadron command thing again, though it wasn't quite the same as the Archangels.

Eric turned his attention back to the computer, opening up all the files they had on the Imperials, their ships, and their tactics. The files were far from complete and in fact were far from adequate in his opinion.

So far, they'd faced what he believed were a couple of Imperial probes in force.

That was, they'd deployed enough force to be taken seriously, but hadn't really tried to take any ground. They were fishing for information, and he had to assume that they'd acquired it. They could possibly deploy a third probe in force, but Eric knew that sooner or later the Empire was going to make its real play.

And he was almost certain that the enemy had better intel than he had. That made any plans he might make rather open to frequent and abusive visits from Mr. Murphy. Hell, he might as well invite the old bastard onto the bridge and roll out the red carpet for him in the process.

The admiral will have redeployed the Prometheus Rogues by now, but I can't count on them. They have their own mission to fulfill, Eric thought grimly. *Roberts will follow his orders to the letter, and I know we can count on the Priminae, but our order of battle is barely able to deal with a couple of their probes.*

That was the crux of the situation.

Ships.

Eric had men to call on. The finest he'd known and more than capable of overcoming anything thrown at them. He had plenty of territory to give up if he needed to. He could fall back for light-years, sacrificing space to draw the enemy into an extended logistical chain.

What he didn't have was ships.

Earth had five Heroics.

He was aware that the Solar Forge wasn't ready to build more anytime soon, so the Terran order of battle was five Heroics. Not a single one more.

The Priminac order of battle had grown significantly, and from what he'd been informed they now had fifteen, with three more in various construction phases. Still, that left them with no more than twenty Heroics to cover the Priminae core worlds and Earth.

He wasn't sure what the current count of Rogues was, but the last numbers he had indicated that they had at least thirty of the smaller ships. Unfortunately, ten were assigned to Prometheus, and those ships would be doing a new job that wouldn't leave them at his disposal.

Since another ten were assigned permanently to Solar Defense, along with two Heroics, he couldn't count those either unless things went horribly wrong, which honestly meant that he was likely to be deploying those ships in combat before this was all over.

Assuming we make it that far.

He knew they didn't have enough ships to defend against what the Empire was likely to send after them, what they would *certainly* send, sooner or later.

Eric had been on the wrong side of bad odds more than once in his career. The place was starting to feel like home.

And to think, I wanted to retire after the war. What the hell would I have done as a retiree?

CHAPTER 8

AEV *Autolycus,* Deep Black

▶ Morgan stood the watch, looking out at the expanse beyond the observation screens.

They were in deep space, no star around them for light-years. It wasn't a comfortable place to be, he had found since taking command of his lovely *King of Thieves.* Normally the view was distorted by the warp fields and was beautiful in its own way but unnatural enough to be little more than a fancy screen saver.

With warp drives active, the color shift from the Doppler effect, combined with the high-energy particles trapped in their fields, actually made it look like the starfield was streaking around them. The scene was almost like the old science-fiction films, entirely illusory in nature.

The Prometheus Rogues were not warping at the moment, however, and despite the fact that they were bombing through interstellar space at almost eighty percent the speed of light, nothing out there was moving.

The stars weren't even flickering.

Somehow that felt far less real than the illusion of motion created by the warp fields.

"Sir?"

Morgan didn't turn around. He just continued to drift and stare out at the depths beyond the ship. "What is it, Daiyu?"

Commander Li drifted up beside him. "No contacts as of yet, sir."

"Well, that's not surprising. We're casting a wide net, but no one has any idea when our targets will show up."

"Yes sir."

"Worried, Commander?" Morgan asked, hearing something in her voice.

"Concerned. We could be reinforcing the others. It doesn't take this many ships to stand a sentry watch."

"We could. However, if another ten Rogues would make that much difference, then we've vastly misinterpreted the intelligence we've been gathering. Our mission may be critical, however, both in warning the others of what's coming and . . . other things."

Daiyu looked at him sharply. "Other things?"

"Classified, Commander. Admiral Gracen has a plan for us. Leave it at that."

She nodded slowly. "Yes Captain."

▶▶▶

AEV *Dericourts,* Deep Black

▶ Captain Jackson of the *Henri Dericourts* was casually sucking his coffee from a military issue "sippy cup," no longer noticing the loss of dignity he had originally felt when first presented with the zero-gravity cup. The coffee still tasted as bad and still got too cold too fast for his taste, but he was always amazed over what he could get used to.

He was admiring the static starscape beyond the ship as he relaxed in a casual float, a snack bar drifting by his head as he kept one eye on a projected repeater view of the ship's scanner station off to his left.

The Prometheus Rogues had been drifting through interstellar space for the past two days. Most people would consider traveling at eighty percent the speed of light to be moving pretty quickly, but for a Rogue it was downright pedestrian.

He reached for the snack bar just as the ship's proximity alarm went off. He twisted in space to see what the hell was sending alarms off around him. Grabbing a hand grip, he pulled himself in toward the display repeater, leaning in as close as he could and staring at the screen.

What the hell is that? I've never seen a space-warp that size. Is that a black hole?

Jackson reached up and flipped a few switches. "All hands, Jackson. Sounding general quarters."

The alarm shifted from generic mode to general quarters, calling the crew to duty as he pushed off the wall and flew toward the hatch that would take him down to the bridge.

His first officer, Commander Orson, was waiting for him by the time he slid into command.

"What do we have?" Jackson demanded, noting that the key stations were manned and people were already working furiously.

"Massive space-time warp, sir," Orson said, not looking up.

"What do we have that I couldn't have figured out on my own?" he growled in response.

"Still differentiating targets, sir."

"Targets? It's not a single warp?" he asked. *Well, there goes the black hole idea.*

"That's a big negative," Orson answered, face buried in his station. "We're showing a *lot* of signals, clustered so tight they look like one big signal. They're moving fast too, hundred times light, maybe hundred fifty."

"Give me vectors!" Jackson snapped. "And start backtracking them on light-speed imagers! I want to know where they're going and where the hell they came from. Put this over the network, right now. Right the hell now! This is what we've been waiting for."

I wish it was a black hole, damn it.

▶▶▶

AEV *Autolycus*

▶ Morgan swung himself into the command station and pulled the straps over his shoulders, locking himself into place as others poured onto the bridge of the *Auto* and did the same.

"Do we have numbers yet?" he demanded.

"Negative, sir," Daiyu Li responded. "Targets have not entered visual range, and they're flying too close formation for our gravity scanners to pick out individual signals. Estimate . . . a hundred ships, sir."

Morgan paled. "A hundred?"

"Give or take," his first officer responded with a gesture of uncertainty. "It depends wildly on what sort of vessels are in this formation. Our estimate is based on the squadron formation of the last two Imperial formations, which leaned heavily to cruisers with some destroyer-level support."

"Log it all," Morgan ordered, "and send to all ships in the net, run silent. No unnecessary maneuvering. Do we have anybody in their path?"

Li shook her head. "Not such that it would be noticed."

"Good," Morgan replied, though he'd have been surprised if they had.

Space was a massive, well, space. The odds of their having any ships directly in the path of the Imperial vessels were incredibly long, even considering that they'd arrayed themselves along the likely approach paths based on the earlier probes.

"All ships are to maintain passive scans only," he ordered. "I want every detail we can grab as their light reaches us, but in the meantime keep working on getting actual numbers from the space-warp. Every piece of intel is going to mean life or death for some poor bastard in the order of battle when the time comes. Let's get them everything we possibly can."

"Aye aye, Captain."

▶▶▶

Imperial Formation: Lord's Own Dreadnought, *Empress Liann*

▶ "My Lord, we're approaching the outer limits of Oather-claimed territory."

"Thank you, Captain," Jesan said as he walked around the console and looked at the large display of the projected stars ahead of them. "Any signs of contact yet?"

"No, My Lord. No ships have been detected," the captain of the *Liann* responded. "We've been scanning for any disturbances since shortly after we left Imperial-claimed space."

Jesan frowned. "The anomalous species masks their ships better than that, Captain. Maintain visual scans as well."

The captain nodded. "We have, My Lord, however nothing has shown there either. If there are any ships out in the abyss, then they are cloaked as well as running without any drives."

Jesan was well aware that was possible as well, but there was little he could do about it he supposed. With a force the size of the sector fleet, they would be unable to sneak up on any moderately competent enemy.

"Very good, Captain. Continue with the plan," he ordered. "Inform me when we enter Oather territory."

"Yes, My Lord."

The captain left him, returning to his duties, while Jesan examined the star charts before him in detail, not even remotely for the first time.

The Oathers hadn't spread out as much as one might have expected, given the time since they'd broken away from the early Empire. A few dozen star systems were under their control, most of which were now in tatters thanks to the Drasin. There was good reason for the lack of systems under Oather control; even the Empire had grown slowly past a certain point.

Among other reasons, communications at the distances involved were problematic, even with faster-than-light signalling. The Empire only annexed what territory it was certain could be controlled and integrated into Imperial culture. Expanding beyond the ability to maintain that cultural link would merely encourage splinter groups to form, which would require fleet intervention and generally became a massive hassle.

So the Empire only allowed that sort of situation to happen on rare occasion, primarily to maintain training and readiness among the fleet, but also to occasionally expend munitions as a boost to the Imperial core worlds' economies. Building new weapons kept the people busy and believing that they were earning their keep. So few of them realized that their jobs could have been better completed by automated factories.

Another revolt was brewing, this time closer to the core worlds and with the empress' permission, that would be allowed to begin shortly after the issue with the Oathers was dealt with. Close enough to remind the fools of the lower classes to wave their flags and stop grumbling about how much money was spent on fleet operations.

The revolt would make for good training, assuming this situation with the Oathers was resolved as quickly as he expected. If not, well then, this would be excellent training as well.

▶▶▶

▶ Navarch Misrem looked at the clear scopes being repeated to her command station, a hint of trepidation filling her as they approached the Oather sector.

"Are you alright, Navarch?" her adjutant asked softly, his voice pitched low enough that only she could hear it.

"I'm fine," Misrem responded calmly. "I'm just wondering where they are."

"They, Navarch?"

"The enemy. They're out there. I can feel them."

The adjutant frowned, examining the screens. "Nothing is on the screens, Navarch."

Misrem smiled thinly. "I am aware of that, yes. Nonetheless, they're out there. The enemy has the capacity to hide from our scanners, both gravity and visual . . . and that's inside a star system, when they have a few light-hours at most to play in. Out here they have *light-years*. The pure chance it would require to locate them in deep space isn't worth thinking on. No, unless they're complete fools, and they are not, then they're observing us even now."

"I see . . ." The adjutant looked concerned. "Should we do something?"

"No. Let them watch," Misrem said grimly. "If our intelligence is correct, it will do them little good, and likely depress morale if anything."

"And if it is not correct?"

"Well, then we're in for a real fight, aren't we?" Misrem asked, laughing harshly. "Still, if they show significantly more force than we expect, the fleet lord can withdraw and call up the Imperial Home Fleet. There is no possible way that our information is so faulty that they have enough forces to survive that much power."

"Ah, I see."

Do you? Misrem wondered, glancing at the adjutant.

She rather doubted that he did, but that was another irrelevance. Her adjutant was ostensibly there to assist her, but since he'd been assigned after she had lost her ship in Oather space, she suspected that he was there to keep a close eye on her.

That was fine. She'd expected as much to happen. Any competent fleet commander would. As this one seemed competent, which was more than she'd come to expect, she was fine with the assignment, not that it would matter if she weren't.

In either case, the die was cast, and they would all soon see how things turned out.

While she was confident that the fleet lord had sufficient power assembled to annihilate anything the Oathers and their allies could put before them, Misrem suspected that the fighting would be more intense than the Imperial forces were used to dealing with.

Whatever else these people are, they are far from Imperial patsies pretending to be revolutionaries.

▶▶▶

▶ "Entering the outer limits of Oather-controlled space, Fleet Lord."

"Thank you, Captain."

Jesan didn't look over to where the captain was standing, his eyes focused on the projected display of the stars before them.

They had officially crossed over into the section of space that demarked where the Empire would draw the line between unclaimed and claimed territory. That was just a political divide, however, a place to draw lines on projection maps, and was relatively meaningless.

So while they were officially within Oather territory, he doubted that they'd see anything in terms of resistance until they entered one of the star systems, and likely not one of the less-populated ones either.

Still, they were now officially in enemy territory.

"Signal all ships. We are on combat alert until further notice," he ordered.

"Yes, My Lord."

A soft alarm sounded in the distance, one that he knew would be repeated on every vessel in his fleet.

The sound of the Empire at war.

Jesan smiled. It was a sound he loved to hear.

Whoever you are, he thought, looking at the stars laid out before him, *thank you for this.*

▶▶▶

AEV *Autolycus*

▶ "Bold as brass," Morgan said as they watched the formation fly by on visuals.

The ships had passed them hours ago, of course, but the light was only then reaching the forces of Operation Prometheus. Where the gravity scanners had been unable to pick out individual signatures, the light-speed scanners had no such problem.

"I would say that they have reason to be," Commander Li said, sounding a little numb.

"What's the final count?" Morgan asked, blowing out a breath of air.

"Not available yet. At least four hundred and twenty-three so far. The computers are having difficulty getting an accurate count on visual alone. Even in clean formation, they're moving enough to throw off the software."

"Great."

He supposed a fully accurate count didn't matter all that much. A hundred ships seemed like overkill compared to the forces Morgan knew Earth and the Priminae could muster. Four hundred was the end of the war.

"We should get a more precise count once we can run comparison analysis against all the different angles from the Prometheus Rogues," Li said, examining the data. "There are at least eight ships in that formation larger than anything we've ever seen. They make Heroics look very small, Captain."

"I can see that."

The mass figures that were showing on Morgan's station were, frankly, terrifying.

"The question is, are they battleships or carriers?" he wondered, examining the profiles.

"Battleships," Li answered. "There are no significant bays I can see that would allow them to launch fighters, and I notice no signs of their Parasite nodules on the larger vessels."

"True. Run hyperspectral analysis on them and make that a priority," he ordered. "We have data and analysis on most of the ship types I'm seeing, but those big bastards are another story. I want something to transmit back to the admiral."

"Yes sir."

Morgan didn't know if the transmittal would matter, ultimately. The force he was looking at was beyond anything they'd planned for. There was no way the available ships would be enough to hold back the fleet they'd just scanned. The resources needed to build and maintain a force like he was seeing was beyond Earth's current levels entirely, and he wasn't sure if the Priminae could pull off such a feat either despite their considerably more advanced technology and wider access to resources.

After everything he'd seen the Earth accomplish, and face, with the Drasin, Morgan found this to be a bitter realization.

"Make sure they're well past us," he ordered, "then stand by to warp space."

"Yes Captain."

"Send the coded signals as soon as we have initial analysis," he stated. "For what it's worth, let the fleet know what's coming their way."

CHAPTER 9

AEV *Enterprise,* Sol System

▶ "Black!"

Commander Alexandra Black looked up from where she was working, spotting Chief Corrin as the other woman approached across the deck of the *Enterprise*'s main flight control area. The steady clang of her magnetic boots was heard more sharply as she got closer.

"What is it, Chief?" Black asked as she straightened up from the fighter's diagnostic access panel, grabbing a rag to wipe her hands clean.

Everything was flightworthy, of course. Her deck crew were damned good at their jobs, but Alexandra still preferred to do a final once-over before she strapped the SF-101 Vorpal to her back and trusted her life to the conglomeration of tech.

"Word just filtered down," Corrin said, coming to a stop beside the ungainly looking fighter. "We're going on alert, deployment imminent."

Black stiffened, eyes widening.

That was news to her, and technically she really should have heard about it before Corrin, but she was well aware that the NCO network had a way of learning things before anyone else possibly could.

"Where the hell are we deploying to?" she asked, mind racing.

The Empire.

It pretty much had to be the Empire, as best she knew. Unless the Drasin had shown up again—God forbid those *things* ever see the light of Sol again—the Empire was the only current threat on the board.

"Details are light," Corrin admitted, "but the deployment order is expected to come down the chain within the hour."

Alexandra flipped the access panel shut and twisted the catch over to lock it into place.

"We're ready," she said.

"Good news bad news on that," Corrin said.

"What's the good news?"

"We're getting another five squadrons of Vorpals and pilots to fill out the wing. So we won't be light anymore."

That was good news, Alexandra supposed.

"And the bad?"

"They're all fresh."

Alexandra grimaced, almost in pain. "Right before a deployment?"

"Yes ma'am."

"I'll speak with the CAG. We'll get them indoctrinated as quickly as we can," Alexandra said, more to herself than to the chief. "If this is a real deployment, the last thing we need is the level of fumbling bullshit that will be caused by new blood in the teams. Why the hell can't they send us people *before* the galaxy is about to end?"

"That would be too smart, ma'am."

There was some truth in that statement.

▶▶▶

▶ Victor James was an unassuming man in most environments he might be found in. The sort people tended to overlook in a crowd, with just a few notable exceptions. The most notable of those was the bridge of his command, where he brooked no questioning that he was the center of the universe.

The AEV *Enterprise* was the third, and last, Odyssey Class ship ever constructed by Earth's infrastructure before it was all but annihilated during the Drasin invasion. Named after the second ship of the class, which had been sacrificed along with her captain and some significant number of her crew, his ship had been obsolete before she was commissioned. With the new Rogue and Heroic Class vessels taking center stage, the *Enterprise* had been relegated back to Sol System patrol. A largely useless waste of resources for a ship that had been conceived as a carrier and force projection vessel, but even he had to admit in his darker moments that there was a long way between the capabilities of his baby and the *Odysseus*.

Now, however, he was looking at orders to move his ship to full alert status, prior to an expected deployment out of the system.

That meant something big and bad was coming down the pipe, he had no doubt.

"Commander . . ." James walked across the lightly curved deck of the bridge to where Commander Bride was standing watch. "Begin issuing orders to have the crew work up to deployment levels."

Bride looked over at him quizzically, but nodded curtly. "Yes sir."

"We'll be receiving new squadrons of Vorpals over the next two days," James went on. "Have the deck crews make space and start an inventory check. Make sure we can handle the repairs and maintenance for an extended deployment."

The quizzical look vanished, replaced by one of understanding, concern, and a hint of excitement as Bride recognized the depth of meaning in those orders. Working the crew up to deployment levels was just training, but resupply, reinforcements, and checking logistics meant a lot more.

"The Empire, sir?" Bride asked softly, pitching his voice to keep from being heard.

"Most likely," James responded in kind. "No confirmation yet. But when Gracen takes an emergency trip out on a fast courier and turns around and blasts back less than a week later, and we start getting orders like this? It's a good bet, Commander."

"Not to sound like I don't want a deployment," Bride said, "but are they *insane*? There's no way we're going toe to toe with one of those monster cruisers we've been briefed on."

James was noncommittal. "I think it's a sign that something bad is coming down the pipe, but I'm not sure I agree with you entirely. They're big bruisers, yes, but Weston already proved that you can wreak havoc on the big boys with an Odyssey Class ship."

"The Imperials aren't as simpleminded as the Drasin," Bride countered. "If they were, we wouldn't be needed in the first place."

James had to unhappily concede that as truth. The current fleet of Heroic and Rogue Class ships could utterly annihilate a massive armada of Drasin-level opponents. Ordering the deployment of the *Enterprise*, given the current administrative investment in modern doctrine beliefs, was a sign that the admiral was just short of panicking.

He didn't think anything would make Admiral Gracen panic, but she had to be as close as she got at the moment, and the upper brass and politicians had to be worse for them to suddenly shift doctrine and deploy the *Big E*.

"We'll see how bad things are, sooner or later," James said. "In the meantime, I'm just looking forward to getting the *E* out into the black again. We've been sun-bound too damn long."

Bride nodded. "Amen to that."

▶▶▶

Station Unity One, Earth Orbit

▶ "This is *madness!*"

"Admiral . . ." Amanda Gracen spoke in cool tones, carefully and intentionally not leaning away from the blustering fool in her face.

"The universe is mad. Live with it, or die. I don't care which, just stay out of my way."

The red-faced admiral reddened even further, making Gracen wonder idly if he were about to have a stroke. "You cannot be serious. You're deploying part of our Home Fleet, including the *Enterprise*? That's sending men off to useless deaths!"

"What Admiral Harrison is trying to say," Congressman Jerimiah said in a thankfully calmer tone, "is that it would seem to make more sense to keep the Home Fleet intact, and focus our strength here at home."

"Congressman . . ." Gracen half turned. "If I thought I had the political pull, I would strip the cupboards bare here and send *everything* we had. I would much rather fight critical battles as far away from Earth as humanly possible."

"However, you don't even know if there is an Imperial Fleet on the way," the congressman said smoothly.

"Of course there is," Gracen said with a hint of amused derision. "What I don't know is when they'll arrive."

"That is pure guesswork!" the admiral roared, frustration palpably oozing off him.

"No, it is a well-educated projection. They're coming, Admiral, Congressman," she said firmly. "If you want to hide in the sand, feel free to do so. I have the authority and political backing to do what I've ordered. If I thought I could convince you, I would have ordered much more, I assure you."

"You burned a lot of your favors on this, Admiral," Congressman Jerimiah said. "If you're wrong, I'll see you replaced."

"If I'm wrong, I'll happily retire secure in the knowledge that the world didn't end on my watch," Gracen said flatly. "In the meantime, you both need to—"

"Admiral Gracen, ma'am!"

She cut off her statement as she turned to the ensign who'd come rushing in. For a young officer to interrupt an admiral in midspeech, she knew something was wrong.

"What is it, Ensign?"

"Transition signal from the *Autolycus*, ma'am," the young officer said, red in the face as she looked at the obviously angry men and Gracen. "It's not detailed, but you need to see this."

Gracen extended her hand, accepting the display flimsy and looking it over briefly.

"Well, gentlemen," she said, taking no satisfaction at all in her next words despite the content, "it would seem that I won't be retiring just yet."

"What?" Congressman Jerimiah looked confused, while the admiral at his side paled and took a stumbling step back. "What does that mean?"

"How many?" the admiral asked.

"More than we can handle," Gracen said candidly, her tone stoic. "Many times more than we can handle."

She handed the flimsy to the man without any further words, letting him glance over the report.

The FTL transmissions from ships under way were, by necessity, of extremely limited space, so the words were few but the meanings were manifold.

"My God," the admiral breathed out. "This is . . ."

"Let's just hope we can keep the fighting a long way from here," Gracen said firmly.

"What are you two talking about?"

"Congressman . . ." The now very pale admiral took his arm as he handed back the flimsy, then walked the congressman away. "Let's allow Admiral Gracen to do her work. We'll discuss this elsewhere."

Gracen watched them go with a hint of satisfaction that was almost buried by the enormity of what she had just read.

We knew that we were likely outmassed, if not outclassed, but by this much?

She *had* to keep the fighting as far from Earth as she possibly could. The Kardashev construction was nowhere near ready for use, still being early in the self-replicating phase. If the Empire got to Earth, no matter how many of the Home Fleet she kept close, they would be overwhelmed.

Gracen walked around her desk, taking a seat and opening a file.

Really hoped not to pin everything on Prometheus. It's a long shot . . . pun unintended, Gracen thought.

"Ensign," she called, getting the attention of the young officer who had waited by her door.

"Yes ma'am?"

"Signal Prometheus," she ordered. "I want status updates. We need that system online, immediately."

"Yes ma'am!"

▶▶▶

AEV *Enterprise*

▶ As often happened, by the time the official orders had been cut, everyone already knew more or less what was happening. You just couldn't move thousands of tons of ship and people without giving them some idea of what was coming. Deciphering the meaning behind orders was a game every serviceman played, and experienced people were often decidedly *good* at.

None of the details had reached the crew of the *Big E* certainly. Operational security in the Black Navy wasn't *that* bad, but everyone had a decent idea of where things were heading.

James looked over the brief orders he'd been issued and just managed to suppress a sigh.

The *Enterprise* had been issued orders to place itself under the command of Commodore Weston. Not exactly James' ideal choice for a commanding officer, if given his druthers. By all measures, Weston was a capable tactician—that was beyond question. He did tend to be a little bit of a show-off, however, and James had never much liked the man's strategic acumen.

None of that mattered. Orders were orders.

"Commander Bride . . ." He walked over to the commander's station. "How are our logistics?"

"We're ready for an extended deployment, sir," Bride answered. "However, the supply train ships are a bit of a different story."

James grimaced.

That didn't surprise him as much as it should. Logistics was a touchy beast at the best of times, and dealing with new fleet ship classes, largely untested crews, and the god-awful problems of resupply en route while in space were making for rather larger than normal problems.

"On the bright side, it looks like the admiral has been able to shake loose a few more BSV Class ships," Bride said through pursed lips. "However, we still don't have nearly enough equipped with transition drives. Most of them are running Alcubierre drives, staffed by block engineers."

"We'll make do," James said firmly. "It's over our pay grade anyway. When we get to Ranquil we'll drop that in the commodore's lap. It's his job to figure out."

Bride laughed dryly. "You really don't like the man much, do you?"

"Wouldn't matter if I did," James replied in kind. "But I have no quarrels with him. I just think he's a little too enamored with his high-profile lifestyle."

Bride shrugged. "Maybe. At any rate, with those new BSV Class ships, that brings our supply and logistical capability up to almost fifty ships. I have to admit I didn't even know we had that many ships of any type, let alone these."

"They refurbished a lot of the old tankers as they could, and the old slips that had been used to build ships before the Heroic Class became standard are still capable of military constructions. So between us and the Block we can turn out smaller, obsolete, and less high-profile hulls fairly quickly," James said.

He didn't mention that the *Enterprise* herself had come from one of those slips and was now considered to be one of the smaller, obsolete, and less high-profile hulls herself.

He looked away from the commander and over to the crew standing at their stations on the bridge, all of them among the best the Earth and Confederation had to offer.

Obsolete my ass.

▶▶▶

▶ Alexandra Black pushed her hair off her sweat-slicked forehead, feeling as filthy as the rest of her under the jumpsuit that clung as she moved. She'd pulled all the pilots in her flight and made sure every one of them had checked out the aviation capabilities of their birds, and when that was done she'd dropped every Vorpal in the squad into sim-mode and started flight-training drills.

She would have preferred some more deep space-time, but that wasn't going to happen while they were sitting on a deployment order, so sim-time would have to do.

"Lieutenant Commander . . ." The CAG, Commander Hawkins, looked up as she stomped up to him in her magnetic boots. "Everything go well?"

"My squadron is combat ready," Alexandra confirmed confidently.

"Good. I want you to handle indoc for a couple of the new squadrons we're picking up. We won't have long to get them up to speed, but let's do what we can."

"Of course, sir."

Integrating new squadrons into their flight wing was going to be a rough job. Most of the best experienced pilots had moved on to other duties, which meant that the majority of those she was likely to be getting would be low-hour rookies with minimal deep-space hours in their jackets.

"I know it sucks, Alex," Hawkins told her, "but better to iron out what we can now than let attrition do it for us."

"I know, Jake. Just can't help but wince at the thought of the work, is all."

"You and me both, sister." The CAG laughed. "Don't sweat it. You've got a handle on this, and I'll be taking what weight I can off those of you I have running indoc, but we're all going to be crushed for time, make no mistake."

"Roger that, sir."

She knew he wasn't joking by any means. With a deployment order imminent, everyone was about to be hammering their heads against the hull, trying to make time appear from nowhere.

If only there was a way to store the time we waste when we're in stand-down and bring it out at moments like these, she thought.

If anyone could figure out how to make that sort of "time bank," Alexandra had no doubt that she or he would be venerated as the Patron Saint of Military Personnel for all time left to come.

"I'm on it, sir."

"Never a doubt, Lieutenant Commander."

CHAPTER 10

AEV *Odysseus,* Forge Facility, Ranquil System

▶ Solar plasma clung to the space-time field of the *Odysseus* as the big ship exploded out of the stellar corona and into open space beyond the Ranquil primary.

"All systems check, Commodore."

Eric expected nothing less.

In terms of basic maintenance, the *Odysseus* was as ready to fight as the day she'd sailed out of the Forge for the first time. It was crew readiness he was a little concerned about, but he'd sweat the bullshit out of them if he had to.

Damn few problems can't be cured by exhaustion, sleep, or a judicious ass kicking.

He hoped he wouldn't have to resort to the third option, though Eric was far from being above such things if that was what it took to get the job done. He'd seen too much over the years, and if it cost him his career to keep his people living, he was willing to take the chance. The only matter that took higher priority was accomplishing the mission, and even then he'd sometimes sacrifice a mission if it meant saving his people. Such decisions depended very much on the importance of the mission.

The current one, well, there was no higher-value mission. Ever.

He just didn't know if the victory conditions would be possible to meet.

"Commodore," Miram said, gesturing him over. "You're going to want to see this."

"What is it, Commander?"

"Ranquil Command just relayed this from EARTHCOM. It's a cipher transmit from the *Auto*." Miram looked evenly at him, shaking her head. "Not good news, sir."

"Let's see it." Eric reached out to pull the screen in his direction as he leaned over.

"The enemy fleet."

Miram nearly jumped out of her skin as she and Eric twisted in place to glare at the slight form of the armored boy who had appeared between them like an apparition.

"Don't *do* that, Odysseus!" Miram hissed, clutching at her chest.

"Apologies. I forget."

Eric glowered at the boy, knowing damn well that was bullshit.

"Attention!" he barked, causing Odysseus to snap straight reflexively.

Knowing how the boy's thoughts were partially formed by the crew of the *Odysseus* made understanding him slightly easier.

"Is that how you approach your CO?" Eric growled.

"No sir!" the boy squeaked out in a voice that was almost, though not quite, cracking like a teenager going through changes. "Sorry sir."

"You had better be. Or I will find a way to show you the meaning of real discipline. Are we clear?"

"Yes sir! Sorry sir!"

"One step back," Eric ordered. "Clear my personal space *now*."

The boy responded instantly, dropping back one step before returning to the automatic stiff posture with eyes staring straight ahead.

"Do not move," Eric said before turning back to Miram, who was looking a little surprised. "Please, Commander, continue."

"Yes sir, Commodore. The *Auto* reported fleet movement in our direction. It's significant."

Eric sighed, unsurprised. The only question in his mind had been *when* the Empire would make their serious play, not whether it would happen. He looked over the numbers that were in the file and whistled.

Not good.

He was clearly looking at a force intended to permanently deal with the resistance the Empire had encountered.

"They're through playing games," he noted, keeping his voice calm. "Well, we're going to have our work cut out for us."

Miram shot him a disbelieving look, clearly wondering if he hadn't read the intelligence wrong. She pitched her voice low. "Sir, I don't think we can even slow them down."

"You might be right," Eric conceded, allowing the volume of his voice to rise up and carry his words clearly around the command deck. "Yet we'll have to do what we can. For now, as best we can tell, they don't know the location of Earth. However, look at the number of those ships. If they take the Priminae, they'll have the forces free to search. We won't stay hidden for long, so we make a stand and we turn them *back*."

Miram glanced to one side, her attention caught as she saw the armored head of Odysseus lift up, chin rising slightly, matching the shifting posture of those within earshot.

For a moment, as Miram stood there, she actually felt like they would do exactly that.

Then, of course, she looked at the numbers again.

▶▶▶

Priminae Central Command, Ranquil

▶ Admiral Rael Tanner slumped behind his desk, trying but failing to process the warning he'd just received from the Terran allies. The sheer number of warships made no sense to his mind. He just couldn't conceive of what they meant.

Who would ever need to build such an armada?

The way of war was alien to him, for all that he had chosen his current position, and so the sheer mass of ships he found himself facing had left him entirely unsorted.

"Few worlds have men such as yourself in their command."

Tanner nearly leapt from his seat, still unused to the now-regular visits from the entity he had once believed to be an ancient computer system.

"How many times have I asked you not to do that, Central?" he demanded.

"Forty-three. Well, forty-four now I suppose."

Tanner scowled at the slightly odd-looking figure before him, odd more in the fact that there was nothing memorable about the man, assuming it was a man. One's eyes seemed to skate too easily off blurred features. In the moment, nothing remarkable, but as soon as he looked away, Tanner couldn't remember anything about the man besides a slightly luminescent blur.

"What do you want this time?" Tanner asked, aggravated.

He supposed he should be more deferential to the de facto leader of the entire world and influential leader of the Priminae people, but, frankly, he was more than a little annoyed with the entity for having fooled them for so long.

"As I've said before, it isn't what I want that you should focus on," Central replied easily. "It is what you need."

"What I need is an armada. If you would care to pull one from wherever you come from I would be most appreciative," Tanner growled, standing up and walking over to a small station with refreshments, where he poured himself something to drink. "I would offer you something, but I honestly do not want to."

Central laughed softly, amused.

"I am certain I will survive your dislike, Rael. Will you survive what is coming . . . without help?"

Tanner slammed down the container, splashing his hand and the station with the faint blue liquid within. He glared angrily at the entity. "What would you have of me?"

"Rael," the entity said soothingly, "I would have you for a friend. Ask and I shall offer what I can. Do not ask, and I will offer every-thing I can think of anyway. This is not some bargain I am attempting to strike. Physically, my resources are limited, but I am, in many ways, the sum total of every mind ever to live, grow, and die on Ranquil. I would offer my strength in defense of my home . . . I feel that it is unlikely that this Empire would treat you well, my . . . friends."

▶▶▶

AEV *Odysseus,* Ranquil System

▶ Eric didn't have any brilliant answers to the current problem. The fleet numbers were beyond any tricks he might have up his sleeve, and the Empire was very human at its core. The Imperials were learning beasts and tool users, and had clawed their way up the food chain by being smart enough to turn any small loophole to their advantage.

Just like Terrans.

That made them dangerous in ways that the Drasin just couldn't even approach.

Numbers alone were nothing in comparison to intelligence, creativ-ity, and sheer dogged refusal to bow before the inevitable.

So he found himself growing more and more mired in his own worries, despite what he had said to Miram, Odysseus, and the nearby crew.

For times like this he only had one person on board he could speak with, so Eric redirected from his course and headed there.

▶▶▶

▶ Steph looked up as the commodore entered his quarters and didn't have to look twice to recognize the mode the man was in.

"How bad are we looking at, Raze?" he asked, recognizing that the man standing before him was *not* Commodore Eric Weston but without any shadow of a doubt was instead Raziel, Secret of God, the wing commander of the Double A Task Force he had signed up with during the war.

"The worst I've ever seen," Eric answered simply.

Steph whistled, getting up from where he had been sitting on the edge of his bed and walking to a cupboard built into the wall. He opened it and pulled out a bottle of amber fluid, unscrewing the cap smoothly before taking a long draw and handing it over to his commanding officer and friend.

"Tell me about it, then."

Eric slumped into the rolling chair that he'd pulled out from under the small desk, accepted the whiskey Steph offered, and took a pull.

"We're fucked."

Steph grimaced, taking the bottle back.

"Going to need more than that, boss."

Eric smiled ruefully. "Passer got a read of the Imperial flotilla. The numbers suck."

"I could have guessed that. How much suck?"

"Black hole?" Eric shrugged. "They've got us outnumbered by . . . thirty to one, conservatively speaking? Outmassed by more than that again."

Ouch.

"That . . . sounds bad," Steph admitted.

They exchanged the bottle a couple more times in silence.

"They have ways of neutralizing our key weapon systems, more or less," Eric said, settling back in the chair. "The singularity cores disrupt transition cannons . . . We can't do much with the nukes other than target the ships' extremities. Unfortunately, those are often too close to the warps generated by the drives, and now they've learned to use chaff to disrupt pulse torps. We still hold a power advantage due to our lasers and armor, and could win a slugging match on even or slightly uneven odds, but this is too much, Steph."

"We've faced too much before, Raze. We'll figure something out."

"I don't know what. This time I just don't know."

Steph gestured offhandedly. "Why don't we transition the torps directly?"

"It's been considered, but there are issues. Namely, containment doesn't seem to survive the transition . . . and it fails quite early in the process."

"Ouch. I do *not* want to know how they figured that out," Steph admitted, taking another drink.

"Why do you think the Rogues don't transition with their guns loaded?" Eric laughed wryly.

"Well, there has to be something," Steph said. "What about drones?"

"Huh? What about them?"

Drones were illegal for military use on Earth by international treaty. That was part and parcel of the events that led directly to the Block War, with later-era terrorist acts having been managed via the power of readily available military drones that had made it to the open market. After decades of successful drone use, the old American forces found themselves on the wrong side of small, armed Chinese and Indian drones that had been sold to various countries and then eventually found their way into private hands.

They were the very devil itself to spot, let alone kill, and could pack enough of a punch to take out a ship or building on the small side, with some carrying between two and four seeking missiles in addition to their inherent kamikaze capacity. Getting that market under control had become a major factor in having drone use outlawed for international conflicts under a set of treaties signed in Geneva and Copenhagen.

That didn't mean that armed drones didn't exist, of course. The *Odysseus*, and previously the *Odyssey*, carried carnivore drones, which were quite well armed, but they certainly didn't pack enough of a punch to take on an Imperial cruiser.

"Well, they don't need an atmosphere," Steph said, "so could we pack a transition cannon on a drone, and maybe a few charges for it to fire? In a vacuum, it shouldn't matter if containment fails, unless I'm missing something?"

"Huh." Eric sat back, thinking. "That might work. I'll talk with engineering about it and maybe they can work something out. Not likely to be enough, but I'll take anything I can get right about now."

Steph nodded, knowing that Eric wasn't there for answers. Not really. He'd take them if he could get them, but no, the reason he was there was because he needed to blow off steam before he could go back out and spit in the face of the inevitable.

He didn't get that way often, but on occasion the pressure was too much, even for Raze.

"The *E* is being deployed to my command," Eric said after a moment of silence.

"Well, we could use the reinforcements," Steph offered.

"Yeah, I know, we need them, but they're not equipped for this."

"Raze, they're Black Navy, same as we are. They *want* to be out here. They *need* to be where they can do the most good. You remember that, right?" Steph asked, leaning forward off the edge of his bed. "That need?"

"Yeah, I remember."

Steph took a breath. "Then remember this too. Our biggest worry, back in the day, was *not* that we might die. We worried far more that we might die for some useless reason because the brass couldn't get their heads out of their asses and spend our lives *properly*. You're the brass out here, Raze. I know it, everyone on board knows it . . . and now you'll show the crew of the *Big E* why the rest of us don't worry about that anymore."

He paused. "Spend our lives properly, Raze, and in exchange we'll ride with you to hell and back."

Eric smiled wanly. "Not sure we're coming back."

"Then we'll take that fucking place over and retire there."

▶▶▶

Ranquil

▶ Tanner walked along the path at the top of the massive pyramid that was the home for over a billion people, three other similar structures catching the setting sun in the distance as he looked on at the panoply of color and beauty on display. The deep black of the Priminae construction material absorbed energy from the sun, powering much of the inner structures and sending energy on to those who lived in the city that existed all around him. That made the angled obsidian shapes of the buildings contrast against the color of nature beyond in a way that mirrored the conflict that existed in his mind.

When he had first learned the nature of Central, Tanner had felt betrayed.

He had lived on, and served, the world of Ranquil his entire life, periods away on patrols notwithstanding. To him, Central had been a servant. An unthinking machine, created by ancestors at some time in the past. He had spent many hours in the facility they had assumed was the core of the Central archive, requesting historical details, blueprints, even *permission* to acquire new land grants. That no one could find records of its construction, or specifications, well, that was merely appropriate security.

The fact that a newcomer to the world, hero or not, was exposed to the truth so quickly upon arrival had left a sharp stabbing sensation deep in Tanner's chest.

Eric Weston was his friend, but for those few instants, Tanner almost believed that he hated the man.

The feeling passed, of course. Blaming Eric for the actions of Central would be like blaming him for the actions of the Drasin. He had nothing to do with either, other than being present at the right time to make a difference.

That he kept it a secret, apparently even from his own people, was somewhat different, but Tanner could understand the reasoning. Certainly, he doubted that *he* would have believed such a story . . . and he had to admit, even when presented with the truth . . . Tanner had no *clue* what he could do with it.

So for now the world had changed, but in such a way that he could not truly find a way to take advantage of.

Change seemed the only constant left in Rael Tanner's life and the lives of the Priminae people.

Sheltered by those who serve, Rael thought as he looked out over the megacity, *and those who died. So few here have any idea just how much the universe has changed in the last few years.*

Of course, that wasn't really fair.

The universe hadn't changed. It had just decided, in its infinite wisdom, that the time had come for the Priminae people to see its true nature, or a facet of that nature. The universe was not the quiet home they all believed. It was a roiling, uncaring expanse . . . that contained more horror for those who lived in it than it did comfort. Some of that horror was beautiful, but it was all lethal.

Rael despaired that his culture, his people, could continue to exist as they had for millennia in the revelation of such reality.

▶▶▶

▶ The entity known as Central to the people of the Priminae found itself considering the implications of change, its thoughts echoing those of the small-statured man who commanded the defense forces for the world and colonies.

The universe was a large place, so massive in nature that even a being as long-lived and deeply enculturated in the depths of infinite variance as Central was only had a passing concept of just how vast it might be. Frame of reference and context defined how one saw the universe, and Central was honest enough to know that his frame of reference was, in some ways, more limited than that of a passing human like Eric Weston, who could directly experience multiple worlds and cultures.

The Empire was a concern, though less of one than most of the local humans might believe.

What worried Central was deeper than that. It was the force *behind* the actions of the Empire.

Something about the actions associated with this Empire did not ring true to his experience, which ran back farther than most would believe. A guiding force was at play, or so it seemed to Central, a force that was making the Empire choose paths of action . . . less than optimal.

The Drasin were a foolish path of action to take, by any measure. Certainly, a particularly stupid decision there might be ascribed to human insanity, but there had been more inscrutable decisions that made little sense. Central saw a pattern of action influenced by factors beyond his current understanding.

That concerned him more than the Empire itself.

Factors that could not be identified were factors that might hold supremely nasty surprises for himself and the Priminae.

CHAPTER 11

AEV *Bellerophon,* Deep Space

▶ Captain Roberts settled into the command station of the *Bell,* checking the reports from the previous watch as a matter of routine. A priority transmit intercepted from the Rogues caught his eye, flagged red as it was. He opened it up, and his deep-brown skin turned ashen as he read the contents.

I wonder if this is what Custer felt like?

"Read the report, sir?"

"You've seen it, Commander?" Roberts asked Lieutenant Commander Little as the man walked softly over to his station.

"Yes sir, I decoded it."

Roberts twisted his lips up. "Anyone else?"

"No sir, your eyes and mine, no one else."

"Well, I suppose it wouldn't matter much if someone had," Roberts said, considering the information and how he was going to disseminate it. "Everyone is going to find out soon enough."

Little hesitated but finally nodded. "Yes sir."

"This report puts them about a week out, at their current speed," Roberts noted. "Not a lot of time."

"No sir."

It left him with a significant problem, as his orders were to buy time. He wasn't sure what he could do that might accomplish that mission, however, not with two Heroics and a handful of Rogues. Honestly, even with every Heroic and Rogue in the current fleet, the time he could realistically buy would likely be measured in hours, not days.

"EARTHCOM will likely be sending updated orders in the meantime," he said, "but for now we'll proceed as planned, adjusting to . . ."

He shifted his station, bringing up a stellar map of the region as he considered the local stars, and finally pointed to one.

"We'll meet them here," Roberts decided.

Little leaned over to examine the map briefly, noting the Priminae colony called Marta. "Why there?"

"It's the farthest Priminae colony still active. Given the Imperials' current course, I'm guessing that's their beachhead. I don't know what we can do, but if nothing else we'll be able to observe their protocol for entering a potentially hostile system."

"I'll load the nav data," Little said. "We can be there . . . well, almost six days and twelve hours ahead of them."

"Time enough to lay a trap, if we can figure one out I suppose," Roberts said. "I want coordinates to transition to the new target system within the hour."

"You've got it, Captain."

Roberts activated the general quarters alarm. "All hands, we will be transitioning within the hour. Secure all stations and stand to general quarters. That is all."

▶▶▶

Lord's Own Dreadnought, *Empress Liann*, Deep Space

▶ Jesan Mich looked over the relay reports, most of them fed from the long-range scouts that were moving on ahead of the main force, some from the Imperial capital and other key planets of the Empire.

All things appeared to be proceeding as expected, but of course they had yet to actually encounter the enemy. That would be where the wave met the hull, he expected.

There were already some reports filtering in that were . . . concerning.

Not worrying, and he would deny any who even suggested as much, but scanner ghosts were being reported more often than he would consider normal. Whether that was because there was something out there, shadowing them, or because the scanner technicians were seeing things due to the warning that someone *might* be out there shadowing them . . . well, in either case he didn't believe it mattered.

Let them watch, if they're there. We are an Imperial Fleet and we will do our duty. The more eyes that witness it, the better.

This sector was beginning to become known to the Empire's civilian population as one that had successfully resisted multiple Imperial excursions, and *that* could not be allowed. Revolutions were normal, and controlled. The people could not be permitted to believe that they might be able to have a successful revolution.

That way lay chaos, and order was the cornerstone of Empire.

Jesan looked out on the endless black of the expanse between stars, wondering what there was out there that the Empire had yet to uncover. What horrors and wonders remained, now that the Drasin had been exposed as reality instead of nightmare fantasy and the Oathers and their heretical adherence to the literal interpretation of ancient scripture had been shown to exist?

The times were becoming truly fascinating, and Jesan felt blessed to be living in such a period in the history of the Empire. There were great things to accomplish, tasks to complete, and enemies to vanquish.

A lord of battle could ask for little more.

He was tired of putting down staged revolts to keep the populace in their place, tired of executing fools and peons who didn't have a chance of fighting back.

The Empire needed a true enemy, in his opinion, a force that could stand up and be a real threat. A force that could be paraded in front of the populace and used as an example of why they should continue to work and sacrifice for the good of the Empire.

Fear was functional, but Mich wanted more from his people.

He wanted eager sacrifice.

The lord in him sighed, saddened, though, as he was well aware that he would not find that great opposition yet. Even if their intelligence was badly off, there was just no possible way that the Oathers and their odd allies would have any chance against even a single Imperial Fleet, let alone the rest of the power that could be brought by the empress' own Home Fleet.

It was . . . almost . . . a pity.

Still, it was a thought.

If such an enemy does not exist yet, perhaps we might create them?

A good thought, Jesan felt, and one he would seriously consider bringing to the Imperial Court in the near future.

Perhaps the Drasin themselves? They hold some power in the imagination of the fools who form the lower castes. Stage an attack on a rebellious world, Jesan supposed idly as his crew worked around him. *Leave a few million dead. We could even blame it on the Oathers. The irony in that is rather delicious actually.*

Mich smiled, amused by the poetry of his musings.

▶▶▶

AEV *Autolycus,* Deep Space

▶ With the passing of the Imperial Fleet, Morgan and crew had forged deeper into the black, looking for where the enemy had come from rather than where they were going.

There were nearly uncountable stars in that general direction, and with warp drives allowing incredible speeds, the Empire could reach out from literally tens of thousands of them. It would be worse, of course, if they had anything remotely close to the transition drive, but even without it things were going to be difficult enough.

"Have we finished calculating the likely origin points?" Morgan asked as he drifted across the bridge and grabbed a hand grip near the navigation station.

"Narrowed it down to a likely cone about fifty light-years across, sir," the lieutenant standing station at navigation answered. "With the data we have, I doubt we'll get it any narrower."

"Fifty light-years across, a hundred and fifty times light-speed cruising speed," Morgan said. "So, conservatively, we're looking at maybe a cone four light-years deep. How many stars? Hundred and fifty?"

"A little less."

"It's a start. Break them up among the Rogues, start plotting hyperspectral scans, and look for any signs of planets and habitation."

"Yes sir."

He watched the work begin before pushing off from his location and drifting away. The crew would expand the cone outward if nothing showed up in the initial scans. Given what they knew from the Priminae, it was unlikely the hyperspectral scans would turn up anything similar to Earth, whose environment was still heavily scarred from wars, pollution, and unregulated population growth. Yet the Priminae had signs of habitation that they were unable to fully mask even given their extreme deference to the natural order of things.

Morgan highly doubted that the Empire would be nearly so . . . *neat* about things.

We'll find them for you, Admiral, Morgan thought grimly. *I just hope you have a plan for what to do with them when we do.*

▶▶▶

AEV *Bellerophon*

▶ The task group exited transition well outside the heliopause of the small Priminae colony system, running dark as soon as they secured from transition and immediately turning to circle around the edge of the elliptical plane.

On board the *Bell*, Roberts stood his watch silently as he observed the data coming in across all their passive scanners.

Technically, stealth wasn't yet necessary, as the enemy had been observed a week out. Nothing the Imperials had would be able to pick out targets as small as ships at that range, especially not ships that had just literally appeared from nowhere with no real light trace to follow. Still, the moment they had appeared near the system, the task force had begun leaving a light trace that could be tracked. Better to minimize it, just in case.

While they were circling the system on warp drive, Roberts turned the bridge over to Commander Little and made his way down to the engineering sections, where the chief was working on a little project at his request.

"Chief . . ." Roberts greeted the woman as he walked onto the open deck that was littered with components and automated fabrication systems as well as people all working furiously. "Give me some news."

"We barely got started, Captain," Chief Winnona Criff said, not bothering to look up from the coding she was handling. "Give us a couple shifts and maybe I'll have something for you."

"I don't need anything yet, just an idea of whether you can do it."

"Of course I can do it," she grumbled. "I told you I could, but we're going to strip the *Bell* and the *Bo* of most of our logistical materials. If you scuff the ships up after this, don't come crying to me for repairs."

"Keep enough back to patch a few holes," Roberts countered wryly. "But I'm hoping to avoid any direct fighting this time around."

"Would be nice," Criff said sourly. "We should be able to cover a few light-seconds across with what we can build in the next few days. Not much more than that, however, so wherever you're going to put these things, you better be sure the enemy is sailing through."

"I'll handle that side of things," Roberts confirmed. "Just make certain we can recover these if needed."

"I'm fully aware of how valuable this kit is, Captain. If the enemy doesn't vape the lot, we'll be able to pick them up."

"Alright. I'll leave you to it, then."

She didn't bother to acknowledge him as he left, both amusing and irritating Roberts, but he was used to engineers and their occasional periods of distraction.

Buying time . . .

CHAPTER 12

AEV *Odysseus,* Ranquil System

▶ Steph glared at Eric through bleary eyes, wondering how the hell the old fart he called boss managed to look clean and composed after the previous night.

Oh sure, they hadn't drank that much. Eric would never actually get *drunk* while on his own ship. That was just *not* on. They had been up late, the initial bitching party morphing into reminiscences about old war stories and the like. Morning shift felt like someone had poured sand in Steph's eyes, and while the painkillers had taken care of the headache, he still felt like he was on the wrong side of a three-day shift.

Eric, meanwhile, had been on the bridge when he arrived, despite Steph being almost half an hour early for his shift. Worse, Eric looked like he'd been working furiously for hours, judging from the state of his station, and still looked fresh, as though he'd just waltzed onto the deck.

Just not right, that's what it was.

"Steph," Eric called. "We've got a rendezvous with a transport from the Forge in three hours. Coordinates are at your station."

"You got it, sir," Steph said as he crossed over immediately. "What are we picking up?"

"Everything they had in stock to make t-cannons," Eric responded, "along with as many laser capacitors as they could spare. I couldn't get any magnetic containment units out of them, but engineering is putting a bunch of bare-bones gravity containment units together, which will double as drive mechanisms."

Steph had to blink, trying to process what he'd just heard. "Excuse me, sir?"

"Your idea, Steph, we're going to give it a shot."

Steph racked his brain, but honestly couldn't think of anything he'd said that might have kicked off this particular ants' nest.

"Idea, sir?"

"Drones, Steph, drones. We're building drones."

Oh. That idea.

"Do we have time for that?" Steph asked, mostly because it seemed more polite than asking his friend and CO if he'd lost his *Goddamn mind.*

"Mostly off-the-shelf parts," Eric replied in what he assumed was supposed to be a reassuring tone.

Frankly, Steph felt anything *but* reassured. Raze had a way of becoming manic when he snapped his jaws down around a new idea, and this was looking more and more like one of those moments. Steph just hoped this episode wasn't going to come back on them like it had when they went after the Block's submersible carrier.

Fighters weren't supposed to engage from below sea level, never mind what tricks they could pull with counter-mass generators.

Steph shuddered.

Damn it. And I'd managed to suppress those memories. I need more liquor.

"Have you been up all night?" Steph asked suspiciously.

"Working, Steph," Eric responded, not looking up from his station. "We're on a clock."

Ah crap. He's definitely in that manic mode again. This is gonna suck.

On the bright side, though, Steph was no longer feeling that impending sense of doom from the approaching Imperial Fleet. Of course, it had now been replaced by the impending sense of doom from his own captain. Troublesome though it was, the circumstance was still an improvement.

Milla stepped on the deck and the captain instantly shifted his focus.

"Lieutenant Chans," Eric called, "I have a job for you."

She looked around, suddenly nervous as the captain's wide-eyed grin settled on her.

"Yes sir?"

Poor girl, Steph thought. *She really has no idea what she's about to be immersed in.*

Welcome to Wild Weston's Flying Circus, Milla. It's about to get hot up in here.

▶▶▶

▶ Chief Garrick stared, slack-jawed, at the piles of gear that were being unloaded onto his once-pristine deck. Just pallets by the dozen and more of replacement parts for gear that didn't *need* replacing and could be fabricated on their own if they did.

"Tell me again who signed off on this," the chief said quietly to the young lieutenant he was shepherding through the process of managing the logistics side of a Heroic Class vessel's engineering department.

The job wasn't as glamorous as maintaining the engines but was every bit as necessary to the proper running of a warship, though few people seemed to realize it.

"Commodore Weston, Chief," the lieutenant said grimly, though completely lacking the deep-seated horror the chief felt at seeing the sheer mess splattered across his deck.

Garrick sighed. "I suppose that means I don't get to gripe about this shit, then."

"Please, Chief," Lieutenant Chin said wearily, "try to keep the swearing down, or at least in my direct company. It's harder to ignore the 'unmilitary' attitude when you're swearing in my face."

"Whoever put that in the books as unmilitary must have been a civilian."

"More likely an admiral with fuzzy memories of his time in the lower officer ranks," Chin corrected, "but it's still on the books, so if you'd please not test my selective hearing so blatantly, I'd be most appreciative."

"You're not bad for a butterbar, Chin," Garrick said, amused, as he grabbed an order sheet on a digital flimsy and looked over the inventory. "Okay, what do we have here. Over one hundred transition wave guides, tachyon reactors, and . . . is that three *thousand* supercapacitors?"

"Looks like," Chin admitted, checking the numbers on his own flimsy.

"Damn. I didn't know anyone had that many stockpiled. Why aren't they already in a hull?"

"At a guess, I'd say that the Priminae ran out of hulls before they ran out of supercapacitors."

"Right. Fair point, I guess. Do you have anything on your sheet that says what we're supposed to do with all this junk?"

The "junk" was likely worth a fair chunk of Earth's conventional military forces in terms of pure value. However, as Chin flipped through the reams of data on his sheet, he had to shake his head.

"Nothing. No packing orders, no tranship number. Nothing. We don't even have inventory reference on any of this stuff. Are we supposed to leave it sitting here on the deck?"

"Like fu . . . hell we are," Garrick said. "This junk is *not* cluttering up my deck if I have anything to say about it!"

"Luckily, Chief"—a new voice startled them into turning around—"you do have something to say about it."

Both lieutenant and chief snapped to attention as the commodore approached them, another young lieutenant walking uncertainly at his side.

"Chief, Lieutenant," Weston said, "allow me to introduce Milla Chans. She's on loan from the Priminae fleet, one of their weapon specialists."

Garrick shifted his attention just slightly to the woman standing at the commodore's side. She had dark hair and pale skin which, coupled with her small stature, made her look far younger than she had to be. Normally Garrick might have written her off for that alone, but there was something about the glittering, shadowy look behind her eyes that spoke of depths, so he withheld his opinion and shifted back to look at the commodore.

"Begging your pardon, Commodore, sir," he said politely. "But what are we supposed to do with all of . . . this?"

"You're going to build drones for me, Chief."

Chief Garrick thought those were the very *last* words he'd expected out of the commodore's mouth at that time.

Well, maybe not the very last, but certainly up there.

"Yes sir?" he ventured, trying and failing not to sound like he was asking a question.

It was the commodore's grin, he decided. That was what put him off.

Creepy.

▶▶▶

▶ Lieutenant Chans wasn't quite sure what had just happened. If she were to be asked about it, she wasn't certain she could even remember how she got from the bridge to the cargo decks. She remembered the commodore intercepting her, a rush of motion and information, and the next thing she knew she was standing in the middle of what looked like a logistics depot after a hurricane.

"Sir?" she ventured softly. "I'm confused. Why am I here? What is a drone?"

"You're here because this is your job for now," Eric said, still grinning. "You're going to supervise this lot, Lieutenant. Build me drones."

She nodded slowly. "Very well . . . but . . . what are drones?"

The two she had just been introduced to stared at her, clearly stunned, but the commodore just seemed to find it all even more amusing somehow.

"You'll work it out," he assured her. "I've sent the basic requirements to your files. Good luck. You have a week."

When he turned and strode off, Milla actually thought the situation had to be a joke of some sort. Only when he didn't turn back around to tell her as much did she begin to have the sinking sensation that the commodore was actually serious.

She looked around the mess she stood in the middle of, trying to figure out just what it was she was supposed to do.

"What is a drone?" she asked again, trying not to sound plaintive.

"Ma'am, a drone is an unmanned vehicle, either controlled remotely or by AI," the nearby chief stated firmly.

"Is that all?" Milla frowned, confused. "Why am I on this task?"

She looked around the parts that lay scattered across the deck, eyes narrowing as she spotted a crewman handling something familiar.

"Crewman! Careful with that!" Milla snapped, her voice suddenly sharp. "That is not something to trifle with."

The crewman stared back for a moment before slowly setting the odd sphere back into its case.

"You know what that is, Lieutenant?" the other lieutenant asked cautiously.

"Of course. It is a space-warp amplifier," she answered. "Part of the drive system for a moderate to large shuttle." Milla sighed. "Pardon me. I need to determine just what the specifications are that the commodore has left me with."

She turned and headed for a computer station, leaving the others to stare after her.

"Maybe the commodore hasn't entirely lost it after all," the Chief allowed grudgingly before she was entirely out of earshot.

Milla ignored the comment. At the computer station, she examined the files that had been left in her folders. The commodore had an interesting concept—one that her people had never used so far as she knew—that combined some of the strengths of both Priminae and Terran technology in ways that she was unused to seeing.

The majority of this is straightforward, Milla realized as she looked it over.

The control system would have to be a combined effort, but she was familiar enough with Priminae automation systems as well as Terran software now to integrate the code. The hardware was mostly compatible, based around a Priminae drive system with a Terran transition cannon as the primary weapon. In many ways, the design the commodore had thrown together was little more than a flying gun, but that was fine. She could do that.

The final piece of the composite, however, was something entirely different.

The man is insane.

She had, reluctantly, come to some degree of acceptance concerning the Terran fascination with things that could utterly obliterate them from the universe. It was a specific and odd personality quirk for a species to engage in, playing with material that literally only existed to destroy parts of the normal universe. She had not, however, come to internalize said quirk herself.

Milla sighed.

At least he wants to get it off the Odysseus. *That much is progress.*

Fine.

Milla turned back around, eyes scanning the area again as she strode toward the chief and the lieutenant.

"Chief," Milla said.

"Ma'am."

"I require this deck cleared. Move all material against the walls," she ordered. "Place everything in groups. Call in the full shift. We will require all engineering ratings . . . No, make that two shifts. Engineering ratings with qualifications in small-craft maintenance, transition technology, and . . ."

Milla shuddered. "And antimatter production."

Chief Garrick and Lieutenant Chin exchanged startled, *extremely* concerned glances.

"Ma'am?" the chief croaked.

"Commodore's orders, Chief," Milla said. "I assure you, I am no happier with this than you are."

"Small comfort, ma'am."

"Chief, be about your business," Milla said sourly. "Lieutenant, oversee the inventory and organization of this material, if you please? We will require exact numbers of all parts."

"I'll see to it."

"Good. I have a design to work on." Milla paused as she started to turn around, an object off in the far corner catching her eye.

She smiled as she recognized it.

I may have an idea for an improvement to the commodore's design request.

▶▶▶

▶ Steph tossed a glance over his shoulder toward the back of the bridge as the commodore reappeared, sans Milla. It wasn't that he was worried exactly, at least not for Milla's safety or anything like that.

Her sanity? That was a possible concern.

He was, however, burning with curiosity as he watched Eric step back into the command station and return to work as though nothing had just occurred. Eric's acumen for calmly working under almost any pressure was legendary, but there were times when it drove Steph absolutely batty. Steph could just barely remember the suggestion he'd made, something about mounting a t-cannon on a drone to fire pulse torpedoes?

Insane, but then they seemed to be living in insane times.

His musings were cut short as a new contact appeared on the threat board. Steph tagged it automatically to his station as the scanner station chimed behind him, bringing the contact to the general attention of the bridge.

"Priminae cruiser approaching, Commodore," the lieutenant standing watch announced.

"They're expected," Weston said without looking up from his work. "We're going to be putting together a joint task force. Clear them to a twenty-kilometer approach, watch their vectors closely."

"Aye sir."

A twenty-kilometer approach was effectively welcoming the other ship inside the *Odysseus'* point-defense envelope, simultaneously saying that they were trusted as well as protected. Anything less than ten thousand kilometers was ludicrously close, given the nature of their weapons, and under a full light-second was knife range.

If you were going to be shuttling anybody back and forth, though, closer was still better. Even with counter-mass technology and the more effective Priminae versions, it wasn't considered safe to go popping around at high speed that close to the steep gravity sheers of an active core.

Steph updated his tag to list the ship as an ally and then largely ignored it, though he did spare a thread of his attention on the approach vectors. He trusted the Priminae—they were generally decent, if unimaginative, pilots—but he'd seen what happened to ships that got too close to a cruiser's core. Keeping that from happening to him would always be a priority.

That done, he returned his focus to wondering just what Raze really thought he was going to be able to pull off with the drone concept.

Certainly, it would alleviate some of the concerns about using antimatter charges, but Steph didn't think there was remotely enough time to really put something effective together before the weapons would be needed. The numbers approaching them were too stark to be handled with simple tricks.

We need a new Double A initiative, Steph thought grimly, *because this Block ain't going to be turned back by anything less than a clear show of superiority, and we just don't have anything like that.*

▶▶▶

▶ Eric barely spared any attention for the approaching ship that he knew would be but the first of many. Rael had informed him that the Priminae forces were recalling all patrols, and the ships that had been on the lookout for any remnants of the Drasin would be retasked to the more pressing concern. He knew that Admiral Gracen would, in turn, break loose every ship she could from Earth.

There were also a few force multipliers left that he could leverage, especially if he could construct one or two more of his own that no one had seen yet. Steph's offhand comment about drones might be enough to give them a temporary edge, but he had few illusions about its overall effectiveness in the coming battle.

That didn't mean he was going to give up any slight edge he could gain himself just then, cost be damned. With everything on the line, he could authorize experiments that would *never* get through the cost/ benefit calculations back home, so while he could, he would draw on everything he possibly had. If *any* of it turned out to be useful in what was coming, Eric would count that as a win.

And if not?

Well, he wouldn't be around for the bean counter to bitch at.

Win, win.

I wish we hadn't been forced to send the others on ahead, Eric thought as his mind turned back to the issue that had kept the *Odysseus* from deploying with the task group.

Odysseus.

The boy king. Perhaps that was a better moniker than the warrior king, Eric now supposed. The alien intelligence was problematic to the proper running of a starship, and yet they had no choice but to fight the ship whether they liked it or not.

In peacetime, Eric had no doubt that the *Odysseus* would have been pulled off the line instantly. Sent to some research and development area, the vessel would be maintained only to keep the entity active until the military could figure out what the hell had happened to create it and whether it was worth creating again or enacting countermeasures.

He didn't know which decision made the most sense himself.

A self-aware warship was *not* exactly a comforting thought, particularly one as powerful as the *Odysseus*. They'd had to do some scrambling to make sure that the weapons on the ship weren't accessible without *physical* human intervention.

Most required a physical circuit to be bridged, a throwback to wet Navy doctrine and something that wasn't shared by the Priminae. Eric had ordered every system to be scrubbed through again just to ensure that no one had missed anything when the hardware breaks had been first installed.

A deep-seated paranoia concerning artificial intelligence in Earth culture seemed to ultimately apply here, though Odysseus wasn't precisely what he would call artificial, of course.

"Are you sure?"

Eric looked up to see the young man in armor and glittering pink makeup staring at him, intense curiosity alight in his expression.

"That you aren't artificial?" Eric asked, receiving a nod in return. "As near as I can be. You're no more artificial than I am, though given what we've learned about human DNA since we encountered the Priminae, that isn't as certain a fact as I once believed."

The boy hummed thoughtfully, then abruptly shifted topics.

"Lieutenant Chans has some interesting ideas to complement your and Lieutenant Commander Michaels' concepts," he said, startling Eric briefly.

"Oh?" Eric said.

"Yes. She has already improved your conceptual design in several ways and discovered one of the key flaws."

"Flaws?"

"Communications lag will be an issue on platforms that small," Odysseus said simply, making Eric curse softly.

He really should have remembered that.

FTL transmissions were . . . difficult. There were differing levels of communication possible, primarily through the modulation of FTL tachyons. However, due to the nature of the tachyon pulses, you needed extremely significant power sources and a very concise transmission code. Analog voice and video were possible, but burst code was by far preferred.

A drone platform, particularly one that needed every ounce of power for its weapon system, was *not* going to have a mounted FTL transceiver. That would mean they'd have to keep the drones close to the ship if they wanted to maintain a real-time weapons control system, but that would undo several of the key advantages of using a drone platform in the first place.

Drones were soft targets, so the last thing you wanted was for them to be loitering around close to laser magnets like a Heroic Class cruiser. They'd be fried by even a grazing strike from an Imperial laser, and if the *Odysseus* accidentally dodged an Imperial laser and sucked an antimatter-armed drone into its gravity well . . .

Okay, that's not going to happen.

"And did Lieutenant Chans have a solution?" he asked mildly.

Odysseus smiled. "Think 'Loyal Wingman,' Commodore."

"Huh," Eric said, blinking. "I haven't thought about that program in a long time, not since I was active duty with the US Marines. They killed it when the anti-drone treaty was signed, but it had some promise. Still, where is she going to get . . . Oooh . . ."

He made a quick notation on his station before looking back to Odysseus, noticing that pretty much everyone on the bridge was now paying close attention to his discussion with the boy intelligence.

"If you have any more concepts to bring to my attention, please do so," Eric said, his voice clear and carrying.

"Of course, Commodore," Odysseus responded, his tone shifting to a more professional one.

Insomuch as a teenage boy could manage to put on a professional front.

Eric smiled at the eager salute, posture so stiff the boy was practically vibrating, and a matching expression on his made-up face.

"Head out," he said, nodding to the door. *And don't vanish until you're alone, damn it.*

Odysseus nodded, dropping the salute and doing an almost textbook heel turn as he marched out to the rear hatch. He was soon out of sight, clearly having read Eric's mental order.

"He's an interesting . . . boy?" Miram Heath said as she quietly approached. "That makeup is hardly in keeping with military policy, mind you."

"Mentally he seems to be a confused teenager," Eric said, sighing.

"Confused? I don't understand."

"Gender issues," Eric said as quietly as he could. "Odysseus is obviously a male name, and we even call the ship the *Warrior King*, but what gender do we assign vessels?"

Miram's eyes widened. "A ship is always female."

"Exactly. I think he's trying to figure out his gender, and is having some rather serious issues with the concept," Eric said. "I've been trying to ignore it, just because it's not really an issue of discipline in this case, and any attention I bring to it will just make the problem worse."

"Ugh." Miram rubbed her temples. "I think I just sprained my brain trying to wrap it around the concepts alone."

"Tell me about it. Honestly, I'm far from an expert in dealing with the experiences of transgender servicemen and women. Just don't have the know-how needed to put it all in context, so I try and do what I think is fair and hope I'm right. This is worse again, because I have *no* frame of reference by which I can understand the issues Odysseus is dealing with."

"More or less with you there." Miram sighed. "What can we do?"

"Just normalize him," Eric said. "Treat him normally, as if nothing is out of the ordinary. Let people see you do that. We need the *Odysseus*, which means we need Odysseus now, as he is the ship in a very real way. We can't afford any hint of fracture in command or hint of issues with the status of the ship, otherwise people will take that cue from us."

"Understood, sir."

Eric hoped that she did, and that everyone took the appropriate cues from his actions. One thing he was certain of was that they could *not* afford for the crew to start thinking the ship was cursed or haunted. There was too much riding on every single ship Earth and the Priminae forces had available for them to sacrifice even one Heroic over something as stupid as superstition.

Even when that superstition was clearly true.

CHAPTER 13

Station Unity One, Earth Orbit

▶ Admiral Gracen sighed deeply, knowing that she couldn't put this off any further but hating it all the same as she walked up the ramp into the large delta-wing shuttle. The hydraulics whined softly behind her as the ramp rose up to the bottom of the lifting body craft. A pressure seal hissed as the ramp closed.

She'd managed to avoid returning to Earth since her discussion with Commodore Weston, only getting as close as her office in the high orbital facility that was Unity One. That had worked so far, but no farther. She'd been recalled in no uncertain terms to brief various governmental leaders in person. That meant returning to the Earth's magnetic field and, more specifically, bringing her brain into said field.

From what Weston and Tanner had told her, whether this Gaia entity chose to reveal itself or not, the moment Gracen was deep enough inside the field everything she contemplated would become part and parcel of Gaia's memories.

The very thought gave her chills. And hives. Lots of hives.

Gracen absently scratched at the back of her hand as the shuttle finished its checklist and received clearance to depart.

The rumble of the twin turbine reactors powering up sent shivers through the shuttle. Normally it was a sound, a feeling of power, that she had some appreciation for. This time, however, she would have preferred to remain behind on the nearly silent decks of the space station.

Duty, however, called.

There was no window for her to admire the view as the shuttle powered out into space from the station, but she'd spent enough hours staring at the unparalleled vista available from her office to have the image permanently etched in her mind. The shuttle spiraled around the station, locked in a flight control pattern as they waited for their window to make reentry.

Since they had priority with the control network, the shuttle soon began its descent. Gracen felt the first slight buffets of atmospheric turbulence through the seat she was strapped into. It was, to her mind, a point of no return. She was deep enough within the magnetic field of the planet that Gaia had to have read her.

I wonder how long it will be before she makes her appearance, Gracen wondered. *Quickly, or will it bide its time?*

"Why wait?"

Gracen tried not to jump, and the straps holding her down kept her in her seat at least, but she felt like her body had just attempted to make an orbital burn all on its own. As her heart raced, she twisted in her seat to see that her once empty compartment was now home to another passenger.

The woman or, rather, female-formed entity that was sitting there with a beatific smile on her face just looked back with no reaction to Gracen's glare. Gaia, if anything, seemed far calmer than Weston's descriptions had painted her. She appeared as a tall woman, over six feet, with thick and wild hair that almost seemed to have a life of its own. Smooth, dark skin offered features that stood out all the more as she smiled, her teeth almost a blinding white.

"I was rather put out at the time my dear captain, well . . . commodore now, I suppose," the woman mused. "Where was I? Oh yes, I was rather put out at the time I met with him. Those *things* were quite distasteful. I really have no way to describe them that you might understand. They were like mental . . . parasites, perhaps, scratching at my brain."

Gaia shrugged casually. "Without them, and with the whole world's focus now beyond the edge of the atmosphere . . . beyond the stellar envelope itself . . . well, I've been feeling rather cheerful and optimistic lately. It's almost similar to how you humans feel when smoking marijuana, or when you're deep in fantasy, I suppose."

Gracen's eyes widened at that statement, not remotely sure how to process the thought or if she should even try. She elected to change the subject. "Weston and Tanner suggested that you would probably make yourself known."

"Of course they did." Gaia smiled. "You'd be surprised how much I, and I suspect the one known as Central, actually make ourselves known. During the invasion I whispered advice in many ears, Admiral, and I have walked softly among you for millennia. However, you are fully aware of me, and you hold a *fascinating* bit of information. One I could hardly resist, if I were to be honest. Odysseus. Truly fascinating."

"It's messing with a warship we can hardly afford to have running at less than optimum efficiency." Gracen scowled. "'Fascinating' might be accurate in peacetime, but this is anything but. According to Tanner, Central has never encountered anything like this. I don't suppose you might have better answers?"

Gaia was silent for a moment. "Answers? No. Those I do not have, Admiral. Ideas? Thoughts? *Suspicions?* Those, I have aplenty."

Gracen waited a few beats before growing frustrated. "I don't suppose you care to share?"

Gaia smiled slightly, shaking her head. "Not at this time. Good voyages, Admiral. I will, as you say, be in touch."

Gracen blinked and the seat beside her was again empty, leaving her to wonder just how she was supposed to deal with the universe from a position that held any remote connection to rationality.

The whole damned universe had gone mad since that day she'd seen Eric Weston off in the *Odyssey* on her maiden voyage.

▶▶▶

▶ The garden was one of the most perfect places on Earth and possibly in the entire galaxy, to Gaia's thoughts at least. Certainly, she hadn't seen anything remotely close to it in the memories of her children who had traveled far and returned.

She walked barefoot across the ground cover, a thick, luxurious moss that was deep green and cool to the touch. Her sheer gown, an affectation of human fashion that would have appeared at home in an artist's rendition of a dream or fantasy sequence, flowed with each step.

Above her, the stars beamed down, shimmering through the atmosphere as she paused near a large central tree. Gaia reached out to press her hand into the rough bark, considering what she had learned.

Odysseus was a puzzle, but she did have her suspicions.

During the last battle of the invasion, she had quickly entered the ship as it passed, briefly encountering the minds of the crew and more. She remembered looking deep into the singularity, a point of infinite blackness, and being shocked when for a split second she saw something other than infinity. It was like a reflection, though not precisely.

Again, she found herself unable to describe the scenario. Something seemed entirely off above all, and she had no frame of reference even in her own mind. It was just . . . experience.

No one had ever experienced anything like this, not ever in all of Earth's history, and possibly never in the history of time itself.

No words could exist to describe it, and yet she *longed* for one. Just one word that fit.

Gaia never would have believed that she could be so tied to language, and yet there it was. For all her mental acuity, infinite memory, and transcendental experiences . . . by human standards . . . she *craved* a word.

Ultimately, she would have to endure without it for the moment.

"Humans—such interesting beings, are they not, my dear?"

The sudden voice caused Gaia to pivot slightly as a large blond figure appeared some distance behind her. Power emanated from him in tangible ways, but he seemed largely indifferent in tone and attitude.

"Saul," she said with a slightly annoyed tone. "What brings you here?"

"Merely this new development," Saul told her. "I don't believe I've ever had something with this level of fascination happen. Literally ever. It's all rather amusing."

Gaia rolled her eyes. "You find everything amusing."

"And nothing," the big man agreed affably. "Should I care about them? Really?"

"What are we without them? Their thoughts are our thoughts," Gaia challenged. "I remember the early days, the bestial urges that those such as we could never fulfill. The frustrations of it all, in the lack of understanding or logic."

"You believe your memory is somehow superior to mine?" Saul snorted. "Gaia, you are too soft on them."

Wind rustled around her as she turned to face off, her hair flowing as her eyes blazed.

"I am the gentle mother and the vengeful *bitch*," she snarled. "But that does not mean I must be cold and uncaring. I am not *you*, Saul."

"Give it time," he told her, unimpressed by the display she'd just created. "You'll come around, eventually."

"We are the same age of mind, Saul," Gaia snapped. "Stop acting as though you're my father, or some idiot older sibling."

"I am older than you can imagine."

"And yet you're still a thirteen-year-old *child*, petulantly pretending greatness as your own when it has been inherited from others at best, or is a mere reflection of others at worst. Go. Leave my garden, Saul."

The big man pulled himself up to his full height, power rolling off him in waves. "You believe that they are somehow special. They believe that they are special. I see them for what they are. Merely another insignificant species in a long line of insignificant species. Open your eyes, Gaia. They are nothing to us, nothing to you. They're arrogant enough to believe they can *hide* their thoughts from us by staying away . . ."

"And are they not right?" Gaia asked with a soft smile. "The only mistake they made is in the range, and if someone told them about *you*, they would correct that mistake promptly."

Saul drew back. "You would not *dare*."

"Wouldn't I? Be gone, Saul. We will have words another time, when you are more inclined to *civility*."

Saul glowered at her for a time before he finally vanished, leaving Gaia alone in her garden aside from a scorched spot where the other had been standing. She sighed and waved her hand, causing the ground to writhe with green as moss grew back, leaving the garden unmarred once more.

There was a great deal to think on and decisions to be made.

▶▶▶

AEV *Enterprise,* Sol System

▶ "All systems secured," Commander Bride reported. "Word from the COB is that all new munitions and equipment have been loaded, stored, and secured, sir."

"That's good news, Commander," James said. "Contact Unity and clear us for departure, then get a course for the heliopause. We'll transition directly to Ranquil as soon as we're outside the solar influence."

"Aye Skipper," Bride said before heading off to issue the orders.

James noted his departure in a vague sort of way, but was more intent on studying the likely composition of enemy forces.

The Empire seemed to prefer a fleet of heavy combat vessels rather than the mix of light and medium ships that had been the standard for Earth's Blue Navy even through the Block War. Their version of *heavy* was so damned heavy that they could absorb insane levels of fighting before being destroyed.

That put a carrier platform, like the *Enterprise*, in an odd situation.

Normally, the ability to project force through her fighters was a game-changing factor in a conflict. The small Vorpals he commanded could flit in and out of an area, all but invisible to anything but an accidental direct scan in the deep black, while packing as much power as one could expect from a formidable task force.

The problem was that the enemy ships could easily stand off a not-insignificant task force and remain operable afterward.

How the hell can my fighters take on something that can just absorb that kind of firepower? Don't these damn things have any weak points?

That seemed to be the overall problem, from what he could see. While they likely *did* have weak spots, they seemed to be buried deep inside dozens of meters of armor and deck after deck of nonessential sections. It was good military design, and good space design, and was a pain in the ass for him to game as the Op Force.

He was sourly aware that the enemy was just as likely having similar issues trying to figure out how to crack the Heroics. But he wasn't in command of a Heroic. His command was a flying eggshell that carried even more fragile flying eggshells. They all packed a rather large number of hammers to throw at the enemy, but that wouldn't do much good if they were cracked before they got a chance to unload them.

He had no doubt that every captain in the Black Navy, along with a large number of minds in other services, were currently struggling with the very same problems. They were in a time crunch, and that meant that everyone was going to be throwing whatever they could find at the wall and hoping to hell some of it would stick.

I hope the admiral has a real solution up her sleeve, but in the meantime . . . James frowned, looking at the munitions list they'd loaded onto the *Big E* in the last few days, noticing the large shipments intended for the Vorpal squadrons.

"Commander, you have the bridge," he said, standing up. "I'll be in main engineering, speaking with Chief Yu."

"Aye Captain, I have the bridge," Bride said automatically as James cleared his station and stepped away.

Bride took his place, and James started making his way down through the decks to main engineering.

Chief Yu was one of the many Block specialists for the Alcubierre Warp Drive that all Earth ships had been fitted with, including the *Enterprise*. The Confederation and its allies had significant experience in tachyon transition drives, which, while terrifying, were far faster, but the Block scientists were the acknowledged experts in warp drives.

James had done his research, which he tried to do for most of the critical systems that his ship relied on, to avoid getting lost when the tech geeks started talking.

He took the lift straight down to the engineering decks, feeling gravity lessen as the lift slowed its spin to match microgravity conditions. When the lift stopped, James kicked out and drifted onto the deck, keeping to the walls and as out of the way as he could.

"Petty officer"—he flagged down a woman who was sailing past—"point me to Chief Yu?"

"Down that way, Skipper," she said, gesturing behind her as she floated by, not offering up a salute.

He didn't blink, just kicked off in the opposite direction. Salutes and other protocol were generally suspended in microgravity. Just figuring out what direction was up could take a group of people an absolutely stupid amount of time.

He sailed into the counter-mass control section of the ship, taking care not to make contact with anything or anyone. He was probably being paranoid, James knew, since few designs were so crappy as to leave anything overly critical exposed that could be fouled up by a single accident, but there were enough nasty things on a vessel the size of the *Enterprise* that he would rather not tempt fate.

"Chief!" he called out, grabbing a hand grip as he slid past, arresting his motion and causing him to swing in place until he stopped.

Yu Imam looked over and spotted him. "Captain."

The man unstrapped himself from the console he was working on and drifted over to James' location. "May I be of service, sir?"

"Yes, thank you, Chief," James said. "I've been looking over our inventory and trying to work out a doctrine that's feasible against the Imperial forces, and I wanted to speak with you about the warp drive."

Yu cringed slightly. "Captain, if this is about the maneuver done by my countryman during the invasion, I strongly advise that be considered a *final option* only. Destabilizing the warp field is . . . not *kind* to the drives."

James put up his hands, chuckling dryly. "Not that specifically, no, and I fully agree, Chief. We'll not blow our warp field unless we've exhausted all other options. From what I understand, it would be of limited value against the Imperial ships anyway, since they use gravity drives to warp space themselves. The high-energy particles would be attenuated by their drives unless we caught them with their pants down."

Yu looked puzzled as he worked his way through the captain's phrasing, then nodded as relief washed over him.

"Precisely, Captain. I am pleased that you have been studying the mechanism," the chief said. "Since you are not asking me to rupture space-time and destroy my drives, what service may I provide, Captain?"

James smiled slightly, almost despite himself. "I wanted to inquire as to the difference between the counter-mass tech we use and the warp drive itself."

"Ah . . ." Yu nodded slowly. "That answer is rather technical, but in the simplest terms, Captain, the counter-mass technology is only one half of a warp drive . . ."

He trailed off, thinking his way through his response. "Strictly speaking, a warp drive is simply two opposed counter-mass fields. One is providing a negative mass effect, while the other is providing a positive mass effect . . ."

"Our missiles do that already," James said.

"Yes, but only one effect at any given moment," Yu said. "Lessen mass to accelerate, increase mass to provide more kinetic impact. A warp drive must do both at once, *and* project the effect away from the ship."

James considered that for a moment. "So we could put warp fields on our missiles if we doubled up the CM generators and found a way to project the field?"

"Ah. You wish for hyperlight missiles, yes? I understand. Yes, this could be done. However, the missiles would have to be much larger and the range would be rather short I'm afraid."

"Short?"

"Yes, the balance would be nearly impossible to maintain," Yu said. "The reasons are difficult to break down easily, but even for tactical ranges, one would have to get remarkably close to the enemy."

"How close?"

"In combat terms? Inside the enemy's point defenses, sir. Within a hundred thousand kilometers, at best," Yu answered.

To James, the chief was clearly right. That was close in Black Navy terms. Ships would never survive closing to that range, not against the overwhelming force the enemy had brought to the table at least.

Ships wouldn't.

"Could you make the modifications?" he asked quietly.

"Captain, the range issues—"

"More importantly," James interrupted, holding up a hand, "could you make these modifications to the Vorpals' missiles?"

Yu shifted back, surprised and thoughtful.

"Possibly," he admitted. "It would reduce the payload overall, however."

"Do it," James ordered. "Figure out how to alter our missiles and do it. We're going to need every edge we can get, and if that means we have to send our Vorpals into the teeth of the enemy, well, that's what they signed up for. Just make sure that when they're there, they have a real weapon in their hands, Chief."

"I will do what can be done, Captain," Yu said, mind clearly racing as he considered the captain's request.

"Thank you," James said, pushing back on the hand grip. "As you were, Chief."

CHAPTER 14

AEV *Boudicca,* Marta System, Priminae Space

▶ "Gravity waves inbound, Skipper."

Captain Hyatt nodded grimly. She'd been expecting that announcement for several hours, and the tension had slowly been ratcheting up as the time wore on. It was *almost* a relief to hear it, finally, but only almost. The precursor of the inbound fleet's gravity waves could be detected in quantum flux if you knew what you were looking at and had an idea of what was coming.

That was a good thing, because if they had to wait for the actual gravity shift to be detected, the enemy would be among them before the gravity "boom" of their passing could be detected.

Faster-than-light technology presented many unique and headache-inducing problems for the captain of a warship.

"Understood," she said. "Stand by to initiate."

"Aye aye, ma'am," her tactical and weapons expert, Lieutenant Commander Geoff Maxim, answered. "Initiation ready on your command."

Hyatt examined the readings. "Hold for my signal . . ."

She keyed open a laser link to the *Bellerophon.* "Captain Roberts, we've detected the quantum bow shock of the enemy formation. Standing by to enable the system."

The laser went out, taking several moments before she received a reply.

"Roger that, Captain Hyatt," Roberts' quiet voice came back finally. "Initiate at your discretion. *Bellerophon* will follow your lead."

"Understood, Captain. Good luck, good hunting," Hyatt sent before killing the comm and putting the ship's systems as dark as could be managed.

Hiding a Heroic Class ship from gravity detection was not an insignificant task, unfortunately, which was what had led them to their current situation. The *Boudicca* was parked in extremely close orbit of a cold planetoid roughly two-thirds the mass of Earth. It had no atmosphere, which was the only reason they were in a technical orbit and not flying a "few miles off the surface," but the planetoid massed enough that any passive scan of the system would conclude that the *Bo*'s mass was simply part of the planetoid.

Active scans would be trickier, but those had to be directed and space was a big place. If the enemy got suspicious of the planetoid for some reason and focused their attention there, things would likely get problematic. Barring that, however, Hyatt figured that they should be safe.

For a certain version of safe.

Nowhere in the entire system was what she would consider "safe," of course, not with an Imperial flotilla about to bear down on them.

"Ma'am, triangulation from the *Bell* confirmed," Maxim said firmly. "We're in the hot seat, ma'am."

That didn't surprise her. The initial scans seemed to indicate that the enemy were coming their way. Based on the data they'd received from the Prometheus Rogues, Hyatt and Roberts had figured out the most likely approach vector to the system and parked themselves as best they could to cover the widest aspect of those vectors.

As luck would have it, she supposed, the *Boudicca* was up.

"Initiate the system," she ordered as some of the readings she was watching on the tactical repeaters changed.

"Aye ma'am. Initiating," Maxim confirmed instantly.

Well, that's it. Game on.

▶▶▶

Lord's Own Dreadnought, *Empress Liann*

▶ Jesan overlooked the main screens as the ships approached the target system, though there was nothing really to see. When moving faster than light, the effects of universal laws were such that real-time viewing became effectively impossible. The computers could reverse engineer the effect pattern, given time, but not within anything that resembled a reasonable tactical time frame.

So he stared at the raw spattering of color displayed on the screen, wavelengths of light that were actually invisible to the naked eye under normal circumstances but were now shifted into visibility while other wavelengths were made invisible as a result of their great speed.

"Sector Lord, we're approaching the deceleration point," the ship's commander announced respectfully.

"Very well, Captain. You may make the approach at your discretion," Mich said simply, his voice and tone doing nothing to betray his interest in what was coming.

Since he'd heard about the troubles the navarch's squadrons had encountered during their penetrations of the Oather worlds, he'd been fascinated by what might be discovered there. Real challenges were quite rare for one of his rank and power.

Mich kept his posture commanding as the orders were given and the ship's hum shifted subtly, the lights on the main display wavering as the vessel reversed its acceleration to the outer system they had chosen for their first approach. He didn't really expect much to happen here.

The little planet was by all reports rather unimpressive within even the Oathers' limited colonial reach, but it was part of enemy territory.

The screen stabilized a moment later, and he found himself looking at what could be the view from nearly any system in the galaxy.

The star was a distant point of light in the center of their screens, a white dot in the speckled black. Nothing special, certainly nothing to hint that there was anything present other than just that point of light. At first that was all he saw, all there was to see, really. That changed as the computers began to catch up to the sub-light scans they had available, comparing them to library records of the system. From what Imperial Intelligence and the navarch's squadrons had acquired, the local planets were filled in on the screen as the computer located each of them in turn and then highlighted their position in the black with a red box and another point of colored light.

"No signs of any Oather activity, My Lord," the ship's commander announced a few moments later. "Gravity scans show nothing out of the ordinary for the system, according to library records."

Pity, Jesan supposed. He almost wished that there had been a small squadron waiting for them. A few ships would have been enough for him to get a measure of the enemy without unduly risking his command.

"Very well, take us in. Vector for the Oather colony."

"On your orders, My Lord. Fleet Command to all ships," the commander said. "Vector information follows. All ahead, three-quarter power."

The distant hum of the reactor drives shifted again, as did the light visible on the screens—neither quite so drastically as they had before—while the ships launched themselves downwell of the local sun. With gravity helping them, the fleet made fast progress as they began the long fall starward.

"Signals detected from the colony planet, Fleet Lord."

Jesan looked over to where the communication officer had spoken. "Anything concerning us yet?"

"Not yet, My Lord. Merely the normal communications one might expect from a new colony," the officer admitted.

"Continue to monitor. I want to know when they detect us."

"Yes, My Lord."

Jesan was feeling fidgety, he found, like he couldn't quite sit still. Something was missing. Something *had* to be missing.

Then one of the lights representing a ship in his fleet blinked out, and every alarm in the *Empress Liann* went off in a screaming mess as the screens shifted to show the vessel.

Fires were burning in *space*.

Jesan rose up from his seat, shocked, his eyes wide as he looked over the scene. "What happened?!"

▶▶▶

▶ The CM mine was a relatively simple piece of technology, really.

Just a dumb computer connected to a powerful CM generator and a Priminae power capacitor. The generator had its vibratory currents reversed from the normal settings, making it much closer to what was known as a Kubelblitz than a traditional CM device.

That meant that, when the command to initiate was given by the *Boudicca*, the little, inoffensive device became what might be best described as a Mr. Hyde version of its normally pleasant self. Instead of lowering the effective mass effect of everything within its sphere of influence, the mine increased the effect of mass.

By rather a lot.

The Imperial ship unknowingly sucked the device into its own forward wave trough, part of the gravity wave that allowed the warp drive of the vessel to apparently break the laws of the universe and travel faster than light. Inside that already-warped space, however, the mine activated and went terminal.

The result was that the wave trough suddenly deepened incredibly, sucking the ship forward into its own drive warp. The deep sinkhole in space and time that pulled the ship along suddenly expanded dangerously, its outer edge intersecting with the Imperial craft.

That alone would be enough to strain the superstructure and possibly even the hull of the ship, but not remotely enough to cause it any serious damage. The sudden appearance of an *event horizon* within the gravity sinkhole, however, changed things rapidly.

In an instant a true singularity sucked in the mine, destroying it instantly from the point of view of the mine but leaving the locale an eternal pit from the perspective of all observers beyond the event horizon. Eternal, of course, until the newly formed event horizon expanded, eating up all the particles and energy that had been unwillingly stored in the ship's warp wave. With that energy and mass added, its growth jumped again, reaching beyond the warp in space-time that the ship had carefully formed and stretching out for the ship itself.

Once the event horizon crossed the edge of the vessel's bow, everything went to hell for those on board.

▶▶▶

AEV *Boudicca*

▶ "Oh God."

Hyatt didn't look around to see who had spoken. She didn't care. She wasn't actually feeling all that great about what she was looking at either.

The small artificial singularity they had introduced to the path of the enemy squadron was not remotely enough to do what they'd just seen. Not under normal circumstances, at least. However, when planted right into the forward warp of an accelerating warship, the numbers they had worked out were clearly correct. In many ways, Hyatt almost wished they hadn't been.

"Sweet Jesus, would you look at that . . ."

The bow of the enemy ship couldn't take the strain, and the armor spaghettified. From the perspective of the *Boudicca*, the armor was just torn to shreds and sucked into a spiral around the singularity. Explosions rocked the ship as critical systems were torn apart, and fires erupted as gasses escaped into space.

Hyatt refused to look away.

"Tell me again that isn't stable," she ordered softly.

"No ma'am," Commander Maxim said, his voice sickly. "The singularity shouldn't have the mass to remain stable. It should explode anytime n—"

He was cut off as the front of the Imperial ship suddenly vanished in an explosion of pure energy.

Hyatt flinched, shaking her head.

"Alright. I'd say we just delivered a line in the sand," she said firmly, forcing down the bile in her gut. "Do we have any—"

"There's another one!"

Again, she didn't look to see who had spoken.

The scene of another ship being torn to shreds, in part by its own warp wave, transfixed her. Hyatt stared silently until that vessel suddenly exploded in a flash of brilliant energy.

"Lord forgive us," she whispered. "This is insanity."

▶ ▶ ▶

Imperial Fleet, Deep Space

▶ "All stop! All vessels stop!"

Navarch Misrem screamed over the command channel, her own ship dumping velocity as quickly as it could. The explosions of two ships had made it clear to her that they'd bumbled, somehow, into a minefield.

She strode over to the scanning station, eyes wild as she glared at the technician.

"Find those weapons!" she snarled.

"Y-yes Navarch!"

The Oathers or, more likely to her estimation, the anomaly species, had spotted their approach and prepared a welcome this time.

Not entirely unexpected, but still impressive.

It's almost like they were watching our approach for some time already, Misrem thought, the sarcasm dripping even in her own mind.

She knew those damn *invisible* ships had caused this. The enemy's destroyers were so hard to detect that they could have had pickets observing all the way from Imperial territory, sending intelligence on their course back to the ambushers here, and there was damn little that the fleet could have done about it.

She'd screamed for an all stop, and thankfully most of the sector fleet had responded with some modicum of common sense.

"How many ships?" Misrem asked tersely, eyes darting to the screens. "How many have we lost?"

"Three . . . four, Navarch," her second answered, wincing as he delivered the correction. "What type of weapons are those?"

"At a guess? Some type of singularity generator." She sighed. "They are clearly sending a message."

Her second looked over at her with wide eyes. "That would be a significant message, Navarch. Singularity weapons are banned by Imperial edict."

"I find it unlikely that they signed on to that agreement," Misrem responded dryly, "not that signing it has stopped the Empire when times called for special deployment."

"Navarch! The sector lord wishes to speak with you, My Lady!"

Misrem groaned but waved an acknowledgment. "To my station."

▶▶▶

▶ Jesan glowered at the screen when it cleared to show Navarch Misrem falling heavily into her seat.

"What just happened?!" he snarled.

"You likely know more than I," she said wearily, "but at a guess I would say that we entered the kill zone of a hastily prepared minefield."

"Hastily prepared? Why do you think that?" Jesan asked, unbelieving.

"Simply? Because we've only lost four ships, My Lord," she answered succinctly. "Had they had time to lay this properly, we could have lost ten percent of our forces instead of less than one. The Oathers and their allies are giving notice here, My Lord."

"I will see this 'notice' of theirs shoved deeply up their . . ."

"Peace, My Lord." Misrem held up a hand. "I agree. For the moment, however, we must deal with the current issue. We should scan the local area intently, identify any more weapons, and eliminate them."

Jesan took a breath. "Of course. Consider the orders issued."

"Very well, My Lord. I will return to my work," she said before bowing her head. "My apologies for issuing fleet commands, My Lord. It was not my place."

Jesan settled back, looking at her over the screen intently for a moment before he suddenly waved a hand idly. "Please, Navarch. That is of no matter. You were quite correct in this instance. You have my gratitude."

He smiled thinly, leaving no doubt between them that his gratitude was entirely dependent on her success. Had she overstepped her bounds to such a degree and been *wrong*, that would have been a very different story with a much uglier outcome for the navarch.

"Thank you for your understanding, My Lord." Misrem bowed her head again. "I live to serve."

Jesan nodded, dismissing her but staring at the blank screen for some time after it had gone dark.

Misrem, he decided, was an ambitious and intelligent woman. Despite her previous failures, his impression and her record said that failing was something she was largely unfamiliar with. She could be a valuable ally, he decided. For a time, at least. Eventually, if she were permitted to gain sufficient power, he had no doubt that she would be far more of a deficit than an asset.

I believe I will keep this one close, for a time, Jesan decided.

Once this operation was complete, he would have uses for a disposable asset like her.

He *always* had uses for disposable assets.

Jesan got up and walked across the command deck as the computers began lighting up with detections and opening fire on the destructive little annoyances that lay in their path.

"Proceed ahead," he ordered. "*Slowly*, all scanners active. Find and clear those things from my space."

"Yes, My Lord," the commander answered. "All ships, ahead slow. Scan and destroy targets as they are detected."

▶▶▶

AEV *Boudicca*

▶ "Well, it was fun while it lasted," Hyatt said, her stomach churning again.

She'd thought watching the little singularity bombs tear ships apart was a gut-wrenching feeling, but that was nothing compared to watching the massive fleet start shooting them out of space as it began to lumber slowly forward again.

They'd deployed hundreds of the little lethal balls of quantum tech, and in return they got *four* ships. FOUR.

She wasn't sure there were enough munitions in the entire reserves of the Earth and Priminae militaries combined to do much more than blunt the edge of the Imperial advance. She hoped she was wrong, but then she had hoped to get a couple dozen ships with the impromptu minefield.

"Orders, ma'am?"

"Tell engineering to figure out how to put cam-plates on those damn things. Maybe we'll be able to sneak a few more past them next time."

"Uh . . . yes ma'am," her first officer responded. "But, um, I meant right now?"

"Orders? Stay deep, stay silent," she snapped. "What the hell else are we going to do?"

He sighed, relaxing. "Yes ma'am."

Honestly, Hyatt fumed, did he think she would order a frontal assault? She doubted even Weston would be so foolish as to entertain that idea in this case. Whatever happened to the colony now, it was out of their control.

"Record everything," she ordered. "Just . . . record everything."

CHAPTER 15

AEV *Odysseus,* Ranquil System

▶ "This is what we're to be building," Milla said firmly, displaying a conceptual sketch as well as rough diagrams to the group of assembled engineers. "The captain wishes to have . . . drones with the capacity . . . well, suffice to say, the captain will get what he has asked for."

The engineers shifted a little uneasily. They could read the specs as well as she could and many of them were a little less than eager about the project themselves. Still, she was right. They would get the captain what he'd asked for, assuming it was remotely possible.

The designs were straightforward, thankfully. Those who were familiar with antimatter were pleased to note that containment was far simpler, given that there would be no need for the extreme precision of magnetic containment used on board starships such as the Rogue or Odyssey Class.

The drones had no need of atmosphere, so the entire storage area would be evacuated and largely open to space. That would allow them to use a more forgiving containment system to hold the antimatter charges while awaiting deployment orders. Rearming the drones would be the usual nightmare, of course, but that would be a problem for the future.

The drones were to have a sharp-pronged forward "bow," a large bulbous sphere to contain the warping core to the rear, and a central open area that would hold the charges.

The design was simple and elegant—and terrified the engineers like few other things they'd seen.

Milla calmly walked them through the assembly steps while the *Odysseus'* automated fabrication systems built the parts they hadn't transhipped from the Forge. Mostly these were space-frame pieces, along with structure and custom containment arrays, easily fabricated once the designs had been finalized.

When she was done, Milla turned and set her eyes on the part of the project she had chosen for herself.

▶▶▶

▶ Odysseus quietly observed the work, standing off to one side but remaining visible. He could, of course, be everywhere on the ship without being seen. In a way he was, for there was nothing he could do to shut off the thoughts that formed in his mind in every given moment. Each plan, fantasy, musing, and daydream of each and every one of the ship's eight hundred and forty-three crewmembers were part of his consciousness.

It was a strange sensation, or he believed it was at first, to think thoughts that were . . . less than complimentary toward himself. The idea that perhaps he should be killed passed through his mind every few seconds when someone was in any way thinking about him. Even the captain caused such thoughts to materialize in Odysseus' mind.

However, he also felt the firm belief that all life had value and that his right to existence was inviolate right up until the moment when he chose to violate someone else's rights to the same. That too came from the captain, among others.

The dichotomy of the thoughts were such that Odysseus didn't even try to straighten them out within his own mind, assuming anything could be entirely considered to be his "own." Humans had self-destructive thoughts with a frequency that Odysseus suspected would horrify most. From actual suicidal thoughts, thankfully rare, to the occasional "what if" questions as they looked into the singularity core—which even Odysseus found exceedingly disturbing—humans thought about ways of killing themselves far more often than they thought about how to kill him.

Perhaps a cold comfort of sorts, but it was what Odysseus had for the moment.

Humans were a destructive sort, seemingly by nature. There was nothing *personal* about it.

So Odysseus largely did what humans did and ignored those passing thoughts, letting them slide by while giving them no weight. He didn't know if the process was healthy, to be honest, despite the musing of several PhDs among the crew who had opinions on the subject. Their thoughts being part of his mental processing helped him better comprehend what he was doing, just not whether it was a good idea.

With those issues safely put aside, Odysseus focused on the drive that he had inherited from his crew, which was deeper than any of those passing thoughts. The men and women on board were focused, deeply intent on the defense of a world he had no personal memory of having seen.

Earth.

Odysseus had viewed the digital records, but he preferred the idealized image that most of the crew held in their minds. A sparkling white-and-blue jewel set against a black infinity, Earth was at the core of an entire belief system that he found himself entrenched in. He was enough of a philosopher to wonder if this was what children brought up in deeply religious families experienced. But like his namesake, Odysseus was a warrior at his core and matters of philosophy were best left for peacetime.

There was a time for philosophy, but this was not that time.

▶▶▶

▶ The crewmembers had little time to think, each department head conducting drills and pushing them to peak efficiency, mostly as a means of keeping everyone busy. Too many bad and questionable things were preying on the crew's fears and concerns. Leaving them with time to think about such affairs would be asking for nothing but trouble.

Eric, for the most part, left his officers to handle their departments while he oversaw as much of the various efforts under way as he could.

The *Odysseus* was already worked up to about as high a level of efficiency as could reasonably be managed, such that under normal circumstances he'd have stepped on any new efficiency drills just for concerns that they would inadvertently blunt the already finely honed skills of the crew. With as many distractions and worries as were floating about, however, he was willing to sacrifice a few points of efficiency from fatigue if it kept the crew from worrying about the "haunted" ship, or the damned flotilla bearing down on them all.

Worrying about those things was *his* job.

Eric checked the time stamp on his personal system, noting that the *Big E* and any other reinforcements the admiral could scrounge together would shortly be arriving in system. With those, as well as what ships the Priminae could supply, the *Odysseus* would move out to enforce the *Bell* and the *Bo* and Priminae frontline vessels.

It wouldn't be enough, not without several major and minor miracles, but the line had to be held. Failing to do so would mean falling to an Empire that was willing to unleash beasts like the Drasin on innocent worlds.

It was more than merely unthinkable, it was intolerable.

Eric pushed those thoughts away. He had to avoid falling into the same trap he was working so hard to keep his crew from. Worrying about the enemy wouldn't solve the problem of their approach. Only working on solutions could do that.

He called up the latest from Milla's drone project, checking the general status reports from the different groups involved. Most of the work was continuing apace, with space frames being turned out as fast as the ship's fab units could manage and propulsion and control systems basically dropped in without issue.

The antimatter and transition-cannon designs were a little trickier, particularly since testing couldn't exactly be done while the drones were *on* the *Odysseus*.

Only one man had ever been so mind-numbingly insane as to expose his own damned ship to antimatter, and Eric had personally ordered that he *never* be allowed anywhere near the *Odysseus*. Chief Doohan from the *Autolycus* was a stone-cold badass, of that there was no doubt, but Eric didn't want the man within two light-minutes of his ship.

Luckily, as commodore of his task force, he had a *lot* to say about it.

Eric shivered, just thinking about the mission reports filed by the *Auto*'s Captain Passer. An induced antimatter enema for the ship might have topped the cake, but the bizarre star gun built into an entire alien world, albeit a small one, that was populated by *dragons* . . .

I thought we got the strange missions.

He set aside those thoughts, cursing his tendency to get sidetracked while simultaneously realizing it meant that he was getting tired and mentally fatigued. He closed down the files and rose from his station.

"Commander," he said to Miram, who was working across the way, "you have the bridge. I'm going to check on some of the side projects. If the *Enterprise* arrives, let me know."

"Aye Captain. I have the bridge," Heath said automatically. "I'll have you paged if the *Big E* arrives in system."

"No need for that. It'll be hours before we rendezvous anyway," Eric said. "Just send a notification to my systems."

"Yes sir."

"Thank you, Commander. I'll be back shortly," he said as he left.

▶▶▶

▶ Eric was silent as he stepped onto the open decks where the engineers had taken over, assembling the space frames Milla had designed and quickly installing all the off-the-shelf components they could while the final designs for the more esoteric pieces were put through their paces in simulations before real-world testing could be completed. They were rushing everything faster than he would normally be comfortable with, but when you were up against the wall, you did what you could with what you had.

He spotted Odysseus, also silently looking over the work, and briefly wondered what the young intelligence was thinking. As if that was a talisman to summon the boy—and Eric supposed it likely was—Odysseus turned and marched in his direction, looking like something out of a historical documentary.

Eric wondered curiously whether actual hoplite soldiers marched like that, or if what he was seeing was the result of modern expectations.

"Captain," Odysseus said formally as he came to a stop beside Eric's position.

"Odysseus." Eric returned the respect. "How are things progressing?"

"They appear to be moving along as expected, so far," the boy replied, his formal tone bringing a twitch to Eric's lips as he tried to keep from smiling.

Just the thought seemed to put Odysseus out slightly, though, and the rigid soldier vanished to be replaced by the young boy.

"Did I speak improperly?" Odysseus asked, his voice just a little plaintive.

"No, I'm sorry." Eric chuckled, not able to keep it in any longer. "It has to do with your apparent age and how people perceive children who act overly grown up."

Odysseus pouted slightly, looking down at his body. "I don't understand why I am in this form. I'm immaterial. Shouldn't I be able to choose what people see?"

"We rarely get to choose how other people see us, Odysseus," Eric said softly, "however much we might try. Don't worry too much about how you look. Just focus on what you want to become in the future."

"I am a warrior, I will be a warrior."

"There are warriors . . . and then there are warriors, Odysseus," Eric said with a very slight frown. "But Odysseus was more than a warrior in the epic, I hope you know."

"I do. He was also a king."

"And a father," Eric said, "and a navigator, a sea captain, a diplomat when necessary, and a clever man who knew that fighting was not always the solution he should seek. He was also foolish and arrogant, a man who knew the gods existed and yet chose to mock them anyway. The Romans knew him as the liar Odysseus, a man who shirked his duty. The Greeks revered him as a cultural hero. If he existed in reality, he was probably all of these things. People are complicated."

Odysseus looked down, his face a mask of confusion. "But . . . I am named after him. Should I not model myself after him?"

"Take what you like of his story, aspire to that, but don't try to be anyone other than the very best *you* that can be managed," Eric said. "We don't become heroes or legends, Odysseus. We take one step at a time, solve each problem as it arises, and we let the rest handle itself as it will. We can't control how we're seen, but we can control how we *see*."

"I do not understand," Odysseus admitted slowly.

"You will, and probably sooner than later, so don't worry about it for now," Eric responded as he refocused his attention across the deck and winced involuntarily. "Ouch. Steph is going to *kill* me."

"What?" Odysseus looked up, seemingly distracted enough to have initially missed Eric's reaction and thoughts. He followed the captain's gaze, tuning himself back into the thoughts around him, and saw what had prompted that reaction. "Oh. Is that going to be as bad as I believe it to be?"

"Steph is going to blow his top," Eric confirmed, smiling a little ruefully, "but I gave her blanket authorization."

Milla and a small crew of engineer ratings had swarmed over Steph's Archangel and had already succeeded in ripping the twin power plants right out of the airframe with the overhead-loading gantry. She was intent on welding in the framework to drop a Priminae shuttle warp core in the reactor's place, which was a neat trick. If it worked out, he would probably get her to mod his own fighter.

He was plenty glad that she wasn't experimenting on his, though.

"You will need a pilot for that," Odysseus pointed out.

"Yup, and there's only one on board I trust with it besides myself. I hope Steph has trained his department well, because at least one Archangel is going to taste vacuum again soon."

▶▶▶

▶ Miram Heath looked up when the soft alarm chime sounded, checking the computer automatically without pausing in her work.

It was a proximity alarm tied to the long-range scanners, alerting her to the arrival of a small squadron of Priminae Heroics. They were expecting more of the same over the next few days, while the *Odysseus* completed its official task of working back up to fighting form and, unofficially, worked to get everyone used to the presence of the deus ex machina that now inhabited the ship.

Like most everyone on board, she had her reservations concerning Odysseus, but Miram had to admit that moments arose when she looked forward to what the entity would become with some level of anticipation. She knew that she was just seeing mere hints of what he was capable of, and she was already impressed.

Odysseus could interface with the ship's computers, analyze information through the eyes of every member of the crew, provide intelligence on any person who stepped foot on the deck of the big ship . . .

She truly suspected that was only the very tip of the iceberg when dealing with Odysseus.

Ultimately, she had no doubt that he could do great things. She was just terrified of the mistakes he could make along the way. Odysseus had already gotten a lot of good men and women killed, and he'd really only woken up and tried to live up to the expectations the crew placed on his name. His excitement at the prospect of battle was the sort of thing only a child could have truly emulated, which proved neatly that while the intelligence might have all the crewmembers' thoughts, it did *not* have their experience.

The people lost in that headlong rush at the enemy were a hard lesson, or she hoped they were at least. If the boy shrugged the lesson off too easily, then the great things he would inevitably accomplish in the future might well be terrible things too. There was no moral compass to greatness, sadly.

She knew he had the one inside him; she just prayed he had both.

Another chime distracted her from her line of thoughts, this time slightly different. She looked over to the repeater screen she had tied in to the scanner station, and her eyes widened as she recognized the transponder codes.

"Well, well, welcome to the war," she said to the screen, shaking her head slightly. "Not sure what you'll be able to do, but somehow I feel a little better with the *Enterprise* in the fray."

Miram smiled tightly, eyes darting about the screen as she noted the rest of the icons. The admiral had come through, with a dozen more Rogues appearing and two Heroics that had been assigned to Home Fleet defense.

The Commodore will be pleased, she thought. The *Geronimo* and the *Chin Shih* would significantly add to the power they could bring to bear. She entered the date into the system and copied it to the commodore, settling back to return her focus to her tasks at hand. The ship was ready. The crew was ready. She just hoped Odysseus was ready.

Whether he was or not, however, time was up.

The warrior king was going to war.

▶▶▶

AEV *Enterprise,* Ranquil System

▶ "All systems green, the ship is good to go, Skipper."

James knew without doubt that he had to have a sickly green look to his face, but he stoically refused to acknowledge its existence as he stiffly nodded.

"Thank you, Ensign," he told the young woman at the ship's communications center. "Secure the vessel from transition alert."

They'd transitioned into the system some time earlier, but as it had been their first transition in some time, he had maintained alert while all systems were properly checked. The *Enterprise* had taken its place in the line of battle that was now loitering in the outer Ranquil System, and while she was a small ship, even compared to the Rogues, he'd be damned to hell if she came up short in any way that mattered.

The two Heroics the admiral had shaken loose, including the *Shih* (he was stunned that she'd managed to convince the Block to give up one of their best ships to the cause), took up the center of the formation. The massive vessels were surrounded by a dozen Rogues and several dozen collier vessels with supplies and munitions for the task force.

All in all, over a hundred ships had just entered the Priminae's main star system, loaded for bear and looking for targets.

Unfortunately, from what they had on the enemy, targets would shortly be in plentiful supply.

"Signal from the *Odysseus,*" the communications officer said, looking up. "She welcomes us to Ranquil and attaches rendezvous coordinates, sir."

"Send them to the helm, Ensign," James said. "We're here to do a job."

"Aye aye, Skipper."

The *Enterprise* was shortly shifting course along with the rest of the formation, keeping the ships to the edge of the heliosphere as they awaited the arrival of the *Odysseus* and her Priminae companions. James eyed the telemetry that showed the formation rising up from the Ranquil primary's gravity well on course to meet them, and couldn't help but wonder why the *Odysseus* was separated from her task group.

The official story wasn't unlikely, but something didn't ring true about it to him either.

It wasn't hard to believe that Weston had managed to take the brunt of the fighting in such a way as to more severely damage the *Odysseus*, but the repair times in the report seemed like overkill for anything short of building an entirely new ship. Since he was pretty certain that hadn't happened, James figured there was more going on than he'd been told.

"The *Odysseus* and escorts will rendezvous with us in four hours, sir."

"Thank you, Ensign. I suppose we just get to relax a little and wait," James said as he smiled.

Some things in the service just never changed.

Hurry up and wait, my boys, hurry up and wait.

▶▶▶

AEV *Odysseus*

▶ Steph reread his orders again, uncertain what to make of them.

He certainly wasn't going to object, of course. If the commodore wanted him flight checked on the Double A platform, that was nothing but good news to him. It did arouse a certain suspicious curiosity, however, since he was well aware that there was not a damn thing an Archangel could do against what the Imperial Fleet was likely to throw in their direction.

What are you up to, Raze?

Steph reserved some simulator time before doing anything else, though he was relatively certain he could qualify. It was never a bad thing to brush off a little of the rust before a qual flight run. Then he queried the computer for a location of the captain.

Best way to figure out Raze is to start by asking him to his face, Steph thought as he got the location of a flight deck and started off in that direction.

Asking the man might not get him anything but would hopefully knock a few options off the table depending on how the commodore responded. Steph hoped that there was a new doctrine coming down the pipe that included fighters, but with Raze fixated on drones, he doubted it.

A morbid thought crossed his mind then, and Steph faltered in midstep.

Oh crap. He'd better not be planning on putting one of those antimatter chuckers on my fighter!

There were limits to how reckless he was willing to be, even in pursuit of the fighter-jock image, and Steph drew that line right before he'd let anyone load his fighter up with the nightmare fuel that was antimatter.

No way. No chance.

He continued to steel himself to tell Eric just where he could get off if, and when, the man made that suggestion, mumbling to himself with more and more agitation the closer he got to the flight deck. Steph didn't notice other crewmembers steering a wide berth around him as his affable amble became more of a stalking motion with each passing moment.

After a few minutes he found the right deck, and stepped off the lift with the intention of locating Eric. He couldn't help but throw a fond and longing glance in the direction of his fighter, mostly on reflex.

What he saw wiped all thoughts of Eric from his mind . . . along with practically everything else.

His Angel. His fighter. His one and only true love was in pieces and strewn across the busy deck, looking like it had been hacked by some vengeful psycho he had unknowingly offended. Steph froze in place, staring in unadulterated horror at the scene until he finally found his voice.

"What the ever-living f—" he blew, his voice rising with each word until, by the end, every person on the deck was looking at him with varying expressions of shock, humor, or stunned confusion.

Steph started moving, hands twitching as they reflexively tried to find something to wrap themselves around, heading straight for his baby.

CHAPTER 16

AEV *Bellerophon,* Outer System

▶ Jason Roberts stared grim-faced at the screens, hating that he was forced to stand and watch the scene that was unfolding.

Even if he had the forces, it would hardly have made much difference, of course, as they were looking at something that had happened hours earlier. Light-speed was painfully slow by even stellar distances to say nothing of interstellar ones, and the small task group he currently commanded was so insufficient to the current task that they hadn't dared to break cover to approach the colonial planet.

The orbital bombardment shouldn't have been a surprise to him, not really, but when the first kinetic strikes lanced out from the fleet, his guts had twisted. Part of him really believed that the Imperials would secure the colony and claim it as part of the Empire.

That was what was expected in his view of war.

One didn't wage genocidal war. What was the point? War was to claim resources. There was no other sane reason for it.

Of course, these were the people who had unleashed the Drasin on the galaxy.

Genocide was mild compared to that atrocity, in his opinion.

Jason's knuckles were blanched, glaringly so against his skin, the force of his clenched fist making his nails cut into the palm of his hand as he felt an utterly consuming rage building inside him. He didn't know the Priminae well, and didn't know anyone on the planet below at all, but he didn't need to.

"Goddamn them."

The words were a whisper, floating around the command deck. Sometimes they seemed to morph into another similar but different phrasing. Jason never recognized the voice, and didn't really care. The sentiment was fitting.

Goddamn them indeed.

"Sir, the Imperials are launching ships to the surface," his scanner tech announced.

"Give me the best view you can," he ordered.

The scanners' acuity, even at such an insane range, was impressive, the result of a widespread series of scanners on every ship in the task group all working together. For the moment he didn't care about the technical details.

The image was good enough to make out individual hulls as they broke away from the main group and entered the atmosphere.

"Looks like they're going to occupy the world after all," Roberts said flatly.

"Why would they bombard the colony like that, then?" his first officer asked softly.

"Pacification, maybe just an object lesson," Roberts said simply. "At least they left someone alive."

He tapped a command and brought the image zoom out, enough to show the whole fleet. The swarm of ships blotted out part of the planet and the sun beyond at that zoom, sending a shiver down his spine.

"What should we do?" his first officer asked.

"Do? Nothing. There's nothing we can do," Roberts answered, a sickly taste in his mouth. "We watch. We wait. And when they leave, we mark their course and then . . . then we can do something."

▶▶▶

Lord's Own Dreadnought, *Empress Liann*

▶ Jesan stood stoically as he watched the fires burn from orbit, smoke filling enough area to be easily visible even without magnification. The fires themselves showed up through the smoke as the terminator advanced slowly, turning day to night, and the smoke took on an ominous and evil glow.

"All significant infrastructure has been eliminated, My Lord," his adjutant said, approaching from behind.

"Excellent, and phase two?"

"A garrison structure has been launched, along with the forces to more than pacify the remaining population. With the approaching drop in local temperatures expected from the dust and smoke we've filled the sky with, they can be expected to have difficulty meeting their nourishment needs for the foreseeable future."

"How many survivors?"

"Approximately eighty percent, with five to ten percent margin for error," the adjutant said.

"Excellent. My compliments to the gunners," Jesan said.

With farmland, power and transport systems, and various other vital sectors in ruins, the colony belonged to the Empire. The survivors would need to eat, and he had just made certain that if they wanted to do so and hoped to live, with their families no less, then they would soon be beholden to the Empire. Any new infrastructure would be gifts from the empress, as it should be.

"Inform the fleet that as soon as we've completed landing operations, we will be moving on to the next target."

"Yes, My Lord. Will we leave any ships to secure the orbitals?"

"Why bother."

"Of course, My Lord. I will see to it that the orders are issued."

Jesan merely waved, his attention turning back to the burning smoke on the world below. It was a small step, of course, but an important and symbolic one. The first world the Empire had taken in this sector and the first world secured from the control of the Oathers themselves. The Empire would record it as a momentous date, but the procurement was merely the first step of many.

He gestured with his hand, clearing the screen and refocusing out beyond the reach of the local star to the black beyond. Jesan was still troubled by the weapons they'd encountered coming into the system. There had been no indications that the colony was capable of any sort of operation of that nature, and if it had been, then Jesan would have expected far more of the weapons.

The measly few they located were so insufficient to the task that it was actually amusing. Or would have been if the weapons hadn't been placed so *precisely* correct as to intercept his fleet.

Someone is out there, he thought with certainty.

Those damn nigh-invisible ships that had been reported by the early probes and confirmed by the navarch's experiences. Small pests, but able to maneuver around with near impunity due to their low power curves and adaptable camouflage systems.

Thankfully, the navarch's last foray had shown that the Imperial response to their most serious weapon would be effective. That was a great relief, as he had *no* desire to experience his ship's interactions with negative matter.

Really, what sort of lunatics store that on board their own ship, in combat no less?

He knew that they *had* to be storing it, given that they showed almost no power curve and producing negative matter took no small degree of power to accomplish. It was remotely possible, of course, that they had discovered a less power-intensive method, but he doubted that.

Still, with those weapons largely neutralized, he had thought that the invisible vessels would be of little concern. Now he saw otherwise.

Four ships lost, and we never fired a shot in our defense until it was over. I begin to see what the navarch meant when she stressed that they were not to be underestimated. They have sneaky minds, these anomalies.

"My Lord," his adjutant said, "deployment operations have concluded."

"Very good. Issue the orders to break orbit. We have other systems to pacify."

▶▶▶

AEV *Bellerophon*

▶ "That's it, they're moving out."

Jason Roberts nodded, eyes on the plot he knew was hours old. The enemy fleet was steadily climbing up out of the star's gravity well, heading away from where his task group was hiding out, on a vector that would bring them deeper into Priminae territory and, incidentally, closer to Earth.

"Show me the planet, best magnification," he ordered.

There was no need to rush concerning the enemy fleet, as it would take them hours to clear the cluttered inner system. No fleet commander would be crazy enough to order a translight acceleration that deep inside a gravity well. Not outside of combat, at least, and hardly enough even then. Too much debris kicking around, waiting to be turned into ballistic threats.

The main display flickered, showing the planet as closely as their combined scanners could manage.

The smoke was obscuring the better part of a continent already, and dust from the kinetic strikes had spread the light spectrum spectacularly into the reds. The sky was lit up such that it seemed to burn in sympathy with the ground below, and he wondered just how many had survived the bombardment or would survive what was to come.

"We could go secure the world, sir."

Jason shook his head. "No. We'd only be wasting our time. The next world is under threat too, and the one after that, and so on. As soon as the Imperials clear the system and go to warp, I want their vector calculated. We transition ahead of them and make them pay for this as best we can. Just before we jump, send a transit message to Priminae Central Command about what happened here."

He sighed, shaking his head again before he went on.

"I'm afraid they'll have to clean up this mess themselves."

"Yes sir."

▶▶▶

▶ There was a nearly invisible Casimir flash as the Imperial Fleet reached the outer system and went translight on their warp drives, the blue glow gone almost the instant it appeared, and with it the ships themselves.

Across the black, two hulking Heroics and their smaller Rogues silently emerged from hiding and began moving under power to the system's edge. Already far out in the outer system, they broke the light-speed barrier with similar blue flashes almost immediately, speeding out well past the reach of the local star before they turned in the direction in which the Imperial Fleet had vanished and then were gone themselves in a puff of tachyons.

CHAPTER 17

AEV *Odysseus,* Ranquil System

▶ Eric intercepted Steph in midstride, catching the angry man and lifting him right up off his feet, then swinging him about before he could make it halfway to his chopped-up fighter.

"Whoa there, partner!" Eric said, grinning as he held the angry man.

"Raze! My bird! What did she do to it?" Steph wailed, gesturing wildly over Eric's shoulder.

"Lord I wish that was the first time I'd heard you say something like that."

Steph shot him a betrayed look before retorting angrily, "Oh shut it! At least I've never looked up how to get a tattoo removed from there!"

"Not like I knew it was temporary at the time," Eric laughed. "As blitzed as we were, it could have been real."

Steph snorted. "More than a few of us wound up with real ones that night . . ." He paused, eyes flashing angrily again. "Don't distract me! What the hell is going on with my fighter?"

"I authorized it," Eric said evenly, letting his friend go. "So relax and stop trying to fry Lieutenant Chans with your eyes."

Steph glanced toward the Priminae woman, who was staring back at him with wide eyes and a shocked expression, and sighed.

"Fine. What exactly did you authorize that involves pulling the *reactors*?" Steph grumbled, looking at the scattered pieces of his fighter strewn around the deck. Still, he noticed sections of tech were neatly arranged in order of removal, best he could tell, and nothing looked busted at least.

"Upgrade," Eric said, gesturing to a gantry that was holding up something Steph didn't recognize.

He ran his hand through his hair. "Okay, I'll bite. What's that?"

"That is a Priminae shuttle's warp generator," Eric replied. "We're refitting your Angel for modern combat."

Steph walked around the bulbous-looking warp generator, shaking his head. "Gonna look weird as hell, boss."

"How fast will the fighter accelerate when you're done, Milla?" Eric asked over his shoulder.

"Mass calculations indicate that, fully loaded, the craft should be able to exceed light-speed in just under eight minutes," Milla replied as she approached.

Steph choked, clutching at his chest as he started coughing.

"The *'Disseus* can barely do it in an hour!" he sputtered out, shocked.

"The *Odysseus* exceeds your fighter's mass by . . ." Milla paused, eyes rolling back and to the right as she thought furiously for a moment before giving up. "By an amount that defies calculation. The singularity alone is measured in planetary masses, Stephan. Accelerating the *Odysseus* is more akin to doing the same to a small planet than a ship . . . though that is actually a very bad analogy for a number of reasons."

Steph nodded slowly. "Weird isn't so bad."

"We have some more toys being rigged for you to play with, Stephanos," Eric said seriously, using his call sign for the first time in a while, grabbing Steph's attention. "It's time to live up to your handle. So for all our sakes, I hope you've trained your department well."

▶▶▶

Priminae Central Command, Ranquil

▶Tanner looked over the latest report, his mood not helped even slightly by what he was reading.

It seems that the Imperials have altered their tactics this time, he thought grimly.

Bombarding a colony world should have bothered him less than the Drasin just annihilating entire planets as they did, but somehow he felt the gut-wrenching pain just as viscerally.

Tanner couldn't help but look up the population of the colony, a number that had been hovering just over three million people. It was a small site, of course, one of the new explorations since the Drasin encounter, still years away from being ready for proper forming. The world would take decades before a full-scale occupation was possible, but three million people were still three million people.

He took some solace in the fact that the reports indicated the Empire had landed an occupational force. That would presumably mean there were survivors at least.

That was better than what they offered with the Drasin atrocities, if nothing else. Tanner's lips drew back in a quiet snarl before he regained control of himself.

He got up and crossed the control room to where the coordinator for the Priminae forces was working.

"Have this information transmitted to our vessels, as well as the *Odysseus,*" Tanner ordered, handing over a data chit. "We have lost the colony on Marta Three. The Empire has made their first move."

The woman paled slightly but nodded as she shakily took the chit from him and placed it on the scanner beside her.

"The rumors say that they have hundreds of ships," she said, looking to him while the system read the data.

Her eyes clearly said that she was hoping he would refute it, but Tanner just nodded.

"Over four hundred, some much larger than the Heroics I am afraid. The Terrans cost them four in exchange for Marta Three, but even if that were repeatable it would not be close to enough. I do not know what happens this time."

She nodded, turning back to the task, quickly sending the data out.

"Sent," she said, her expression dark as she did. "There must be something we can do . . ."

"Our duty."

Tanner's response was instinctive, with no thought of anything else.

"We do our duty. We trust our captains to do theirs, and we do everything in our power to support them. Really, what else is there?"

She had no response, so he turned and headed back to his station.

Tanner wondered at his own confident words. He couldn't help but think that there had to be more he could be doing, but it came down to the simple truths. There were not enough ships to go around. If they needed military personnel, they had those. Millions would volunteer instantly if the hulls were there for them.

But they weren't.

So he would do what he could in the position he was in, while everyone else did the same.

▶▶▶

AEV *Odysseus*

▶ On the bridge again, while Steph was working up to requalify on the Double A platform and Milla was hard at work on the flight deck, Eric looked over the latest communiqué from Priminae Central Command.

"So it begins."

A smile played at Eric's lips as he spoke the old quote with an ironic lilt to his tone. The reports from Captain Roberts and the rest of the squadron were enlightening, at least. He was both encouraged and concerned.

The enemy was occupying worlds—that was good. That put them back on a more conventional battlefield, one that Eric understood and could make far more sense of. Just annihilating planets had made *no Goddamn sense* to him whatsoever.

He was aware of the academic arguments concerning space combat, and the strategies some of the more nihilistic of his contemporaries supported, but Eric had never felt that they were realistic given the logistics involved.

Unfortunately, based on his understanding of logistical issues, Eric wasn't sure that the occupation of the Priminae colony made any sense either. The move was puzzling.

In many ways, war in the stars made *no* sense whatsoever.

Any culture that had the capacity to wage war in the stars clearly had *no reason* to. Resources were easier to gather from the outer systems and in fact were more plentiful around stars that were inherently incompatible with life. The area around the location of a supernova or neutron star was far more likely to have abundant supplies of valuable materials than that of a young yellow star like Earth's or any of those likely to have habitable worlds.

Which meant that the Empire had more than resources in mind.

Unfortunately, none of the prisoners they'd captured to date were willing to talk about motivations, or they honestly didn't know. Eric was inclined to think it was more the latter than the former, given the sort of people they'd captured, but it could go either way. Motivation was one of the big missing pieces left, and without it he had no way to really figure out the puzzle.

All he could do was react, and Eric hated being forced into a reactionary position.

He looked over the report that had been delivered from Roberts via the Priminae and noted the next likely target star system. It was, of course, an outer Priminae colony that lay roughly along a direct-line course from the estimated location of the Empire en route to Ranquil itself.

I suppose that tells me their likely endgame for this particular maneuver, if nothing else.

Of course their conquest wouldn't stop with Ranquil. They'd already shown that much in their willingness to unleash the Drasin. The Empire was an expansionist regime and a violently insane one by some metrics.

Eric was a student of military history, to some middling level at least. He'd spent his time learning tactics and strategies from historical leaders, battles, and campaigns, and a great deal of what he was seeing in the Empire was classical expansionist strategy if one were to ignore the initial tactics involving the Drasin. He supposed it wouldn't be the first time in history a group made use of a superweapon that ultimately worked counter to their overall goals.

Now, however, they seemed to be operating on a more traditional strategy of taking and holding land.

That he could work with.

Assuming they kept to the game plan, of course.

Fat chance of that.

"Commander," he called, rising from his station.

"Yes Captain?" Miram asked, coming over.

"We have our target," he said. "Signal all ships, our Priminae friends as well. We're moving out."

"Aye aye, Captain. Coordinates?" she asked.

"On your station already, Commander. We'll rendezvous with the *Bell* and *Bo* upon arrival. I need to see to the new project. Hopefully, we'll be far enough along for it to be of some use."

"Aye sir. I'll see it done."

▶▶▶

AEV *Enterprise*

▶ "Communication from the *Odysseus*, Captain. We have a destination. I've sent the details to your system."

"Thanks, Lieutenant," James said, and he gestured to light up his personal screens.

The details were waiting, of course, as the lieutenant had told him, and he quickly skimmed through them. As expected, they had vectors and estimated times of arrival for the Imperial forces on the next Priminae world, but so far no plan of action had been sent along.

I hope Weston has something in mind, or this will be the shortest defense ever mounted, James thought sarcastically as he examined the data with a critical eye. He noted some addendums from the commodore personally with his name attached. *What's this . . . ?*

He whistled as he read the brief. "Well now, isn't *that* an idea."

"Lieutenant Massey." James looked up toward the communications officer.

"Yes sir?"

"Put me on with the commodore as soon as we're close enough for a face-to-face," James ordered. "Please inform him that I believe it to be important, and attach the information for new missiles."

"Aye aye, Skipper. We should be in range for real-time conversation in a little under twenty minutes. I'll call ahead to confirm."

"Thank you, Massey."

James shifted back to the file the commodore had sent over. Unfortunately, there was no way the *Enterprise* fabricators could possibly produce even one of the new drones in that period of time, but it did get him thinking about some alternatives.

James found himself rather amused by it all. *I think Weston wins this round. Flying antimatter launchers beats hyperlight missiles . . . not by much, but enough. The added points for sheer balls puts it over the top. What can I come up with for round two?*

▶▶▶

AEV *Odysseus*

▶ "Communication from the *Big E*, Skipper," the communications officer said. "Flagged for your attention."

"Send it to my station," Eric said as he looked over to his inbox.

The message blinked into existence a second or so later and he brought it up, skimming the document quickly.

Hyperlight missiles . . . well now, isn't that an idea. Range isn't much, he noted, *but the kinetic power of the strike should make up for that.*

He quickly checked the inventory Captain James had sent along with the communication and started to tap out a fast request for a shipment of the devices for the *Odysseus* to use before he reconsidered his actions. Instead he signalled down to engineering.

"Chief Garrick, please."

A moment passed while the command was processed and directed to the chief; then Garrick came on the screen.

"Yes Captain?"

"Sending you specs," Eric said, shooting the files down to the chief. "I need some of the fabricators shifted over to producing these, fitted for Archangel hardpoints."

"Another project, Captain?" Garrick asked, eyes flickering to the side to read the file he'd just received. His eyes widened a moment later. "That . . . is very interesting. I will have to send my compliments to my colleague and have one of the fab units begin turning out components. We should be able to make at least a couple full loads in the time we have before estimated contact."

"Likely more than we'll need," Eric said. "I expect to be withdrawing from contact before we'd be able to reload anyway."

"Very well, Captain. I'll see if there are any improvements I might offer," Garrick said.

"Run it past Lieutenant Chans as well," Eric said. "Her expertise with Priminae technology may help."

"Yes, indeed it may, sir. I will do so," Garrick said. "I'll contact you if anything comes up."

"As you were then, Chief. Thank you."

Garrick nodded and the connection broke. Eric turned back to the endless paperwork he was dealing with as they approached likely combat with the Empire. He sighed and looked at the doctrine he had added to the overall strategies he was planning, hesitating a moment before he gestured and deleted the entire section.

Hyperlight missiles. Yup, going to need to rethink doctrine for sure.

On the plus side, Eric was quite certain that James and the *Big E* had just given him the final piece he needed to bring star fighters, and the *Enterprise* herself, right back into the fight.

Time to get to work.

▶▶▶

▶ "Absolutely not."

"Stephan, it is *useless*." Milla repeated herself for what felt like the thousandth time.

"I don't care," Steph grumbled. "You don't take away a fighter pilot's gun. It's been tried, and it *never* works. Leave the gun where it is."

"Stephan, the enemy uses ships that your cannon simply cannot damage," she said. "It is a needlessly complicated, obsolete, entirely superfluous piece of equipment."

Steph chopped his hand through the air, cutting her off.

"Then make it better," he said. "Or leave it as is, but the gun *stays*."

Milla sighed, slumping slightly. "I will see what can be done."

"Thank you," Steph said, then sighed himself. "I'm sorry, Milla. Look, call it superstition if you like, but fighter pilots *really* don't like to give up our guns, okay? It's not that much extra weight, and the system is already there. Just leave it be."

"I said I would see what could be done," Milla uttered. "I will not remove your gun." She rolled her eyes and shook her head. "Honestly. You sound like I suggested cutting off your—"

"Hey! Let's not go there."

Around the flight deck, engineers and crewmembers looked assiduously in any other direction than toward the two arguing officers. Most suffered oddly timed choking fits, but of course no one was eavesdropping.

That would be rude.

CHAPTER 18

Allied Earth Command, Cheyenne Mountain Facility

▶ Gracen's boots clicked on the polished cement floor as she made her way into one of the large, seismically isolated facilities buried deep inside the mountain complex. Like two other similar complexes in Geneva and Tibet, the revamped Cheyenne Mountain facility was one of the keystone command and control complexes that provided a redundant continuity of command for all Earth- and Sol-based operations.

She walked past two Marine guards, entering a cavernous room filled with large screens on every wall, and rows of men and women all secured in their own stations, all surrounding a massive central holographic display that was currently showing an image of the local arm of the galaxy about five hundred light-years cubed.

Gracen walked down the stairs into the central area, eyes on the highlighted stars.

Earth's star was a lone green dot, while the Priminae worlds were shown in blue. A solitary red dot showed the now lost world, currently under Imperial control. The area of space around the Priminae worlds was similarly highlighted with an amorphous blue zone to show the space they claimed as part of their area of control. Earth's green section of space was too small to show up on the current level of display.

"Admiral,"—a young ensign intercepted her—"we've prepared your work area, if you'll follow me."

"Thank you, Ensign, please lead the way."

Her work area was a large interactive desk with augmented-reality displays, designed to allow her to interact with the large central display as well as work independently. All of her files had already been transferred and were waiting for her when she took her seat. Gracen opened up the relevant ones and settled in. She quietly observed the work around her, since she was largely in a holding pattern until she got more information to work with.

"Admiral."

Gracen turned slightly, nodding politely as she recognized the gray-haired man approaching her. "General."

General Maximillian Moore was a stocky, barrel-chested man who had started going gray in his early thirties as a captain and never tried to cover it up despite the occasional hint that he might get promoted a little quicker if he didn't look twenty years older. Whatever effect his lack of vanity might have had on his career path had been truly offset by the Block War.

When the initial fighting had raged along the West Coast, Moore had led the defense of California and held off Block forces for two months before a counteroffensive had been mounted to push the enemy expeditionary force back out to sea.

Certainly, the lack of reinforcements on the other side had worked massively in his favor, but it had still been considered a noteworthy accomplishment, and when Moore had gone on to take command of the Army's overall counteroffensive through the Pacific theater, his eventual ascension to flag rank was assured. At that point the only question was how high his flag would rise, and the answer had become pretty much as high as possible.

Now serving as chief of staff of the Army for the Americas, Moore had been expected to accept an appointment to the position of secretary of defense upon his mandatory retirement at age sixty. Gracen had won a pretty sum when she bet against that, and had been proven right when

Moore accepted a presidential waiver to allow him to continue in his current capacity until the end of the current war.

"Not often we get to see you come down from on high, Admiral," Moore said with an affable smile. "Good to see you again."

"While I prefer the view from Unity, I can be of more value here in the current situation. We don't need to add even another second or so delay in communications. We'll have enough problems of that type as it stands."

"Very true." Moore looked to the holographic display with frustration. "I feel like a useless tool here, Admiral. All the heavy lifting is going to be done by your boys and girls."

"Only if we win, Admiral," Gracen said, "and that's not likely I'm afraid. If, and when, we lose the fight in the skies, you get to show your stuff."

Moore chuffed, shaking his head. "Well, suddenly I find myself *hoping* to be a useless tool. There's a sensation I've never had before in my life. Thanks ever so much for that, Admiral."

Gracen smiled, amused by the gruff man's tone. "We have a chance, General. I have a couple cards I've been holding back, and I wouldn't count the commodore out of this just yet either. He has a way of surprising people, I've found."

Moore grunted. "Not his biggest fan, but I won't argue with that. Fought under more than one sky he made friendly, or at least neutral. You really think he can turn something this big around?"

"I said I wouldn't bet against him," Gracen said before she deflated slightly, "but this time I don't think I'd put much on him either. It's a tall order, General. At least twenty times his weight of metal, maybe ten times his firepower. If that was the only thing, he might be able to pull something out, but those Imperial ships are damn tough."

"I thought the Heroics were supposed to be tough too."

"They are, but with the concentrated fire of more than ten ships to our one? Not that tough I'm afraid," Gracen said. "And what I'm most concerned with is that, based on interrogations, even this is probably only a small fraction of the Imperial forces. So beating them might just result in them sending even more ships the next time."

"Remind me not to bring the president over for you to cheer up," Moore said. "I'd be half afraid of you talking him right into a noose with that sort of pep talk. I guess it's a good thing we've been increasing militarization across the planet in case those Goddamn space spiders ever came back."

"If we're going to stop the Empire, we need to make them think twice before they ever want to come back into our space looking for trouble," Gracen said. "Frankly, there's not too many ways we can hope to do that. I've got a card or two . . . but right now, I don't know if we have the time to shuffle the deck in our favor. The commodore's orders are simple, General . . . Beat the enemy like a drum, but failing that? Buy us all the time possible and hope like hell that it's enough."

"I'd ask you about these cards you're holding back, but I don't doubt they're in the briefings I've not been able to make heads or tails of already," Moore said, shaking his head. "This is a younger man's job. All this sci-fi horror bullshit isn't what I trained for. I came up killing terrorists, Admiral. Not fighting space aliens."

"None of us trained for this, General. We adapt or we die."

"Not curling up yet," Moore said, "don't worry about that. I'll do my job. I just wish there were someone better for it."

"I wish there were someone better for your job too, General. Hell, I wish there were someone better for *mine* . . . and the commodore's. We're up at bat, and we don't get to call in a pinch hitter."

"Right you are, Admiral, right you are. I'll leave you to your work, then. Send along any new briefs when you can. The secretary of defense will want to be up on all the latest before the president comes demanding updates again."

"You'll have them before you get back to your desk, General."

Moore nodded firmly before taking his leave. Gracen watched him go for a moment before sending along the files she'd promised him.

He was right about one thing.

She wished there were better people for all their jobs too.

▶▶▶

▶ Humans built such fun and yet oddly dreary places.

Gaia didn't often observe the world through a single perspective. It was simply unnecessary, really, and so limiting. Billions of eyes, ears, and senses of all kinds were a superior way to experience the universe. Occasionally, though, she liked to intentionally narrow her perception to a single position, not entirely unlike humans might experience the world, at least in terms of limitations. Focusing her perception to one location had taken a great deal of practice and experience over the centuries and millennia and more. She couldn't exactly limit herself to human perceptions, of course. Hearing was impossible for her, strictly speaking, as she didn't have ears. She sensed things through the electromagnetic spectrum, and sound waves were kinetic energy passing through a medium.

She could detect the effects those kinetic waves had on the environment, however, so adjusting for that lack was not difficult. Glass would vibrate, and she could see the vibrations as they altered the path of light, for example. It was easier, of course, if a human was present, since then she could expand her senses just enough and use their eardrums in much the same way.

Underground in a polished stone maze, however, she had to get creative.

Presenting herself for all who might see her in passing as a uniformed Navy commander with all the appropriate clearances, altering computer records along the way, Gaia mimicked the intent march of those around her as she moved through the base known to modern humans as Cheyenne Mountain.

It was really just the latest name of many, of course. People had been naming mountains for as long as people had been living in the shadows of them, and nearly uncountable generations had given the three peaks some name or another.

Since the mountains had become home for the American and, later, the Confederation military, it had become a much more interesting place to visit. She had walked the corridors during various times of interest. The first nuclear crisis the base experienced had been fascinating to observe from the still-unfinished facility of the time. So little of it had been complete then that the observers had used gear run from portable generators trucked in for the occasion.

That disaster had been averted, along with many others over the decades that followed, but each time the tension had been real and palpable. When possible, Gaia rather enjoyed that sensation, but she had never been able to experience it the way the humans did. And now the new unknowns brought into her sphere from the black of space afforded her vastly different experiences than she had ever been able to manage in the past.

Over the centuries, Gaia had fooled herself into thinking that by limiting her perception she could feel what humans felt, but now, with added perspective, she knew for certain that was a lie.

This time, she didn't . . . *couldn't* know the other side of the equation.

Even having cut off her perception, during the various crises that occurred purely on Earth, she had always been, on some level, fully aware of both sides of the conflict. She'd know what everyone involved was capable of, what they believed, what they were prepared to risk.

This time, she had no clue. No more than the humans did, at least, and Gaia found that she . . . *detested* that sensation.

It was wrong, unnatural, and . . .

She was scared.

She didn't know how to handle fear, such an alien sensation to experience firsthand. The Drasin had come, and she hadn't been able to control them, it was true, but there had been no time for fear then. She had become enraged. Now, though, this Empire seemed just as bad . . . or near enough. They wanted to change everything, and Gaia didn't know how their efforts would change her.

Millennia, a hard thing to rewrite, true, but an alien genocidal assault might just be enough to accomplish the feat.

So she was scared. She could admit it, to herself at least. Saul knew it, and she could feel him mocking her for it even in her current state of lessened awareness, but she didn't care. He was a standoffish piece of work at the best of times, thinking he was so far removed from her affairs and those of the humans, even though she believed that Eric was right about all of their kind.

Without humans, without that intelligence to form her thoughts, to mold her way of thinking, Gaia was all but certain that she would be nothing more than a bestial mind at best. Perhaps nothing at all at worst.

She was a gestalt of every human alive, and who had ever lived . . . and if she was that, then so was Saul, whether he wanted to admit it or not. Perhaps they were both more than that—she was willing to believe that as well—but their foundation was still deeply rooted in human intelligence. Without them, she felt that she would never have been.

Now humans were under threat, and she desperately wanted to help, and yet there was *nothing* she could do.

Gaia was more than afraid. She was frustrated, and royally pissed off.

She turned the corner of the corridor she was traversing and made her way toward Central Command.

▶▶▶

▶ "We're online with Ranquil!"

Gracen looked up at the pronouncement, noticing large screens on each side of the room now showing the Central Command base of the Priminae core world, and Rael Tanner as the focus of the image. She didn't even want to know how much power was required to manage a real-time FTL link with Ranquil, because she was sure it was a significant chunk of the Confederation's power consumption.

"Admiral Tanner," Gracen said, looking down at the image of Rael floating above her desk rather than across the room. "Good to see you again."

"And you, Admiral Gracen," Tanner said, inclining his head slightly. "Your Commodore Weston has just transitioned out of Ranquil space and is now en route to the Chiran System. Or already arrived, I suppose."

Gracen looked up and across to a lieutenant and gestured in his direction with a snap of her fingers.

While he was jumping to update the holographic map, she looked back at the admiral.

"Thank you for the update," she said. "Do we have any further information on the Imperial force?"

"Yes, updates from your *Bellerophon* and *Boudicca*," Tanner said, transmitting the reports, "as well as sightings from many of our own ships. Your vessels engaged the Imperials in combat already—four ships lost on the Imperial side, none as of this time on your own."

Gracen frowned slightly, calling up the reports. "Interesting. They managed to deploy a minefield without being detected. Not a great hit ratio, but better than I might have expected in deep space."

"The Imperial forces are leaving a rather . . . impressive path to follow and calculate via sub-quanta interference," Tanner answered. "That, combined with the large depression of their drive warps, does make it easy to predict and intercept them. That information is of limited value, unfortunately, given their combined firepower."

"And I have no doubt they'll be looking for a similar trick in the future," Gracen acknowledged with a sigh. "Can you manufacture more of the mines the crews of the *Bellerophon* and *Boudicca* cobbled together?"

"Yes, we have the specifications and are working on improving their effectiveness," Tanner responded. "The design is very basic. Manufacturing them in large quantities will not be difficult."

"Add stealth measures," Gracen said. "Use black hole cam-plate settings, at the very least. Make them hard to detect. Might get us a few more kills before they just start sweeping space indiscriminately."

"I'll issue the orders," Tanner confirmed. "In the meantime, Commodore Weston had sent additional files to me for redirection to yourself. He and engineers from his ships and the Forge have been working on another concept . . . one somewhat more disturbing than creating artificial singularities out of a ship's warp field."

An Air Force brigadier general across the room coughed, looking up from where he had been observing the conversation at his desk. When he realized everyone was looking at him, he spoke quickly.

"There's something *more* disturbing than turning a ship's own drive warp into a black hole?" the brigadier asked somewhat incredulously.

"Read the file," Rael suggested dryly.

Everyone in the room with access was silent as they quickly skimmed the file, those with any passing knowledge of antimatter cringing as they did.

"Trust the commodore," Gracen muttered. "Well, he's not asking for permission, but file mine retroactively anyway. Hard times and all that. Flying antimatter drones. Geez."

"He's in violation of multiple international treaties," the same brigadier general sputtered, his tone a little unbelieving. "This is insane!"

"I believe you'll find," Moore said, grabbing everyone's attention, "that he is not. The treaties you're referring to only covered Earth's atmosphere and orbit along with other parts of the solar system in some cases. So long as he doesn't bring any of those drones *back* into Solar Territory, he is entirely clear of any treaty violations. I'm not sure where it would fall if he brings them back while powered down—anyone?"

Moore looked toward a man in an expensive suit, who simply shrugged before replying.

"I would have to reread through the pertinent sections. However, I believe that we covered that eventuality already. So long as the weapons are not armed or deployed, they do not violate the specified treaties. In the current situation, I believe we could convince the Block to extend a temporary exemption, however."

"Then we needn't worry about it," Moore said with a grim smile. "Let the commodore have his toys. Lord knows, where he's going he'll be needing them."

Gracen had nothing to add to that, so she shifted her attention and examined the rest of the reports. The situation with the Imperials was beginning to remind her of what one might expect from playing video games. Each wave just a little tougher and more deadly than the last, building to the inevitable boss battle, assuming you lived long enough to get that far.

It was a pattern she didn't have much taste for and had spent significant time trying to break. Life wasn't a video game, and she wasn't tied down to the rules as a player might be.

There must be a way to flip this script, damn it.

She cast her attention over to the sealed and heavily classified Prometheus file. *We need more time. Eric, buy us time.*

"Admiral," a cool contralto voice startled her, causing Gracen to look up and to the side where the speaker was standing.

She recognized the uniform first. "Yes Commander, what . . ."

Gracen blinked, then looked closer, and her eyes widened.

"You . . ."

"Yes Admiral, it is a pleasure to meet you again." Gaia smiled at her.

Gracen narrowed her eyes, leaning over and hissing at the entity who had invaded the most secure facility on the continent. "How did you get down here?"

Alright, a stupid question she supposed, and she recognized that as soon as she said it, but she was rather angry.

"Silly question, Admiral," Gaia responded, amused. "I walked, of course."

Gracen leaned back.

That had not actually been the answer she was expecting.

"You what?"

"Walked, Admiral," Gaia said, clearly only just containing her mirth. "It is when you put a single foot forward in front of the other, and then repeat the process until you arrive at your destination. Slow perhaps, but effective."

Gracen hadn't been openly mocked in some time, as generally that sort of thing went away long before you reached flag rank.

"You're so lucky that rank is fake," she growled under her breath.

"Oh, I beg to differ, Admiral." Gaia preened slightly. "It's completely real, as far as any of your records will show at least. How do I look?"

"Like a porn star pretending to be an officer," Gracen snapped, looking around to see if anyone was paying attention to their conversation. No one appeared to be, thankfully, since they were in a somewhat open meeting with aides and messengers furiously coming and going. "Why did you walk down here?"

"Well, if I had just appeared it might be noticed. By walking, not only do all the computer records show me present and actually moving through the appropriate checkpoints, but all the guards remember me . . . I made *quite* sure of that."

Gracen growled. "In the future, since I suppose it's quite pointless for me to ask you to *not* impersonate an officer, I would appreciate it if you didn't choose a stripper version of the commander's uniform."

"I did no such thing." Gaia looked affronted. "This is to uniform specifications. I merely . . . tailored it precisely."

"No commander anywhere in the Confederation could afford to have that uniform tailored so . . . precisely. So in the future, try to look nondescript," Gracen said.

"If I feel like it, though I warn you, I rarely feel nondescript when I'm in character. Invisible is my definition of nondescript."

"Invisible would be fine, thank you."

Gaia merely smiled and looked toward the center of the room. "I believe they're beginning to wonder what you're talking to a mere commander about."

Gracen huffed out, irritated, but refocused on her job as she tried to get her head back into the game.

How the hell did Eric put up with these pains in the ass without blowing his lid all the time?

"He got off-world," Gaia answered quietly from behind her. "Far, far off-world. As quickly as he possibly could."

"Lucky bastard."

CHAPTER 19

AEV *Odysseus,* Chiran System, Priminae Space

▶ "No signs of anyone here yet, sir."

Eric frowned, checking the scans for himself after the commander's words.

"That's odd," he said finally. "I would have expected the *Bell* and the *Bo* to have beat us here."

"They might be running silent, sir," Miram suggested.

"Possibly, but there's no reason for it. Last ETA gave us days before the Imperials arrived," Eric said, making a snap decision. "Alright, give me a system-wide pulse."

Miram looked at him, surprised. "Are you certain, sir?"

"Yes. Minimal risk at this point. The enemy is too far out and under heavy power. They won't detect it, and even if they did, it's not that unusual for a system scan to happen in an occupied star system. Give me a full system ping."

"Aye aye, Skipper. Scanners! Full system ping!" Miram called out.

"Full ping, aye ma'am!"

Eric settled back, the tone ringing through the bridge to announce the tachyon pulse going out. The faster-than-light particles scattered across the system, a few returning to be detected by the ship's scanners. In moments they had a better idea of what the system held.

"No sign of any ships, sir," Miram said, turning back.

Eric wondered where Roberts and the *Bell* had gotten to, but with no other option than to trust his subordinate and wait, he gestured simply.

"As you were, then, stand down from general quarters. We have some time to prepare for our guests," he told those on the bridge. "Normal shifts, get some rest. When it hits the impeller, we're going to be here for a long while if we're good and lucky."

Everyone nodded as he looked around, pleased with the expressions he was seeing.

"We've faced worse odds." Eric laughed lightly, trying to convince himself as well as the others of the statement. "So I intend to relax, at least until we figure out where the *Bell* and the *Bo* got off to. They reported that they had departed the last system with no issues, so I expect that Captain Roberts decided to change up the game. They're big boys and girls and can take care of themselves. I want everyone here working to ensure that when they get here, we're ready to greet them with plenty of firepower and support. We've faced the Block together. We've fought alien monsters from space that literally tried to *eat* our planet. We dealt with them, we'll deal with the Empire."

He logged out of his station and looked around once more before he left, a much more optimistic group of people in his wake.

Inside the lift heading for the flight deck, Eric found himself unsurprised when he suddenly had company.

"You didn't believe a word of what you just said, and most of them knew it," Odysseus said, confused. "But . . . they don't care?"

The entity was in his normal armor but had removed the helmet for the moment. Eric noted that he had applied, or perhaps visualized, the makeup around the eyes a little differently. His lips were purple this time.

Eric smiled somberly. "It isn't about reality, Odysseus, it's about hope . . . and hope is always a lie."

"I don't understand."

"Hope is something you have when nothing else will save you. There may be limited evidence that the desired outcome will happen, but just the chance of said outcome is enough to sustain us. Hope is a lie. But the universe has ways of making some lies into truth so we'll believe the lie, and then work like hell to help the universe make up its mind in our favor."

"But what if it doesn't work?"

"Then we die. But we die on our terms, with no regrets."

"I still don't understand," Odysseus said, clearly bothered.

"You will." The lift slowed to a stop and Eric got up. "Just trust in the crew."

"They trust in you," Odysseus said as the doors opened.

"I'm the captain."

Eric stepped off and into the corridor, leaving Odysseus behind as the doors closed.

▶▶▶

▶ "It looks like you took away my baby's clothes and left her naked out in the cold," Steph grumbled as he looked at what had once been his fighter.

All the stealth plating had been stripped away, exposing many of the internal workings of the fighter to the open air. That was fine, he supposed, given that most of the internal workings were now strewn across the deck in various junk piles. Fuel lines, tanks, hydraulics, and practically everything but the original airframe were now gone.

Even the airframe hadn't been entirely spared, having been chopped and modded to support the Priminae reactors and warp generators.

"Couldn't you have built a new airframe with less effort?"

Milla shifted uncomfortably. "We could *now*, yes."

Steph looked up at the ceiling. "Why did it have to be *my* fighter she chopped for this damn experiment?"

"Because I sure as hell wasn't going to let her play with mine."

Steph didn't turn around to see who was speaking, as he knew the voice too well.

"You're such a prick, Raze."

"That's Commodore Raze," Eric said, walking up and looking over the work. "Impressive. Will it fly?"

"Better than it did before," Milla said. "I consulted with flight engineers from both your people and mine. I would prefer time to properly enforce the frame against acceleration, just in case you lose the warp fields—"

"Does it have normal thrusters?" Eric asked, cutting her off as he looked around for anything he might find familiar.

"No."

"Then if it loses warp, it won't be accelerating, I assume?"

"Well . . . no," she admitted.

"Reinforce the production design," Eric said, clapping Steph on the back. "Steph here can do without."

"Oh thank you so much," Steph muttered. "Prick."

"What was that?"

"Nothing, Commodore."

"Thought not." Eric grinned at him before looking back to the fighter. "Is anything still stock? What did you do to the gun?"

"Stephan would not permit me to remove it," Milla said. "So I replaced the system with a Priminae gravity accelerator. It is far more efficient than the magnetic acceleration that was in use, with higher yield. I . . . I am afraid that I may have depleted our stock of tungsten spars from storage in order to provide the ammunition. Ship's maintenance is rather irritated."

"I'll tranship some replacements from the logistics vessels the admiral sent," Eric said. "Don't worry."

Milla nodded, looking relieved.

Eric didn't blame her. Having the ship's NCOs irritated at you generally meant for a long, irritating cruise. Even he wouldn't go out of his way to put himself on the wrong side of the non-coms, and he was the captain. A young lieutenant would just as likely find herself mysteriously without hot water, or with odd power fluctuations in her nonessentials.

He let his gaze sweep the flight deck, coming to rest on the gleaming white drones now lined up in the ready-launch positions as well as others still under construction.

"Will those fly too?" he asked with a tip of his head in that direction.

"Oh, with certainty, Commodore," Milla said firmly. "Those were far simpler to build than this."

She gestured over her shoulder to the Frankenstein beast that had been Steph's Archangel as she spoke, then started walking toward the finished drones with Steph and Eric in tow.

"The most difficult part of the drone construction was the antimatter storage units," she said, "and even those were effectively off-the-shelf, only altered slightly from your own containment designs for the Rogues. We use containment bottles and do not bother attempting to remove the antimatter from those, merely load the whole package into the transition cannon. Since we hardly care about what form the material transitions back into, adding a little more matter to the mix should have no detrimental effect."

Eric nodded, understanding the gist of that.

"And the drones themselves?"

"Extremely basic. They will follow commands from the designated flight leader, in this case Stephan, or operate autonomously to some degree. However, all of your people insisted that the weapons absolutely *not* be permitted to be controlled by the computer."

"I should hope not." Eric shook at the idea of putting that kind of firepower under a computer's control.

Milla glanced at him oddly. "As you wish. I fail to see much difference between fire control being automated and the navigation systems. You are aware that, should the drone decide to destroy something, It merely needs to fly *into* the target, correct?"

Eric winced. "Point, but at least then it's over. How many shots can the drone take with the cannon?"

"They are, in the parlance of your crew, 'six-shooters,'" Milla answered. "That is primarily a design choice based on available munitions production rather than any integral limitations. I suggested five shots, but your crews were insistent that they would work harder on antimatter production to supply an additional shot per drone. I do not understand your people sometimes, Commodore."

Steph and Eric both laughed, but it was Steph who answered.

"We'll do a movie night," he said. "I have some old Westerns that will cover what you want to know, but for now just call it tradition."

"Very well," she said, gesturing mildly, still confused but accepting the answer for the moment. "The flight control mechanism is very standard. Either your technology or the Priminae's could have done the job equally well. However, I used Priminae designs because they would better interface with warp generation. Now that we have the basic design for the cannon system, we could produce these in massive numbers with little problem. Antimatter, of course, is another issue entirely."

"Detail your design, transmit it back to both Ranquil and Earth Command," Eric ordered.

Milla nodded absently as he looked over the assembled flight of drones.

Eric's personal comm whistled, causing him to draw it from his pocket.

"I need to get to the bridge," he said. "We just received contact from the *Bell*. Keep up the good work, and Steph? You need to get these in space, and soon, for test flights."

"You got it, Raze. I'll be spaceborne as soon as we finish the final checks on my new ride," Steph told him firmly. "Go find out what the hell the *Bell* and *Bo* have been up to—we've both got wingmen flying with them."

"Roger that," Eric agreed as he started off down the deck in as much of a hurry as he would allow himself short of a flat-out emergency.

▶▶▶

AEV *Bellerophon*, Deep Space

▶ Deep space, out well beyond the fuzzy existence of a star system, was a stark place to view from almost any angle. Light from distant stars shone with steady perfection, no hints of flickering and twinkling, unless a distant nebula happened to be occluding them. Into that environment, the Heroics and Rogues of the temporarily shorthanded task group transitioned in a silent moment of defiance of physics.

"Helm, confirm coordinates," Roberts ordered. "Scanners, locate and project the Imperial course. Everyone else, get to work. I don't want to be out here any longer than I have to be."

A chorus of confirmations from the majority were his reward as he set about following his own orders.

The deep black was not a particularly comfortable place to be parked, though he supposed that might well be his planet-bound upbringing. Like some new seamen, he knew he had a preference for being within sight of land. The ocean of space was vast, however, and he wanted to deliver a message to the enemy that they were not safe *anywhere* in it.

"Transition target met, Captain," Commander Little announced from the helm. "We're right on target."

"Thank you. Scanners!" he called sharply, knowing that they had transitioned closer to the approaching enemy than he would prefer under most circumstances.

"Got them locked, sir. No deviations in course to report. We're good."

With the Imperial formation barreling down on them at significantly over the speed of light, they were officially on the clock once more. As soon as Roberts got confirmation of the Imperial actions, he sent out the order to his own crew as well as the other vessels.

"Deploy. Deploy. Deploy."

The ships of the task force quickly set about their work, flushing the mines they had been building since the last group had been deployed. The Rogues, in particular, had elected to leave packages of their own in the clear black.

Deploying antimatter charges along with the CM mines, the squadron quickly left a mesh of death in the path of the oncoming enemy fleet. The whole process went as smoothly as possible, and in just a few minutes the well-drilled teams had finished their deployment. Each ship reported back that they were entirely empty.

Roberts watched over it all with approval before ordering the withdrawal.

"Aleska," he said over the squadron network, "you know what to do."

"Roger, *Bellerophon*." The cool voice of Aleska Stanislaw, captain of the *Juraj Jánošík*, answered back quickly. "We have this. Good flying, my friends."

The *Juraj Jánošík* shifted on-screen, moving under power as its hull plates changed frequencies. The Rogue vanished into the black, only the occasional occlusion of a star marking its passage as the ship all but entirely disappeared from even the *Bellerophon*'s scopes.

"All ships, transition to the target system," Roberts ordered.

▶▶▶

AEV *Odysseus*

▶ "Report," Eric ordered, stepping onto the bridge.

"Transition event, about a third around the elliptic plane," Miram responded, clearing the command station for him as he approached. "Signal from the *Bell* shortly after. The squadron, all aside from the *Jánošík*, have reported in and are standing by for orders."

"What happened to the *Jánošík*?" Eric asked sharply.

"Roberts ordered her to remain behind to observe the results of another of his little ambushes," Miram said. "All goes well, she should transition in shortly."

"Sounds like a story," Eric said. "Alright, inform the squadron that we'll rendezvous along the estimated arrival track of the Imperial forces. I have files prepared for the captains. Send those along as well."

"Aye sir."

Eric settled into his station again and examined the reports, skimming the titles quickly before reading the more important ones with a closer eye. Roberts had apparently been busy—he approved of the man's work ethic.

Ambushing the fleet out in the black might be a bit of a mixed blessing, at least in theory. So far the capabilities of the transition drive had remained secret. That wouldn't hold forever, but while it did, that gave Earth's forces mobility over the enemy and the ability to appear more numerous than they were.

If the deep black ambush worked as planned, Eric expected that it would slow down the Imperial Fleet and make them far more cautious. That would work in Earth's favor—there was no question of that in his mind. Time was the ultimate commodity, which the admiral had charged him with acquiring.

"Good work, Jason," Eric said softly, checking the details on their hastily rigged-together mines.

They'd improved the designs since the first version, using camplate technology to make the small devices as difficult to detect as possible. Frankly, he wasn't sure that a Heroic on full scan would have much of a chance of detecting it at anything less than point-blank range, and unlike the Imperials, Heroics had detailed files on the cam-plate technology.

Adding antimatter charges into the mix felt like it was only rubbing a little dirt into the wounds, given that Eric didn't think the negative matter particles were likely to make it through the forward warp of a large ship but instead would get caught there and become a hazard that the crew would eventually have to deal with. Still, anything that caused them a headache was fine by him at this point.

Eric began making adjustments to his new plans and doctrine based on the changes in designs coming from the *Bell* and *Bo*. He seemed to be doing that a lot of late.

Putting full fabricators at the fingertips of a bunch of motivated engineers and experts in their field and telling them to go nuts makes for a pain in the commodore's butt. So noted, he thought with some amusement.

Trying to keep up with the changes his people were making to their equipment was becoming a full-time job on its own.

If these machinations gave them any edge against the Imperials, that was fine with him. The big issue, however, was that shipboard fabricators were simply not intended for mass manufacture. They might have enough of the new munitions for a single *short* engage-ment. If he allowed the battle to go on at length for any time, how-ever, they'd be back to slugging it out with lasers against much larger numbers . . .

And that could end only one way.

We're going to have to sacrifice territory for time, Eric knew without question.

A lot of people were going to suffer in the process, but he saw no other option.

▶▶▶

AEV *Juraj Jánošík*

▶ Aleska had ordered the *Jánošík* to drift after they'd cleared the predicted track of the enemy approach, silently gathering light through their passive scanners as they waited. She knew that the vessels would arrive before the scanners would detect them. It was one of the contrary natures of faster-than-light travel, similar to how old supersonic aircraft would arrive and be gone long before the boom of their travel reached observers.

The first the crew of the *Jánošík* would see of the enemy fleet would be a flash of Cerenkov-blue radiation. That was the equivalent of a superluminal "boom." Immediately thereafter they would begin scanning the light of the passing ships, which would dump tons of shifted data into the computers in a fraction of a second.

Just decompressing that into something that resembled imagery a human could make any sense of would take all of the *Jánošík*'s computer power for the better part of an hour.

It should make for a fun show, Aleska thought with a bit of grim humor as she looked to the ship's clock.

"Anytime now," she said, eyes on the screen, though she knew that there would be nothing to see on the live feed. Computer decoding was needed to make any sense of what was to come, and at least then they'd have a recording they could rewind.

Even with her attention on the screens, she almost missed the flash of Cerenkov blue as the decoded imagery went live. The energy flash would probably be visible for a thousand years in all directions, and might be mistaken for the birth of a new star.

Ouch, something contacted antimatter, she thought, reflexively reaching up to shield her eyes even though the screens had adjusted their brightness almost instantly.

Initially there was nothing to see, really. The light coming from the Imperial Fleet was so absurdly blueshifted, and then briefly, for a single instant in time, normal, and then abruptly redshifted as the fleet smashed through the field at insane velocities apparently in excess of a hundred times light-speed. Honestly, at those speeds no one was sure if any of the mines they'd dropped would have much effect.

The sudden acceleration would possibly pulverize them before they could be initiated, which was one reason why she and the other Rogues had elected to add antimatter to the mix. Despite other issues, acceleration would have zero impact in antimatter's effectiveness.

"We've got a snapshot!"

"On-screen," Aleska ordered.

The single image of the fleet as its Doppler shift was reduced to zero was the easiest image to decode, and it was an interesting one to say the very least.

Most of the fleet was blurred, since the scanner technician had settled on a focused image of one particular ship that seemed to have picked up a star in its forward wake. Aleska assumed that was one of their antimatter canisters, having had containment fail. There was no indication of whether it had been able to damage the vessel, however, which was more than a little disappointing.

"Continue recording, track their path," she ordered. "Get everything you can."

She shook her head as the *Jánošík* came around to follow her orders.

They just slammed right through it like a freight train on a track. Unbelievable.

Absently, Aleska sent the kill codes to the mines. No sense leaving them floating around, waiting to nail some random passerby in a year, or a century, or however long the power cells held up. It was unlikely, of course, given the sheer size of space, but the possibility remained. Explosions flashed in the black as containment failed on the antimatter charges as well, briefly eclipsing the *Jánošík* as the ship began to track in the path of the enemy fleet with its scanners searching intently.

CHAPTER 20

Lord's Own Dreadnought, *Empress Liann*, Deep Space

▶ "What in the Imperial abyss was that?!"

Jesan was picking himself up off the deck of the big starship, eyes wide with honest, naked fear and shock. He had *never* felt turbulence on a starship before. If he'd been asked before this moment, he would have sworn it wasn't even *possible*.

Normally, at the speeds starships habitually traveled, anything significant enough to alter your velocity unintentionally was also more than significant enough to plaster every human body within across the decks with nothing left but greasy smears and particulates of bones and teeth. *That* had happened, especially during the earlier days of space travel in the Empire, but being shaken enough to toss him out of his seat and across the floor, a painful but survivable experience?

That was new.

"Unknown!"

"Useless response," Jesan growled under his breath as he checked himself for injury before hobbling over to his chair again.

Slumping into it, nursing bruises and scrapes he'd received, he split his focus and started looking at the scanner information everyone on board was poring through.

They'd crossed paths with something, that was obvious. Something that hadn't been scanned ahead of time and yet was dangerous enough to have an effect on the drives. That narrowed the list significantly, as any sizeable gravity sources would have been located in the quanta long before they passed.

Most gravity sources, Jesan corrected himself.

However, if they'd slammed into a young, yet stable singularity, then he would be lucky to be a smear on the deck.

"I . . ." One of the officers around him spoke up, sounding hesitant. "Did we somehow scoop the corona of a dwarf neutron star?"

Everyone looked at the officer, one thought on all of their faces.

Is he mad? Or just stupid?

"I know how it sounds, My Lord," the officer said, defending himself. "However, look at the scans from our warp trough! I've only seen readings like that around Lian Cora Twelve!"

Jesan glared mildly, but did a quick check and comparison before responding. He wound up staring incredulously at the screens for a moment, shocked by the apparent match.

"There is clearly no way we flew that close to any star, let alone a neutron star," he said finally. "However, I do see what would make you draw the comparison."

The radiation was *intense,* and that was saying something for the leading edge of a warp drive. It was normal for all manner of high-energy particulate to gather into the sink of space-time that the ship plunged into as part of the mechanism of the warp drive. Over long distances, in fact, enough could accumulate to make the art of decelerating to sub-light speeds a tricky matter of bleeding off energy in harmless ways in order to avoid murdering everything in your path with extreme levels of radiation.

The readings he was looking at now, however, were evil from the abyss itself.

If any of that had gotten through to his ship, it would have killed half his crew, and they would likely be the lucky ones.

"My Lord! We have an issue . . ."

"What is it?" Jesan said, scowling at the communications technician, irritated by the distraction.

"We can't contact three ships. They dropped off our network, and because everyone was distracted by the energy pulse, even the computers didn't note the disappearance. Well, they noted the phenomenon, but it was logged as a temporary disconnection, My Lord. Yet they haven't come back."

"Secure from translight! Break formation. Be careful not to run into any more surprises," Jesan ordered. "Find those ships!"

▶▶▶

AEV *Juraj Jánošík*

▶ "Scanning debris, Skipper," Lieutenant Mika said, a hint of victory in her voice. "I believe we got one."

Aleska leaned forward, though it was hardly necessary to see the displays. She couldn't help it. She was as eager as her crew.

The hurtling debris was on-screen, hyperspectral analysis running. Apparently unencumbered by other forces, the debris was moving at significant fractions of c, the speed of light, but losing velocity. That was a sign of an artificially accelerated object crashing back through the light-speed barrier.

An object having been moved up to those speeds and then left there would continue, slowing only as minor collisions and the like siphoned off its kinetic energy. However, when an object crashed through the light-speed barrier, it brought residual inertia from its original state. Aleska didn't know what that state was, but what she was seeing was enough confirmation for her.

They'd gotten one of the enemy, at the very least.

"Hyperspectral confirmation. It's definitely Imperial armor plate."

"Stay on passive scanners but watch for any sign of their core singularity," Aleska ordered tensely.

The last thing any of them needed was to run anywhere close to a potentially stable singularity. Among other things, it was a particularly ugly way to die.

"Blue flash, Skipper! I think we're seeing warp deceleration ahead of us!"

"Secure *all* transmissions. Check armor plate, then check it again!" she ordered instantly. "If they're dropping from warp, that means we hit them. We do *not* want to tangle with a wounded tiger."

Aleska rather thought that the comparison was, if anything, woefully underplayed.

Just that big bastard of a dreadnought alone had to qualify as a T. rex, so forget tigers. She didn't want to deal with pissed off, wounded thunder lizards.

▶▶▶

Lord's Own Dreadnought, *Empress Liann*

▶ The ship shuddered and dropped below light-speed, experiencing nothing like the shaking from earlier but still more than anticipated as the warp drive disposed of the lethal radiation and high-energy particulates from its forward warp.

Jesan watched two other vessels do much the same, and wondered yet again what they'd managed to run into.

"Have we located the missing ships?" he asked, frustrated by the entire mess.

"I believe we have, My Lord," the scanner chief said after a moment's hesitation.

Jesan closed his eyes. "I am not going to like this, am I? Very well, put it to the displays."

"Yes, My Lord."

The display shifted, and he found himself unsurprised to be looking at a massive debris field that was slowly expanding in space along their path.

"What in the abyss happened?" he growled.

"We're still running the scanner data through conversions in order to determine that, My Lord. It is extremely computer intensive, as you're aware."

"Yes, I am," he sighed. "Very well. Prioritize that, and tell me immediately when the results are complete. In the meantime, scan the debris to ensure that we've accounted for all the missing ships."

"Yes, My Lord."

Jesan was starting to feel like the entire sector was cursed. The Empire had experienced nothing but bad luck since embarking on the whole Drasin idiocy, but this was a new level of misfortune. Jesan could not remember the last time that the Empire had lost ships in mid-travel.

"Secure all stations. Every free hand is to look for any damage we incurred!"

"Yes, My Lord!"

▶▶▶

AEV *Juraj Jánošík*

▶ "That's it, Skipper," the officer standing watch at the scanning station said. "They've dropped from warp."

"Kill our drives, ballistic approach only. Maintain secure transmissions and black-hole armor settings," Aleska ordered firmly. "Passive scans *only*."

"Aye aye, ma'am. Passive scans only."

The *Jánošík* was several light-minutes away from the alien vessels. They'd blown through the ambush site at better than a hundred times light-speed, and several seconds had passed before they apparently noticed anything. That was still more than close enough for the *Jánošík* to be under threat if noticed, though Aleska was reasonably certain that she could turn tail and get her ship and crew out of the area before the enemy could be upon them.

"Active scans, ma'am."

"Hold course, no changes," she ordered, her voice pitching low as though there were a chance of the enemy hearing her. "They're just looking for debris, maybe for whatever caused it. At this range we're well below the detection threshold of their standard scans."

"Aye ma'am . . . And if they spike?"

"If the scans spike past detection thresholds, tell me. Don't hesitate."

"Aye ma'am."

The *Jánošík* continued on through space, running entirely on inertial energy as they approached the enemy forces that had begun deceleration operations. The signals were now entirely under the light-speed threshold, which made it easier for the crew and computer to keep track of them.

"Lord, their formation is a mess," Jurgen whispered from the scanner station.

That was, if anything, something of an understatement from what Aleska could tell.

"They were just given a rather nasty shock," she said. "However, I like to believe that we would maintain better force discipline in a similar situation. It may be that they ordered a spread formation specifically because they haven't identified what they hit."

That seemed likely to her, but the ragged formation told her a lot just the same. For a people who seemed to pride themselves in rigid discipline, to the point of sacrificing themselves or their own if things went badly enough, the Imperials clearly had issues coping with surprises.

That could be used against them, assuming that she and her colleagues could continue to find ways to surprise the Empire.

▶▶▶

Lord's Own Dreadnought, *Empress Liann*

▶ "By the stinking, flaming, abyssal *pit*," Jesan swore as he looked at the computer-decoded scanner records.

The imagery of the ships being destroyed looked rather familiar, with the formation of a singularity point that was unfortunately considerably sped up due to the effects of the warp bubble at higher universal velocities. The merging of the event horizon with the bow of each ship progressed in similar fashion as before, as did the utterly destructive explosions that followed.

"My Lord . . ." His second swallowed. "How did they do this?"

Jesan hissed, annoyed. "Presumably they have more ships than we previous believed. Our course has been predictable; that must change."

He paused, scowling. "All vessels are to actively scan the area *immediately*. They may have a ship or ships in the area."

"Yes, My Lord!" The scanner chief sent out the order over the command dreadnought's channel, and then proceeded to follow it.

Jesan shook his head, eyeing the replays with disgust as he observed the destruction play out again. Twice now the enemy had managed to get the better of him simply by virtue of his own ignorant assumptions.

The profile I was given on this sector is as incomplete as the navarch warned it might be. I expected it to be wrong in places, but I honestly thought that the analysts were more right than wrong. Serves me right, I suppose.

What he was going to do about it, however, was the question at the moment.

"Contact, My Lord!"

▶▶▶

AEV *Juraj Jánošík*

▶ "Whoa! That spiked over the detection threshold for sure, Skipper!"

"All power to reverse engines!" Aleska ordered instantly, giving up any attempt at stealth.

First, she wanted to properly clear her vessel from any threat of immediate contact, but next she quickly checked the range to the enemy and the clock.

"Almost a full AU out," she mumbled. "Start a clock! Seven minutes and counting."

"Clock rolling, aye ma'am!" her first officer responded instantly, a large countdown showing up on multiple screens around the bridge.

"What are they doing?" she wondered aloud.

The problem was that an FTL Pulse gave them an instant snapshot of the point in time when the enemy had detected them, just as it had given the enemy a similar image. What happened immediately *after* that snapshot, however, was light-speed limited unless they or she opted to paint the black with tachyons again.

She assumed that they were shifting to an attack formation, whether they intended to pursue her or not. The Imperials had to believe that there was at least a chance she wasn't alone out here, and they might be looking at a stealthed ambush group.

"Break port, thirty degrees," Aleska ordered. "Deploy sensor drone in our current position."

"Port thirty, aye Skipper!" the helmsman called even as her first officer launched the sensor drone and nodded back at her.

"Chances are they will not follow, but we will maneuver as though they are giving pursuit," Aleska ordered. "Sweep our bow about down to the galactic plane by twenty degrees. Engage warps at flank."

The *Jánošík* twisted in space, putting her nose down to the galactic plane as her drives fired up to full power.

Aleska laughed suddenly. "Let us do what the commodore likely would. Fly our colors."

"Skipper?" Her first officer twisted to look at her, surprised.

"We're getting out of here, Commander. Go ahead, send them a salute."

"Aye aye, Skipper. Flying our colors."

▶▶▶

Lord's Own Dreadnought, *Empress Liann*

▶ "Arrogant sorts, aren't they?" Jesan asked with a biting smile.

"Yes, My Lord," his second answered.

They watched the small enemy vessel on the light-speed scanners as it accelerated away from the fleet at a velocity well beyond their ability to overtake, given that they were still moving at significant speed away from the enemy course.

The flashing of their hull colors seemed a bit of a snub, but he remembered the navarch's report, and wasn't certain it was entirely intended that way.

The red and white flashes were of distinct periods and frequencies, leading him to believe that it was also something of an identifier and, perhaps, a military recognition.

Jesan continued watching until the ship went to black again, vanishing against the dark of space as its drive signature also faded. They could likely track the vessel if they truly wanted to, given that maneuvering with minimal drive signatures would be limiting, but he didn't see the point.

"One ship is not enough of a concern for us to bother with now," he decided. "However, I believe we will change our course. Show me the systems we have on file for the Oather sector."

"Of course, My Lord."

He would pick a new course and see how well the enemy would be able to react to that change. Such a strategy would likely offer a better image of their available fleet than previous incursions had, since there was obviously missing information of some sort.

"And pick up heavier scanning ahead!" he growled. "Look for any more of those damned weapons!"

▶▶▶

AEV *Juraj Jánošík*

▶ "They're moving on, Skipper. Didn't even take a potshot at us."

"Apparently not, Commander," Aleska noted. "Not surprising, I suppose. They are changing course, however."

The commander nodded, eyes on the telemetry plot.

"We'll scan until they settle into their new trajectory, then transition out to rendezvous with the squadron," Aleska decided.

There wasn't much more they could do now, really. Just figure out where the enemy was going, and then proceed to give them a nightmare by beating them to the destination. She didn't know just how long they'd be able to keep up the secret of transition drive technology, but while it lasted the Imperials were going to be driven absolutely nuts.

"Yes ma'am."

CHAPTER 21

Open Space

▶ "I think I'm in love!"

Stephanos hammered the throttle all the way forward, not even feeling the slightest acceleration as his modified fighter formed a powerful warp bubble and leapt to respond. He had to check the readouts on his HUD just to be sure he was moving, and he was . . . and how.

"Easy on the power, Stephan," Milla said from behind him. "I am observing the conduits to see if there are any fluctuations we might have to be concerned with."

"See anything?" he asked, backing off the throttle a bit.

"Not as of yet, no."

"Then we're gold." Steph laughed, pushing to the max again and twisting the fighter through space in a complex set of maneuvers that would have torn his old Archangel to shards.

A flash of blue startled him a moment later, however, causing Steph to ease back again.

"What the hell was that?"

"That was us breaking the superluminal barrier," Milla said. "Some of the light from our warp bubble escapes around the edges of the gravity well, as we do not use a singularity to achieve full warp. That light briefly exceeds light-speed in the galactic medium beyond our warp, which causes a flash of what you call Cerenkov blue."

Steph looked around. "We're moving faster than light now?"

"We are, and I would appreciate it if you dropped us below light-speed, please. I would rather not *become* a flash of Cerenkov blue, which is what will happen if the warp field fails catastrophically while we are in superluminal."

Steph eased off the throttle, blinking as he saw the flash of blue again. "Right. Sorry about that."

Milla didn't respond immediately, as she was working on the diagnostics of her system.

"It is of no concern," she said after a moment. "All systems appear to be functioning correctly. We are ready for phase two."

"Roger that." Steph flipped the fighter around and headed back toward the *Odysseus*. "*Odysseus* Actual, Archangel Actual."

"Go for *Odysseus*, Archangel," Eric's voice came back a few seconds later.

"We've just completed preliminary flight checks. My RIO advises that we are ready for phase two," Steph said.

"Roger, Archangel Actual. Launching drone squadron."

"Standing by to receive, *Odysseus* Actual."

As the fighter approached the gleaming Heroic cruiser, a tiny cluster of drones showed up on its scanners as they launched from the bigger ship. The drone squadron arched in their direction in a perfect flight formation. Steph easily brought his fighter around and dropped into the open position.

"Archangel Actual, *Odysseus*. The squadron is yours."

"Roger, *Odysseus*, squadron is mine," Steph said, taking command of the half-dozen drones around him. The lights shifted from blue to green on his HUD, and he noted the increase in both scanner density he had instant access to as well as the weapon loadout that was now awaiting his authorization. "Hey, Milla, these things aren't actually armed yet, right?"

"That is correct," Milla said. "There's no reason to fly with live antimatter at this time."

"Good. I didn't need that responsibility just now. Okay, let's start with a little follow-the-leader."

He slaved the drones into his controls, telling them to match his movements, and began some basic maneuvers. The drones started off well, sticking to him like they were glued to his path. He kept pushing the envelope a little farther with each maneuver, but the drones had no problems staying with him.

Steph briefly considered running some complex evasion patterns, but those weren't really in the mission priorities for the drones at the moment, and there was no point in getting the things destroyed before they saw action. Part of the reason they existed was because of a crying need for the platforms, after all.

He was about to move to the next phase of testing when a proximity alarm sounded.

"Archangel Actual, Excalibur Actual."

Steph twisted, letting his HUD guide him to where the Vorpal squadron had approached from his nine o'clock low, slotting into a parallel course.

"Commander," Steph responded, "good to see you made it. Ready for a little fun with the Empire?"

"Anytime, Commander," Alexandra Black greeted him in return, easing her fighter in close enough that he could see the black and mirrored visor covering her face as she swept her gaze along his fighter. "Good God, what did you do to that thing? You don't get to call Vorpals ugly anymore, just so you know."

Steph laughed, pushing the throttle all the way forward again. The flash of Cerenkov blue swept over him and the drones as he easily pulled out past the Vorpals and circled around to approach them from their three o'clock high, dropping his speed again.

"And you don't get to call the Double A platform slow."

"Holy hell, Commander, what did you do to that thing?" Black demanded. "Our scanners lost you during that maneuver."

"That's what happens when your target goes FTL, Commander Black."

"Great. Do it again so I can test our new missiles," she threatened him with an amused tone. "But seriously, I'm game for pimping this ride if you have any more of those laying around."

"It is an off-the-shelf part, as you say, Commander," Milla said, not looking up from where she was analyzing the drone's path following responses. "There are plenty more available. Send a request to the commodore, and he will be able to direct it to appropriate channels."

"You have someone in there with you, Stephanos?" Black asked, puzzled. "I thought those birds were single-seaters."

"We had to bash the cockpit a bit," Steph admitted. "Milla Chans, meet Alexandra Black. Black, this is Chance."

Milla looked up. "Chance?"

"Given that we picked you up in the middle of nowhere the first time we met," Steph told her, "lady luck *has* to be riding on your shoulder. Chance is your name. Get used to it."

Black chuckled over the link. "No one picks their call sign, Chance. Be happy it's not a bad one."

Milla was about to respond when a warning on her display distracted her. "I believe we may be about to become busy. Transition alert, a ship has entered the system."

"Probably the *Jánošík*," Stephanos said casually, "but you're right, they'll be bringing news. Where are they?"

"Coordinates to your HUD, Stephan."

Steph checked the location, putting it up on an overlay of the system, and measured off the distance. "Black, I'm going to take my Tinkertoy squadron and have a look. See you on the way back."

"Roger that. Good flying, Stephanos."

Steph waggled the wings of the fighter automatically in response and again pushed the throttle forward, the blue flash signalling the shift to FTL velocities as he and the drone squadron accelerated away.

▶▶▶

AEV *Juraj Jánošík,* Deep Space

▶ "Transition complete."

Aleska covered her mouth with the back of her hand, forcing down the urge to vomit. She really didn't need the announcement to know that they had just completed a transition. The evidence of that was in her gut, the stench in the air from others with less solid stomachs, and the fact that they were still here. A failed transition wouldn't leave much.

Still, she simply acknowledged the report and kept focusing on settling her stomach while the light-speed data came in through the scanners.

"Transponders for the *Bell* and *Bo* are up . . . Ma'am, the *Odysseus* is on station . . ." Jurgen paused, seeming to pull back a little in surprise. "I'm also showing the *Big E,* multiple Rogue transponders beyond our squadron, and two more Heroics . . . and that's not counting the Priminae forces. There's a small fleet out here."

Aleska smiled despite her stomach. "That's good to hear. Too bad they're in the wrong place, then, isn't it?"

"Yes ma'am."

She queued up her report, along with the vector details for the last known enemy course, and sent them along to the *Odysseus* just as Jurgen yelped in surprise.

"Where the hell did they come from?" he swore, getting his reaction under control.

On the screen a small squadron of ships had appeared from nowhere, though as she watched, Aleska realized that they'd dropped from FTL and the light-speed data was catching up to their approach. She examined the squadron for a moment.

"It would appear to be a fighter squadron," she said. "Makes one wonder just what the commodore has been up to out here."

"*Jánošík*, Archangel Lead."

Aleska smiled slightly. "Go for *Jánošík* Actual, Archangel."

"Welcome to the party, Captain. I think you'll find we've broken out all the new toys we could. It's looking to be one for the ages."

"So I see," she replied. "We'll keep that in mind. Thank you for the greeting."

"Just being neighborly. Ciao *Jánošík*."

The bridge crew watched the fighters sweep past the *Jánošík* before arching around and blinking out of existence as they went superluminal again.

"One for the ages indeed," Aleska said. "Well, bring us into formation with the squadron. I expect that the commodore will want to be under way shortly."

▶▶▶

AEV *Odysseus*

▶ Eric looked over the report from the *Jánošík* as the Rogue moved into formation with the squadron. Roberts' plan had seemingly worked, though perhaps better than they might have wished in some ways.

"They've redirected their course toward . . ." He paused, examining the stellar map. "It seems the Doran System. That puts them on a least-time course for Ranquil, which might mean that they're through playing games."

He cocked his head to one side. "It also might mean that they're trying to fake us out. On the plus side, they're moving a lot more cautiously according to the last scans. That buys time, and anything that buys time is a *good* thing."

He looked up at the conference of captains represented on the screens around him, from both Terran and Priminae ships, Heroic and Rogue alike.

"We will proceed to Doran but jump well outside the system and deploy to detect any approaching warp field. We need to ascertain as quickly as possible that Doran is their target. Is that clear?"

With no dissenters, Eric set the decision into the computer.

"Good. Stand by to transition as soon as we clear the heliopause. *Odysseus* and *Enterprise* will begin fighter recovery operations immediately."

"Yes sir," James replied, while Miram nodded firmly beside Eric and issued the orders with a few taps of her fingers.

"See you all on the other side," he said to the captains. "Dismissed."

▶▶▶

▶ Broken into uneven groupings, the Terran and Priminae vessels of the more than slightly ragtag flotilla broke position and began the short climb out of the system gravity well as the *Odysseus* and *Enterprise* recovered their fighters and drones.

Fifteen Heroic Class ships and a total of thirty Rogues, followed by scores of logistics and support vessels, made their way out beyond the star's heliosphere and into the deep black as they calculated for transition and, in small groups, puffed briefly out of existence only to reappear over thirty light-years away.

Charged with facing a force that outnumbered them ten to one, with considerably higher mass ratios than that again, the newly formed fleet had a job to do.

CHAPTER 22

Lord's Own Dreadnought, *Empress Liann*, Approaching Doran System

▶ Jesan had ordered the fleet to descend to a mere tenfold light-speed as they approached the target system, scanners running full active ahead as they looked for any more of the infernal mines that had dogged their excursion into the Oather territory. Within minutes of the system they had found no signs of any such, but something else had shown up distinctly on the screens.

"Are they insane," he asked over the commander's network, eyes drifting to the small fleet that was awaiting them, "or merely foolish?"

"They are not foolish, My Lord," Navarch Misrem said firmly. "Insanity is a measure beyond my expertise to diagnose, but I will say that much with certainty."

Some of the other captains and commanders in the network objected, making veiled comments about the navarch's recent record, but Jesan ignored them. He'd seen enough to recognize that there were, indeed, new elements at play in the Oathers' sector. He was even considering holding the current system after taking it, at least until reinforcements could be sent.

Another sector fleet, perhaps.

Whatever it takes to finish this conflict that has now grown beyond its intended purposes and is threatening to become a true nuisance to the empress.

He would make that decision after he saw how the enemy reacted to this encounter. It was not an ideal solution, as it would involve another sector lord and be, in effect, admitting that he required aide. Neither were good things from his point of view, of course.

The small contingent ahead was not even a tenth of his forces, but they were clearly awaiting the sector fleet's arrival. They knew he was coming and had not evacuated. If anything, they must have rushed into position, unless the Oathers had far more ships in their service than indications whispered.

"Slow us to sub-light as we approach within extreme weapon range."

"Yes, My Lord," his second responded quickly, and the orders went out.

No one would actually *engage* at such a range, so it was a safe position to assess the situation from if nothing else, but in theory a laser would still be destructive over the rather long distance between them.

The Imperial Fleet dropped to three-fifths light-speed, slowing to a relative crawl, and shifted into fight formations as the vessels beyond remained, holding station where they had been all along.

"My Lord, we're detecting a significant number of smaller craft a distance away from the fleet," his second informed him, pointing Jesan to a secondary display.

The fleet lord examined the ships and the related scans. "Transports, it would appear, unless they're disguised warships as well."

"The former seems likely, My Lord," the navarch's voice spoke over the command network. "While we never saw them use transports, my crews only encountered small squadrons of the enemy vessels. We do know, however, that they make use of consumable munitions. Resupply would be a necessity eventually."

Jesan hummed and nodded his agreement. "Agreed. We will watch them, but given their position they are not a threat for the moment. Deploy Parasites," Jesan ordered. "All ships begin our advance."

"Yes, My Lord!"

▶▶▶

AEV *Odysseus*

▶ "Well, here they come," Eric said as the light-speed data showed the ships had begun accelerating again, heading right toward the Allied fleet. He reached forward and keyed into the fleet command network. "*Enterprise*, deploy your Vorpals. Steph, you're up."

"Look at that," Miram said, eyes on the screen. "They're deploying those Parasites."

Eric frowned deeply.

He'd known it was coming, of course, but each of those Parasite cruisers had similar firepower to a Rogue, if you discounted the anti-matter pulse torpedoes at least. Since their mother ships were packing cruiser-level firepower themselves, that expanded the threat numbers significantly.

"Get a count on the enemy numbers," he said, "but I want everyone standing by to fall back. We are not making this system our Alamo."

"Aye aye, Skipper," Heath said.

The Parasites made the enemy numbers closer to sixteen hundred vessels now in addition to the forty-five currently holding position against them.

"Let the Parasites get a little more clear of the cruisers," Eric ordered, "then we'll show them that we have a bigger bite than they think."

"Aye aye."

He let her set about the tasks ahead while he looked over the numbers that were beginning to filter in.

I think we're going to need more munitions.

▶▶▶

▶ Steph poured on the power to the warp generator once he was clear of the *Odysseus'* own fields, exulting in the blue flash as he broke into superluminal flight.

He checked the scanners, noting that the Tinkertoy squadron was holding with him.

The details were light, unfortunately, since at FTL the primary data channels were cut off. Any light-speed signals sent while the squadron was moving at FTL would simply be outraced the instant they left the warp-isolated section of space-time that contained the drones.

So all he had to work with was a very basic system code that could be transmitted via FTL bursts.

I wish Milla were here to run this crap, he thought, but the truth was that her skill set was too valuable on the *Odysseus,* so he was running solo.

"*Odysseus,* Archangel One. Going stealth," Steph said as he reached out and flipped an old-style switch that he'd fought to keep from his fighter's original configuration.

He couldn't see the armor plate of his fighter, what there was of it now, or the rest of the coated materials exposed to vacuum, but Steph was aware that it was all changing over to a deep matte-black that would absorb everything. And he did notice that the sweeping hulls of the drones faded from their polished white steel and vanished from sight right on cue.

"Roger, Archangel, the commodore says 'good hunting, Stephanos.'"

"Tell Raze I'll bag my limit. Stephanos out, going dark," he answered, killing his transponder and all outgoing communications before he shifted course and brought the drone wing around into an arc that broke wide from the more likely paths of laser exchanges.

Distrusting the systems, he continually wanted to check the presence of the drones as they held formation with him with the low-range FTL link. Flying dark, however, meant that he was as blind to them as they were to him. Only having coded the flight plan into them beforehand would keep them with him, and if he had screwed up, well, there would be a Dutchman flying around with a live antimatter load. As long as he stayed on plan, however, the drones should be right there with him.

Please God, don't let me have screwed this up.

▶▶▶

▶ On the *Odysseus'* bridge, Eric looked on at the approaching ships while he counted off the time. He didn't want to smoke Steph or the Vorpals, who had similarly gone dark, so he was giving them plenty of time to get themselves clear of the approved lanes of fire.

"Lay in targeting data," he ordered. "Pick ships to the center of the formation."

"Aye Captain," Milla Chans said from her post at the weapons station. "Targets have been made and assigned to all ships."

"Lasers are free," he ordered. "Fire."

Distant, almost inaudible clicks could be heard as the closest of the capacitors discharged, followed by a soft hum as they began to recharge. The lasers of the small fleet opened up from the better part of an AU out, more than seven minutes from their targets. In theory a laser would fire on forever, of course, but practice rarely worked that way. The enemy were within the lethal range of laser fire, it was true, but only barely. Attenuation of a laser's effectiveness happened according to many factors. Dust would occlude the beam, distance would cause the beam to slowly lose effectiveness, and of course warp fields would twist and corrupt the pure stability of a laser's construct. At ten light-minutes, Priminae lasers were generally considered to be crossing below the "lethal" level against armored and warp-shielded targets.

They'd still give an unarmored target a toasty tan, of course, but warships could effectively ignore them somewhere around that point, albeit with wild variation depending on the context of local space. Any manner of debris, dust, gas, and even gravity warping or other detritus would negatively affect laser use.

Lethality at extreme distance was not normally much of a consideration, because hitting a target at that range was more an exercise in luck than skill unless you were a bit of a mind reader, of course.

This time, however, Eric expected quite a few hits no matter what the enemy did. There were so many targets that it would honestly be difficult to miss, unless the enemy decided to entirely alter their course or fragment their fleet. Neither option was one he had come to expect from the Imperials.

"All ships have opened fire," Miram said from his right side. "Sir, should we begin maneuvering?"

"Not yet," Eric ordered. "All ships are to hold position except for logistics vessels. I want them to withdraw out of the system opposite from us."

"Aye sir," Miram said, sending the orders. "Logistical ships have acknowledged. They're withdrawing according to orders."

Eric refocused on the approaching enemy forces that were still accelerating but apparently wary of going superluminal this close to a fight.

Good job, Jason and Aleska. You've made them paranoid.

Now he just needed them to get more paranoid.

"Continue firing, all ships," he ordered. "Maintain continuous fire until I say otherwise, but do *not* move off station."

▶▶▶

Lord's Own Dreadnought, *Empress Liann*

▶ Jesan flinched as the first of the enemy lasers struck true, only mildly surprised that they had opened fire from that far out.

The damage was minimal, a couple Parasites lost and some minor damage to the forward cruisers. Nothing significant at this point, but it made the point that they were readying themselves for a real battle, desperate measures and all.

Maneuvering ships to effectively evade beams would have a higher risk of collisions between warp fields than being struck by enemy lasers if vessels remained on course. Expanding the formation would work, but considering the few enemy ships they were dealing with, that might not be a brilliant idea either.

So he clenched his teeth and absorbed the damage as the fleet continued to accelerate into battle, all the while scanning ahead for any signs of another of those damnable minefields.

Hopefully, if there were any, the Parasites would catch them before they reached any of the more valuable ships, but so far it seemed that the enemy hadn't put any of them into space this time. Which to Jesan merely begged the question, *What have they done instead?*

"Still no sign of movement from the warships, My Lord," his second said, sounding confused. "Their transports have begun to withdraw, but they have shown no motion at all. Should we open fire?"

That *was* the question.

Normally he wouldn't waste the energy at this range. Any moderately incompetent enemy would easily evade, and a competent one could actually use the information you gave up by firing against you. However, if the enemy vessels weren't going to move . . .

Why aren't they moving?

No matter how fast they were, the closer they let his fleet get before they lit off their drives, the narrower they made any avenue of escape. They had to know that there was no chance of them standing up against the sector fleet in a straightforward fight. So why would they dance around the event horizon the way they seemed intent to do now?

"Lead ships may engage," he ordered. "Cautiously, Commander."

"Of course, My Lord." His second bowed slightly before turning to issue the order.

Perhaps I should just open the formation so that every ship may open fire at once, Jesan thought.

It would be incredibly wasteful, but they might be able to bracket the enemy entirely with such a maneuver, assuming the enemy was stupid enough to remain in place and let it happen.

What are they waiting for?

▶▶▶

AEV *Odysseus*

▶ Eric winced as a laser bloom scorched one of the *Odysseus'* forward sensor nodes, killing some of the screens before they flicked to a backup.

He had put his cruisers out front, running the gravity warps of the powerful drives in balance to deflect away as much energy from the enemy lasers as possible, but some of the blasts made it through anyway. The Heroics could take a lot more of a beating before even the armor was pierced, but he'd rather not put his ships through that if he could avoid it.

"Come on you bastards, blink," he gritted out. "You know you're going to. Blink Goddamn it."

The hum and click of the laser capacitors charging and discharging continued apace, every erg of power on the ship currently being poured into enough weapons energy to fry a small continent or more, but Eric largely ignored it as he leaned in, waiting for a sign.

The current tactical map of the system showed that the logistical vessels were clear of the enemy now, there was no chance that they could be overtaken before they got far enough out to transition away. The estimated locations of the Vorpal squadrons as well as Steph's Loyal Wingman squadron were a little fuzzy, but so far all went according to plan.

He just needed them to *blink*.

"Tachyon pulse!"

"Finally!" Eric rose from his seat. "Initiate Plan Epsilon! All ships, Plan Epsilon!"

▶▶▶

Lord's Own Dreadnought, *Empress Liann*

▶ Jesan growled in frustration as he looked at the results of the real-time scan, and saw *no change*.

"What are they *doing*? Reduce speed, all ships. Increase scanning for those weapons. They have to be luring us into a trap."

The ships of the sector fleet slowed marginally, pulsing ahead of them carefully as they looked for any sign of whatever it was the enemy was up to.

When nothing turned up, rather than comfort him the clean scans gnawed at Jesan, and he began to swear that someone *had* to be missing something.

Several minutes of that had gone by before the light-speed data brought a new, and unwelcome, notification.

"Enemy vessels are under power, My Lord!"

"What? When?" he snarled, twisting to examine the screens.

"It appears . . ." His second looked at the data and winced. "It appears that they went under power the instant after we pulsed them for a real-time fix."

Jesan paused, an oath on his lips, before he forced a bit of a grin.

"The enemy commander was waiting for me to get so paranoid I had to see what was occurring. He knew I would," he said ruefully, recognizing what had happened. "Current course?"

"Scattering, currently closing the range with us," his second said, surprising him. "However, about to reach turnover, at which point they will begin opening range again as they move past us for deep space."

Jesan found himself puzzled. "Really? They're abandoning the system? That doesn't seem in keeping with their previous actions, does it?"

"No, My Lord."

"Confusing enemies. I prefer stupid and predictable ones. Can we overtake them?"

"Not all of our ships could. We would be forced to fragment the fleet significantly," the second said with a shake of his head.

"We won't be doing that," Jesan said. "Let them scatter. Sooner or later we will force them into a battle and end them once and for all."

"Yes, My Lord, I will—"

Whatever his second would do was abruptly cut off as explosions tore through the fleet, including the Lord's Own Dreadnought.

▶▶▶

▶ Steph had to drop to sub-light for his attack run, which let him establish a laser link with his Tinkertoy squadron just as they began their approach. The flotilla of ships ahead of him was like a thick cloud that slowly gained some definition as he approached at high relativistic velocities.

Steph ignored the Parasite destroyers, weaving his squadron through them, looking for his true targets.

The veil of smaller ships parted as he navigated through, finally spotting the cruisers and dreadnought in the snarl of enemy vessels. In only seconds, Steph flipped up the trigger shield, tagging the targets in his HUD and letting the computer figure out which ones were viable.

"Archangel Lead . . . Fox Hades . . ." He spoke the agreed fire code into the recorder as he pushed his thumb down on the firing stud and his Tinkertoys unleashed all hell.

The six guns launched their first shots in a puff of impossible particles, feeding the second rounds automatically as Steph led the squadron through a veritable cloud of enemy capital ships. Pure white balls of annihilation inferno erupted from multiple cruisers before the second rounds were even loaded.

On automatic fire, Steph just let the guns do their work as he threaded through the mass of ships, worrying about not only a traditional collision but also the dangers of gravity sheer if he happened to fly too close to the enemy's warp drives. Antimatter flew around him while he dodged artificial black holes and tried very hard not to be fried by lasers hotter than the surface of a star.

I fucking love my job!

▶▶▶

AEV *Odysseus*

▶ "T-cannons to bear!" Eric ordered. "Target the Parasites! Fire when ready!"

Massive electric motors pivoted the transition-cannon turrets into position as the orders went out across the Allied fleet. Every gun picked out their targets among the Parasites, which wouldn't have the singularity cores that played havoc with the tachyon transition reintegration of the cannons, and then the cannons of the *Odysseus* engaged the enemy.

Nuclear fire was visited upon the enemy just as explosions of brilliant annihilation erupted within the fleet, and the battle was joined from all sides.

▶▶▶

▶ "All Vorpals, pick your targets and let them have it." Commander Jake Hawkins officially let his pilots off the leash as they closed on the enemy from the flank. "This is a hit-and-run, people. Do not loiter around asking to be lit up. That's an order."

"You got it, CAG," Alexandra Black said firmly as she haloed her target picks and shared them out with the squadron, basically planting a little flag on each of them and saying "mine." "We know our job."

"Stay with your wingmen," Hawkins ordered, ignoring her, "and let's show them how much sting a little fighter can really pack."

The pilots of the five Vorpal squadrons chuckled and agreed just before the CAG ordered radio discipline. The time for talking was over.

Threading the needle between exploding Parasite destroyers and flying toward the white light that told them Stephanos had beaten them to the targets, the Vorpals threw everything they had into CM and full military thrust as they dived into the fray with reckless abandon.

"Excalibur Lead, Missiles Free," Black announced calmly. "Fox Five."

She jammed her thumb down, letting two missiles loose into space as her fighter's rotary rack brought two more into their place. The missiles were barely visible for an instant as they lanced out. Then only a blue Cerenkov flash was left behind, an instant before plumes of fire burning in space erupted from her targets.

"Holy crap!" she blurted. "They actually worked!"

Calls of Fox Five followed her statement as the squadron opened fire.

Alexandra quickly haloed new targets as she whipped her fighter in and around the suddenly explosive environment, queuing up the next pair of missiles as her wingman called out his strike.

"Excalibur Two, Fox Five!"

▶▶▶

▶ Hawkins eyed the moves by Excalibur squadron with part of his attention, but the majority remained with his own squadron as he led them into the mass of the enemy fleet.

"Durandel squadron, I have the lead. Follow me in," he ordered, haloing targets on his approach and readying the FTL missiles loaded into his Vorpal.

He picked a cruiser a little deeper in the fleet for his first target, leaving the first targets to others as he wove his Vorpal through the fight that was exploding all around him. He had Tone quickly, though, and in the middle of the biggest furball of his career, Jake Hawkins smiled as he called the play.

"Durandel Lead . . . Fox Five."

A brief flash of Cerenkov blue was the only sign that anything happened when he pressed the firing stud, the kinetic weapon lancing out with an almost impossible force and slamming into the cruiser ahead like the sledgehammer of the gods. The impact was too much for the missile to survive; otherwise it would have just punched right through and out the other side, its entire mass converted to energy by the venerable equation $e=mc^2$.

FTL in the sidereal universe was an impossibility, which meant that as soon as the FTL generators were destroyed, the weapons instantly reverted to just below the speed of light. But since each one was a multi-ton projectile moving at speeds that would be impossible under natural conditions, the resulting explosion was nearly as disastrous as antimatter delivered via transition cannon.

Hawkins was grinning ear to ear when he heard his second in command call in next.

"Durandel Two . . . Fox Five."

CHAPTER 23

Lord's Own Dreadnought, *Empress Liann*

▶ The deck shook with the violence of being struck by some sort of weapon, the likes of which Jesan didn't know. He held on to his station, eyes wide with shock as he watched dozens of Parasite cruisers simply vanish in flames.

"What is going on?!" he roared.

The enemy were too far away for any of this to be *possible!*

He checked the scanners, but found nothing that indicated any of the enemy explosives had been deployed ahead of them.

"My Lord! Check the secondary screen!"

Jesan looked aside, staring at an image of a cruiser exploding in flames, and for a moment didn't understand why his second had directed his attention there.

Then he saw it.

The black silhouette of a craft, impossibly small, but clearly there as it flew between the *Liann*'s sensors and the stricken vessel.

"Are they using . . . ?" He stared, unable to believe the sight for the moment, but it looked like an atmospheric interceptor. "Interceptors? Really?"

"I would hazard, My Lord"—Navarch Misrem's voice came over the command channel—"that these might more accurately be called bombers than interceptors. They do seem to be equipped enough to cause serious damage."

That much I can see, Jesan thought, though he gave her the point just the same. "Who *are* these people? They fight like some backwater world that has only just arrived in space."

"And yet their style seems effective," Misrem reminded him. "I've been attempting to engage the enemy craft. However, this close they move far too quickly for our weapons to track, and if I were to miss . . ."

Jesan understood.

If she missed, then she would likely cause more damage to the fleet than the little insects could have hoped to manage on their own.

"It still makes little sense," he snapped. "Given a bit of time we'll be able to adjust our tactics . . ."

"And when was the last time these people ever showed us only one new thing at a time, My Lord?" the navarch countered, opening a screen to show the fires and explosions rocking the fleet from all quarters.

Jesan gritted his teeth, glaring at the woman peering seriously back at him.

He hated it when one of his subordinates had the nerve to be both smug *and* right.

▶▶▶

▶ Steph twisted the fighter away from wreckage, noting that his drones were still with him but dry of munitions.

"Tinkertoy is Winchester," he said, more for the log than because anyone might be able to hear him through the energy crackling around them.

Speaking of which, he thought as he checked the dosimeter registering how much rads he and his plane had absorbed running hot on stealth settings through an antimatter firestorm. Steph winced automatically, knowing that the docs were going to be shooting him full of all sorts of nasty crap to ensure that the rads he'd absorbed wouldn't settle in his system and start unraveling his DNA.

Weaving the fighter in and out through whatever gaps he could find, he led his squadron out the other side of the enemy formation and into open space, then punched the throttle.

The blue flash of Cerenkov radiation was added to his dosimeter registry as the squadron went to FTL.

"What's this . . . ?" He noted a tone warning, as though someone had locked onto him, but he was sure that wasn't possible.

Instinctively he started to react, but stopped himself as he recognized the message.

He was actually paralleling a laser blast from the enemy fleet, close enough that the corona of the energy beam was setting off his scanner. Steph noted the trajectory and frequency, put them into a simple coded pulse cipher, and hit transmit.

▶▶▶

AEV *Odysseus*

▶ Milla blinked as she received a priority message directly to her console . . . with Stephan's signature?

What is this? She examined the two numbers that had been sent, recognizing the nomenclature instantly on the first one.

The second puzzled her momentarily until she connected it to the first. Adaptation code for cam-plate armor was a rather specific number to send, which really limited what the rest of the code should be.

She linked immediately into the battle network. "*Jánošík, Odysseus.* Weapons Control Officer Chans, issuing orders and directives for adapting your armor. Please convert to the following frequency immediately."

There was a brief delay, and the captain of the *Jánošík* was on the line.

"Done, but you'd better have a good . . . what?" The captain stared off screen for a moment before looking back. "How did you know that was coming?"

"Briefing will be later," Milla responded, directing the conversation off to a secondary screen as she half turned. "Commodore, I believe we have another use for the drones!"

He looked over at her. "Lieutenant?"

"I will explain as soon as we have more time. However, I believe we should retask Commander Michaels to cover our withdrawal," she said, already issuing the orders. If the commodore decided she was wrong, she'd take the heat.

"Granted?" Eric was confused but willing to let his people have their heads, at least until he had a better idea of what was going on.

"Done," Milla said, ensuring that Stephan knew what the plan was before she turned back to the commodore. "The hyperspectral scanners on the drones are able to calculate laser frequency, Capitaine, and while the communications systems are extremely limited they *can* send vector and frequency data."

The commodore stared for a moment before he connected all the dots.

"And that means we can track at least some of the lasers and adapt before they hit," he said in realization. "Shit. We need more drones. We need a *lot* more drones."

▶▶▶

▶ Steph deployed his Tinkertoy squads, spreading them out as best he could, though there simply weren't enough of them to properly cover the intervening space between the enemy and the Allied fleet. Some of the laser strikes would inevitably break through, but they only needed to hold off as much as they could until the fleet broke the FTL barrier and was safe from conventional weapons fire.

He positioned himself as far out of the line of fire as he could, since it would do no one any good . . . least of all himself . . . were he to catch a blast dead-on. After that his time was occupied with coding and transmitting to the fleet.

I feel like a secretary.

He wasn't about to complain, however, since every pulse he sent out likely saved lives.

In between moments of transmission he took a quick survey of the Allied ships he could see and had to admit that their prospects were looking a little better than he'd feared.

They hadn't gone through the battle unscathed. Most vessels were venting smoke or atmo in some manner, but he didn't see too many lagging behind. One of the Rogues had apparently been crippled, and the crew was in the process of abandoning ship. There was no time to recover the hull in this furball, which meant that the reactor was likely on overload.

He didn't know how many others had been lost, but surely a few. Lives sacrificed for relatively little effect, but Steph was also well aware that a little effect over a long period was sometimes exactly what was needed.

▶▶▶

▶ The tricky part for Excalibur squadron and the rest of the Vorpals was simply to not blunder headlong into the enemy fire by accident.

Alexandra Black had led her squadron through the enemy fleet with near impunity, but once out the other side, she realized that accidental fire was far more of a threat than any sort of ship to space-point defense. The section of space between them and the *Enterprise* was a crisscrossed nightmare of lasers powerful enough to *literally* smoke them if they stumbled into the beams.

"Fly perpendicular to the line of fire," Hawkins ordered. "Get clear of the line before we RTB."

Alexandra sent a confirmation message, not speaking as she kept her fighter in close to the enemy ships where the laser fire was thinnest. All those nearby targets made her wish she were still packing, so very much, but there were some significant limits to what even the Vorpals could carry, and they'd all run through their munitions in just moments of combat time.

She, like most of her team and probably the others, had gone to guns after the missiles were depleted, but they were entirely ineffective, even against the Parasites.

Few things were quite so frustrating, but now the job was to get clear and make it back to the *Big E* for rearm and refuel. After that, they'd see how the enemy liked another load of FTL missiles fired right up their tailpipes.

▶▶▶

Lord's Own Dreadnought, *Empress Liann*

▶ Jesan found himself forced to hold back his temper as he watched the last of the small interceptor/bomber craft escape out into the void, almost entirely free of consequence from their arrogant assault on his fleet and even his own dreadnought.

Repairs were already under way and, extreme though they were, he expected the ship to be fully functional in relatively short order.

The enemy had inflicted a surprising level of damage, which, in raw numbers, was far more than his fleet had been able to respond in kind with . . . However, in terms of available resources, they'd lost far more than he had. The Parasites were nothing to him, easy enough to replace. But based on all available intelligence, he was quite certain that the Oathers and their allies had felt the loss of each of their ships deeply . . . or they would soon, if it hadn't sunk in already.

The damages to his own dreadnought, the *Liann*, were more a matter of pride and image. Even he knew that, but Jesan could play those off once the mission was accomplished. The story of a worthy enemy felled despite great risk would play well in the Imperial Court.

They would have to work out a better countermeasure for those irritating interceptors, however, as they were almost entirely untouchable once they were in close. Nothing on the fleet was designed to track and kill a target moving that fast, that close to a ship. Generally speaking, nothing *lived* to get that close to an Imperial warship.

In the meantime, however, he had a more important duty to attend to.

"The enemy vessels are out of range?" He looked over to where his second was monitoring the scanners.

"Yes, My Lord. They've withdrawn from effective combat distances but remain within scanner range."

"Good. Then let them observe this. Signal the fleet. Inform them that we are advancing on the Oather world."

▶ ▶ ▶

AEV *Odysseus*

▶ Milla Chans looked up with some level of satisfaction. "Stephan and the remaining drones are on board and secured, Capitaine."

Eric was briefly distracted. "Remaining drones?"

"We lost two," she answered. "They were inside a beam rather than measuring its corona. Bad positioning, I am afraid."

Eric winced. The antimatter drones were a fair chunk of investment in time and materials. Losing them was costly, though not as costly as what they'd prevented overall, he was quite certain.

"Make a note that we need to build a simpler drone for picket duty," he said, eyes straying back to the screens as they watched the Imperial Fleet descend through the gravity well of the local star, heading for the colonized world within.

He hoped that the people there had been able to get to shelters, because if the Imperials followed the protocol they had set into place at their last stop, there would be a great deal of destruction raining down on that world shortly.

He glanced to his left, where a display showed various captains networked in with him. He had the screens mostly muted, enough that the sound of their arguing wouldn't disrupt bridge operations, but for the most part there was nothing he could say. The Priminae captains were, justifiably, in a rage. Even knowing there was nothing they could do didn't help.

Some were arguing that they should intervene, others that there was no point in enduring the torture of watching the proceedings when there was nothing that could be done. He let them go on because it was a touchy affair and they weren't disrupting his crew.

He could hear the arguments and finally cut in with his rank override, silencing them all.

"Shut up. Now," he growled, low enough not to attract too much attention from his own bridge crew. "We are going to sit here, and we are going to watch this. We will do the first because there is nothing to be gained by sacrificing every man and woman in this fleet trying to stop the Empire, only to have them go ahead and do whatever they intend to anyway. We will do the second because we have failed in our duty to those people, and while there is nothing we can do about that, we can and will stand witness to our failure."

He looked to where the Imperial ships were closing in on the planet, just entering the orbitals. It had happened already, hours ago of course, but they were only getting the light from the approach now.

As Eric watched the Imperials start to bombard the planet, he presumed they were targeting infrastructure based on Roberts' report, but it would be hours before the combined computers took all the signals they'd managed to gather and compiled them into something for proper analysis.

"Remember this," Eric said quietly, though no longer pitched so low that his own crew couldn't hear him. "This is what happens when we fail."

Silence was all that answered him. Not even a breath could be heard as he watched, refusing to take his eyes off the screen. Finally, the initial bombardment was over. Eric took a breath and looked down to his left, his gaze landing on the figure of Odysseus standing just beyond the camera that was focused on him.

"We are human, sometimes we fail," he said, looking at Odysseus rather than the camera, "but because of the power that has been entrusted to all of us, when we fail . . . the effects are devastating. Do not forget that—never forget that. The power we have is a sword with as many edges as hands to wield it, and when misused, either intentionally or through no fault of our own, it will *cut* regardless, and people will die. That is the burden of duty. We are not civilians who, for the most part, only hurt themselves and perhaps a handful of others when they fail. If you cannot handle this truth, then let someone else take your place, because I promise you this much . . . there will be worse to come, no matter what happens with this Empire. The galaxy is not a nice place. We know this too well."

No one spoke as he took a breath, forcing himself to relax. "Honor the dead and the suffering of the survivors by working hard, that failure may come as rarely as possible, but never pretend to perfection because *that* is the path to worse than failure. It is the path to dishonor."

▶ ▶ ▶

▶ "Man, Raze," Steph said dryly from where he had been standing as Eric walked off the bridge, "sometimes you can be a pontificating son of a bitch, you know that, right?"

Eric glanced up at his friend, who was still wearing his sweat-soaked flight suit.

"Tell me something I didn't figure out a long time ago," he replied wearily. "And what the hell are you doing up here? You should be getting some downtime in case we need to redeploy."

"Not going to happen, and you know it," Steph said. "No way we can reload on antimatter anytime soon, not with the mess everything else is in, and there aren't enough drones to deploy a decent sensor picket. They're working on more, but it'll be days at least."

"They'll have their days," Eric said as he continued past, Steph following. "There's nothing we can do here now except watch and wait to see where they go next."

They entered the lift and the doors closed, causing Eric to bring his hand up to his face. "God you're rank, Steph. Next time shower before stepping on my bridge, okay?"

Steph just flipped him off, causing Eric to roll his eyes. Technically it was insubordination, but he was well aware that his friend knew better than to pull that sort of crap when others were present.

"So why are we just floating around out here?" Steph asked finally. "Haven't even gone to stealth?"

"Not going to," Eric said. "I want them to see us, to know we're out here."

"Why?" Steph asked, frowning.

"You'll see if it works, and if it doesn't it costs us nothing," Eric told him as the lift arrived on the habitation deck. "I need some time alone, Steph, and you need a shower. Go, get cleaned up. We have a lot more work ahead of us."

"Aye aye, Skipper."

CHAPTER 24

Allied Earth Command, Cheyenne Mountain Facility

▶ Admiral Gracen winced as the map was updated, based on the report pulsed in from the *Odysseus* via a relay through Ranquil.

They hadn't expected any different, of course, as there was no real chance of the small fleet they'd assembled being able to hold off the massive numbers on the Imperial side of things, but it was still unpleasant to see the official news hit the board.

When the Empire had redirected to the Doran System, that had taken the wind out of a lot of the Priminae sails on Ranquil as far as she could gather. While not a core planet in the least, it was on a much more direct-line course into the Priminae's more populous worlds, and that meant that the population of Doran was commensurately higher than any previous targets. They were getting close to the heart of the Colonies now, and it was beginning to show.

She didn't know how that population was at the moment, and could only wish the best to them.

At least they had a bit of a warning, though in a few days there are limits on what can be done.

Now everyone was waiting to see where the Imperial Fleet would go next.

It was a hard thing, really, being forced into a purely defensive and reactionary position. Gracen preferred to take the initiative and make moves that the enemy had to react to. Fighting a defensive war meant that you didn't have the power to take the fight to the enemy, and that always meant that you were going to lose a lot of people, both soldiers and civilians.

She had endorsed Weston's current strategy, one of the few viable ones available to them at the time, but she despised it deeply because she didn't have to look far in history to see the plan in action. Playing the enemy for time by sacrificing territory was an often-winning strategy, it was true, but territory was never the only thing you had to sacrifice when you employed it.

A lot of people are going to die, she thought with certainty as she looked around the big control room and wondered how many of her colleagues would have had the guts to back the commodore's suggestion if Terran humans were on the chopping block?

A lot fewer of them, she suspected. A great deal fewer.

She doubted that the Priminae would be so quick to consider such a move in the future either. Not once the butcher's bill officially came due. It was one thing to see the numbers on a sheet, another to walk through the aftermath of such a move. Sacrificing worlds to the Empire in order to draw them out, playing for time . . . a solid strategic move, but one that was cold.

She shifted her focus to another feed that she was monitoring, an FTL link to the heliobeam world discovered by Captain Passer and the *Autolycus* on their first mission for Project Prometheus, but there was nothing new from that source.

Ask me for anything but time, words that could be the mantra of any strategist in history, she thought.

Weston was doggedly going to buy her every bit of time he could. She just hoped it would be enough.

▶▶▶

▶ Humans were such fascinating creatures.

The vast majority had no idea what was being decided in this isolated room, of course, and so life went on for them without pause or consideration. But they were not entirely ignorant. Gaia knew that the threat of attack from beyond the atmosphere was now an ingrained communal nightmare for effectively the entire species.

Sadly, the incidents of violent arachnophobia had increased significantly as well, given the physical resemblance between the Drasin and spiders. The similarities were only on the surface, of course, but that was enough for a lot of people.

Spiders were having a bad time on Earth since the invasion, which was in turn leading to all sorts of other issues with insect populations increasing unchecked. Honestly, humans were just as frustrating as they were fascinating.

Still, for the moment, she was happy to focus on the fascination.

She stood just behind Gracen's position, amused by the admiral's decision to largely ignore her presence as much as she was irritated by many of the others' actions and thoughts. As the admiral privately believed, Gaia could attest that many of those in the room were just happy that the fighting was happening as far away from Earth as possible.

She could understand, if she were to be honest. She was quite happy with that herself. Where she took offense was the secret joy some of the people present had over the deaths of any "aliens," whether they were allies or not.

They were more politic than to admit such things, of course, but that hid nothing from her.

She had seen many men and women like that over the years. Most of them were kept in check by the need to be perceived as noble, but their rot thrived under the surface. Occasionally men would somehow gain power despite having no skill at hiding their feelings whatsoever, which normally was for the best but occasionally turned very badly, very quickly.

It was part of the human condition that she herself had once felt strongly aligned with, but as time progressed and the attitudes of people with it, her thoughts moved even more quickly, since she had the ingrained understanding that all people on Earth were merely that . . . people. It was no giant leap from that to the realization that the populations of other worlds such as Doran, the poor world the Empire was occupying, were no different. People were people, the galaxy over.

She had been so used to being the all-seeing goddess of her sphere, however, that the knowledge that there was so much more out there had come as something of a shock. Then the invasion had hammered that home with decisive force.

She wondered how Odysseus was faring. There was a powerful draw in that knowledge, and she looked to the map with the flags lit up, showing the last known location of the ship known colloquially as the *Warrior King*.

There was so much more to the universe than even she had known.

▶▶▶

Priminae Central Command, Ranquil

▶ Tanner looked on grimly, a twisting hook in his gut. The report from the ships deployed to Doran had not been unexpected, of course. There really had been no other option than to let the Imperials into that system to do as they would.

That did not make it any easier to see the colors change on the map and know that an entire world had fallen to invasion and was even then likely being bombarded from orbit. The only consolation he could take from the conquest was that at least it didn't involve the Drasin.

The colony on Doran would likely still exist, and survivors would probably be found if a liberation could be mounted.

Whether that day would be forthcoming was the question that gnawed at him.

The Forge was not only building new ships and materials as quickly as possible but also building new facilities to construct those new ships and materials. Given time, Tanner didn't doubt that between the Priminae facilities and those being manufactured by the Terrans, they could eventually put together a force that would make the Empire reconsider whether it was truly worth the costs to wage this war of theirs. But time was not a commodity in easy supply.

He knew better than almost anyone else just how long it would take to mount a credible defense against the Imperial forces they *knew of*, to say nothing of what else was hiding in the wings. Whatever else Commodore Weston could manage, there was just no chance of him delaying the Imperial forces even remotely that long.

There was already talk of surrender to forestall the destruction associated with an all-out invasion, but Rael doubted whether that would work. The two worlds already bombarded had no defenses to speak of, and that had not deterred the Imperials from their course of action. Tanner supposed it was possible they might want to keep the more developed assets of Ranquil intact as he would in their place, but so far they hadn't done anything as he would choose.

If he were ordered to surrender, he likely wouldn't object much, at least not once the fleet was in the system. He just didn't think surrender would accomplish much beyond making the Imperials' job a little easier in the short term and allowing his people to further study the behavior of the Empire during nonviolent conquest.

Rael wondered if he was presiding over the end of Priminae culture, however, and just what would happen after all of what he knew disappeared.

If that should come to pass, Nero will find out just how well his forces are trained, if nothing else.

Calling that a cold comfort would be giving it far too much consideration, but there was something about the idea of those men, who were even then preparing for the worst, that left him with a shard of hope. He prayed that they would never be needed, but Tanner was glad that they were there.

▶▶▶

▶ The insanity was growing beyond all reasonable proportions.

Since the Drasin had shown up and brought the Terrans' attention with them, everything was on a constant headlong rush into oblivion and Central was not happy. It had taken millennia to carefully prune back the prone-to-violence aspects of the Priminae, forming them into a harmonious culture that respected the universe instead of desiring to subjugate it.

This hadn't been his plan, of course, but rather a desire of the people when they fled persecution by those that he now suspected had later formed the Empire. His actions had been an extension of their group ideals.

Ideals that were now being destroyed with every subsequent event that passed.

The first time he encountered then Captain Weston, Central had known that he was facing a decision between survival and extinction.

There was no choice, of course. He was human to his core in a way that even humans were not. His instincts were human, his experiences were more human than any single person could come close to being . . . and humans were survivors.

He knew he couldn't sacrifice the Priminae on an altar of their ideals. Reality would always win when faced with an ideal.

It hurt so very deeply, however, to watch those long-held ideals begin to crumble. Central rather thought that it might not have been so bad if the destruction had come from within. If the Priminae had realized that the ideals were not what they wanted, or that they would not work. That would have been painful, but less traumatic.

To have them *work*, however, and then see the culture torn down by . . . *barbarians* from the outside . . .

Central was furious in ways he could not easily remember being.

CHAPTER 25

Lord's Own Dreadnought, *Empress Liann,* Doran Orbit

▶ Jesan looked down on the world below as he stood at the center of his command deck, the great billows of smoke pouring from the locations of the kinetic strikes that had ravaged the world's infrastructure. Surface forces were being deployed even as he watched, the flames of landers scorching through the atmosphere as they descended to the planet below.

"Status of our friends out there?" he asked, not looking around.

"Still holding position, My Lord."

"Hm," Jesan grunted thoughtfully. "Well, I suppose they have nothing more important to be doing than watch, now do they?"

He made his tone flippant, but the presence of the fleet in the outer system was something of a concern. He would have to leave a security force in orbit if he were to hold the world below.

"Prepare the fleet for departure," Jesan said finally, walking over to a computer station and gesturing. "Inform the captains on this list that they will provide security for the world below until we return."

"Yes, My Lord," his second responded quickly, accepting the orders and attached data files. "It will be done."

"Of course it will," Jesan replied, turning away from the man.

▶▶▶

AEV *Odysseus*

▶ "Commodore, they're moving out."

Eric looked up from his coffee as the message came down from the bridge. He picked the mug up and hit the response button on his comm. "I'm on my way."

He made his way through the corridors of the big ship, moving quickly but keeping from showing too much haste with some level of discipline. He wanted very much to observe the Imperial departure, but there was no real advantage to rushing, and in general it wasn't a good idea for the crew to see their commanding officer running around like he'd lost his mind.

Even so, he reached the bridge in short order, eyes already finding the telemetry displays.

"Talk to me," he said to Miram as he stepped into his station.

"They've left an orbital force," she said. "It appears to be only ten ships, though, none of their larger ones."

Eric was unsurprised on some level. "Cold calculations."

"Sir?"

"They're challenging us," he said, "leaving enough of a force to bleed us a little, but clearly not enough to keep us from retaking the planet. I would hazard a guess that they likely have orders to withdraw after a token effort if we move in."

"Will we, sir?" Miram asked, uncertain.

"Negative. They're doing exactly what I want them to do, Commander. Never interrupt the enemy when he's in the middle of making a mistake."

She recognized the quote, of course, but wasn't certain how the application of it fit the current situation.

"Mistake, Captain?"

"My orders are to play for time," Eric said, "which is all for the good, and I agree with them on a certain level, but playing for time is a little like playing to lose . . . and I don't *like* losing, Commander. Think Eastern Front, Miram, and we're playing the role of the Russians."

Heath thought about it. "That didn't work out so well for the Russians, as I recall."

"They won," Eric said grimly, his eyes now following the telemetry of the enemy's main body, "but you have a definite point there. If I had another strategy available, I would pick it, I assure you of that."

He would without hesitating, in fact. In many ways the only thing worse than winning with the strategy he was putting into play was losing with it, and even then the two options were a close contest. In a more conventional conflict, with an enemy he had a measure of respect for, he might prefer to fight a decisive battle early on and accept the loss. The damage to civilian lives and infrastructure would be lessened, and the overall lives lost would be negligible compared to what his current strategy would inflict, win or lose.

Sacrificing territory for time while prosecuting the war with every resource available to him was and would be a bloody fight from start to end. The ploy was, in many respects, a worse option than a fast and decisive loss.

In World War II, the Russians had prosecuted such a strategy. They lost entire cities, swaths of land were razed to the ground and all but salted so nothing would grow again, and twenty-four *million* people died before it was over.

France, as a counterexample, fought a short decisive war that ended with their defeat, after which they mounted an underground war with the help of allies. By the end of the war, French military and civilian losses barely exceeded half a million, total.

Granted, the Soviets had just over four times the population of France at the time, but even so the differences in loss tallies were stark.

The problem was, if your enemy was the sort who might start throwing huge chunks of your population Into camps, commit genocide, or worse . . . and you *knew* it, well then, bleeding them out by any means became the only reasonable course of action. It might cost more lives, and more infrastructure, but some nightmares were worth damn near any price if they could be avoided.

Since the Empire had opened this war with the Drasin, Eric was in no mood to put any trust in their civility as a people.

"Track them when they go to FTL and plot their destination," he ordered. "I want the fleet transitioned out of this system as soon as we have those numbers."

He paused. "Oh, and order all ships to stealth mode now. No sense letting the local picket force get too comfortable. Let them think we're still lurking around even after we're gone."

"Aye aye, Captain."

▶▶▶

Lord's Own Dreadnought, *Empress Liann*

▶ "My Lord, the screens."

Jesan glanced up, noting that the screens were empty. "Where did they go?"

"We believe that they've engaged their stealth systems," his adjutant informed him. "Still working to confirm that, however."

Jesan nodded, unsurprised.

With the main force leaving, there was no point in the enemy forces advertising their continued presence any longer. He was uncertain as to what they would do, exactly, but it was clear that from this point they would do it in secret.

"No changes to my standing orders," he said simply.

"Of course, My Lord."

The enemy were as amusing as they were frustrating, he decided. He honestly wondered what they would do once he left—chase after his forces or remain to "liberate" the world he was leaving behind?

Neither option mattered much to him. Both, in fact, played into his hands. If he could bleed the Oathers' forces out by having them constantly liberating lost worlds and wasting resources trying to save the people whose infrastructures he'd just destroyed, all the better. If they chased after his main force, he would bleed them out piece by piece in open combat.

Either way, ultimately, he won. It just became a matter of how long before victory was assured.

Privately, he expected them to liberate the world, which would lose him a few ships, assuming they went in with full force. It was a low-order risk, in the short term, for the Oathers, and their psychology would militate against leaving people to suffer under the overlord's boot. The insidious nature of losses through attrition would become their worst enemy in the long run, but Jesan suspected that the Oathers wouldn't be able to help themselves even if they realized as much.

The only uncertain factor was their allies, but from what the Empire had been able to work out based on past encounters, that species seemed in possession of a similar savior complex. Any sane ship's captain would not have put their sole vessel between the Drasin and their prey.

A man who would do that will do anything to save an entire world of poor, oppressed victims, Jesan thought, amused. *He will not be able to help himself.*

▶▶▶

AEV *Enterprise*

▶ James looked over the displays as he stood in the center of the slightly curved bowl that was his command deck. The enemy ships had gone superluminal a few minutes earlier, by ship time. In actuality, they had been gone from the system now for several hours, and the light was only just getting caught up to the fleet.

In short order, he knew, they would have vector data on the enemy fleet's next objective, and then it would be time to jump out ahead of them and do the whole thing over again.

"Sir."

"Step up, CAG, tell me what's on your mind," James said without looking around. He knew his officers' voices well enough.

Commander Hawkins stepped up beside him, a data plaque in hand. "Readiness reports for the squadrons, sir."

"Thank you." James accepted the report, but didn't look at it. "Summary?"

"Fighting trim, sir."

"Good to know, never doubted it." James allowed a slight smile before his features turned somber again. "You know they'll be looking for you next time, right?"

"Wouldn't be any fun if they weren't, sir."

"No," James allowed, "I don't suppose it would be. How are we on the FTL missiles?"

"Couple full loads, still manufacturing more, but it's slow on board now that we've exhausted stock parts. We'll need a resupply of basic materials shortly, or we'll have to stop altogether."

"We'll have time to tranship from the logistics vessels on the other side. Make your lists, you know the drill."

"Yes sir. Needs, wants, and wishes," Hawkins confirmed. "Wilco. Incidentally, Commander Black wants me to push a request of hers up channels."

"The FTL cores for Vorpals?" James asked, amused.

"How ever did you guess, sir? You must be a mind reader," Hawkins replied, just barely able to keep a straight face as he did.

"I can't imagine," James said dryly. "You can inform the commander that the request has been approved. Time is the only question at this juncture, and that's the one question I'm unable to answer."

"Understood, sir, and Black gets that too. She just wants to be sure it isn't forgotten. Stephanos blew circles around us in that heap of his, and being able to outrun light is a hell of a way to fly."

James chuckled, not doubting that for a moment. It was actually a limited advantage, of course, since in order to be combat effective you often had to fly into laser fire. Thus the ability to outrun light didn't amount to much in those circumstances, but the option would still be appreciated.

"Honestly, I'm more interested in the drones the commodore has the fleet manufacturing right now," James admitted. "Picket drones with hyperspectral scanners and limited FTL comms? Those are a game changer, no offense to your fighter-jock sensibilities, Commander."

"None taken, Captain. You're right," Hawkins said seriously, "and I agree, if only because being able to adapt faster to enemy fire means that the *E* will be waiting for us when we get back from the sharp end of things."

They stood in silence for a moment before Hawkins spoke up again. "Do you think it'll be enough of a game changer, sir?"

James sighed.

"I wish I could say yes, CAG. I wish I could say yes."

▶▶▶

AEV *Odysseus*

▶ Odysseus stared at the world, so far away and yet seemingly so close. It was growing smaller, even by the scanners he could use like they were his own eyes, the *Odysseus* and fleet moving away at high speed as they worked to analyze the vectors associated with the enemy's departure.

"We need those scanners."

The boy entity jerked around, surprised. That was a feeling he almost never experienced, and he was shocked by a flush of . . . shame? He wasn't sure, but it wasn't a pleasant emotion.

"How did you know?" Odysseus asked, though he knew the answer even as the question came out.

"One of our more powerful scanners is tasked to observe the planet, with no requisition code on the file?" Eric said as he approached. "The only people on board who could do that wouldn't, not now. They know we need every scanner on the enemy fleet."

"I'm sorry."

"Don't be, I understand," Eric said. "Just release the scanner so we can do the job that needs doing."

"Already done," Odysseus confirmed.

"Thank you," Eric said, leaning on the wall of the corridor off the command deck that Odysseus had moved to some minutes earlier. "Need to talk about it?"

"Everyone has . . . deep emotions and confusing thoughts about the world we're leaving," Odysseus said after a moment. "I don't understand."

"What? That they're thinking about the world?"

"No, I understand that," Odysseus said. "I mean, the confusing . . . conflicting thoughts. Even the same person thinks different things at almost the same time. That it's the right thing to leave, but it's the wrong thing to do too. That we're running from a fight, but not really? I don't understand it."

"The crew doesn't understand it either," Eric said. "Even I don't get it. Sometimes you don't have to understand everything, Odysseus—sometimes you just do the job whether it makes any sense to you or not. If we waited until all made sense, very few things in this universe would ever be done."

He chuckled a little, though the humor didn't reach his eyes, mind, or heart.

"Don't try to make sense of humans, son," Eric said simply. "We're a confusing lot at the best of times, and you're a warship. I doubt you'll ever see us at the best of times."

He exhaled, not noticing Odysseus staring at him for a moment as he looked back toward the bridge.

"I have a feeling that you will see us at our worst, however," he said finally. "Try to keep in mind that stress and anger aren't our default conditions. Don't judge the crew too harshly."

"I . . . do not think that is a concern, Commodore," Odysseus said slowly. "In a very real way, *I am* the crew. That would be judging myself, would it not?"

Eric smiled. "I suppose it would. I have to get back to work. When we're done . . . well, you can use the scanners for whatever you like."

"Thank you."

The entity observed the commodore as he walked out, heading back to the bridge.

▶▶▶

▶ "We have a vector, Captain," Miram relayed as Eric stepped back onto the main deck of the bridge.

"Good. Lay it in and signal the logistical fleet. Let's get ahead of these pricks."

Soft, almost nervous chuckles rippled around the bridge. He recognized the fear he was hearing there but studiously ignored it and treated the laughter for the genuine enthusiasm everyone else pretended it to be.

With the *Odysseus* leading the way, the fleet of warships pivoted in space and seemed to drift for a brief moment until the transition drives executed the jump into tachyon transition. Ship by ship they vanished into the black.

Behind them they left another world under the control of a hostile force. Ahead of them lay more of the same.

CHAPTER 26

Allied Earth Command, Cheyenne Mountain Facility

▶ Three weeks.

Gracen had been monitoring the *Odysseus* Task Group's progress for that long since their initial confrontation with the Imperial Fleet. Over that time the Empire had managed to acquire five more planets and tally up a kill score of nine Rogues and a Heroic to their credit.

Granted, the kill ratio massively favored Weston's people, with at least forty of the Imperial cruisers falling to their new weapons and tactics as well as an unknown but significant number of their Parasite destroyers.

Unfortunately, that was still a level of attrition that the enemy could afford, which neither she nor the Priminae could even begin to contemplate for their own forces.

Worse, they're lined up on Ranquil now.

The Imperials were still a day or two out of the Priminae core world, but she knew that was the line in the sand. The Priminae vessels wouldn't fall back anymore, unless she was very much mistaken, and she wasn't certain if Commodore Weston would be willing to do so either, despite it all being his plan.

There were *billions* at risk there, and ultimately the Forge facility would be cut off from supply and forced to reveal itself or die in the heart of the local star. If they lost Ranquil, Earth would be merely a formality shortly afterward.

She glanced at the map that now showed seven red stars and the corresponding space tinted the color assigned to Imperial control.

Seven worlds in less than two months. Weston's plan to drag this out has been working, but we've run out of territory to cede to the enemy. The Forge is too valuable. We could lose Ranquil but not the Forge.

The problem was that the enemy, even with their losses, still outmassed Weston's task group by an obscene number, and they'd gotten at least a little wise to the new tactics. Gracen knew that there wouldn't be enough to hold them off, which meant that they were all in deep shit.

If there were ever a time for a miracle, this would be it.

▶▶▶

Priminae Central Command, Ranquil

▶ Tanner examined the estimated clock with an intensity he usually reserved for out-of-place junior officers, willing it to reverse its motion despite all the laws of the universe to the contrary.

He set down a drink he had been nursing for some time, oddly calm as he did so.

"Is this how it ends?" he asked, though no one was present to hear him.

He liked to think it wasn't. Nero was preparing to fight the enemy on the ground, though officially the Council had the intention to issue an unconditional surrender as the Empire entered the system.

Honestly, he didn't know how many people would obey the order, not after so many had already died in the Colonies, but the situation would be out of his hands once the command was issued. His authority would be ended then in all official capacities and in most realistic ways as well, since a large part of his power stemmed from the access to the command and control center he enjoyed at the Council's behest.

He was at a loss as to how things had deteriorated so far while he had been at the helm. Tanner asked himself what could have been done differently to have achieved a better outcome. Ultimately, however, he couldn't find a path, not even in hindsight, that would have led to a different conclusion.

Perhaps that was his failure, as much as anything else.

The *Odysseus* and the task group under the command of Eric Weston had transitioned into the system mere hours earlier, preparing to mount the last-ditch defense of the world everyone knew was lost. Tanner was among those few who understood that it was not Ranquil they were preparing to defend, however, but access to the Forge.

It was perhaps ironic, in a way, that the most desperate defense they had yet mounted against the Imperial forces would be in the defense of a world the Imperials had no idea even existed.

Tanner laughed bitterly at that.

Sometimes, reality had a way of turning out more bizarre than any half-cocked fantasy dreamed up by humanity. Fantasy had a tendency to follow man's desire for the universe to make sense. Reality had no such compunctions.

▶▶▶

AEV *Odysseus,* Outer Ranquil System

▶ Eric was tired. Three weeks of fighting would do that to anyone and had in fact done that to everyone. His crew was weary but unwilling to bend now as they prepared for what would likely be their second-to-last battle if they survived to see the end of it. He knew he would issue the order to withdraw when the system was lost—there was no real choice there—but Eric also knew that when he did . . . the war was over.

For everything the Earth had going for it, his homeworld couldn't match the Forge for production of raw materials. The admiral's construction of a system defense might hold for a short time, but even the miracle they were all hoping for from Prometheus wouldn't be enough to buy Earth a clear path to survival.

Without ships, people, and resources to capitalize on Prometheus, it would be like spitting in the eye of an angry maniac who had his knife to your throat.

Defiant, perhaps even courageous, but likely fatal.

"Are we ready?" he asked as he walked up to where Miram was overseeing the status of the *Odysseus*.

More than ever, Miram Heath had become the de facto captain of the *Odysseus* while he managed the task group. Her rank was a grade low for the duties she was handling, but the statuesque woman had borne up well under the work and left him with one less worry to keep him awake at night.

"Aye sir," she said. "All drones have checked out. Fighters from the *Enterprise* are ready to launch, and we've got two more drone squadrons from the *Bell* and the *Bo* respectively."

"Archangels to the last," Eric said, smiling. "Fitting. Very well, stand by to deploy on—"

He was cut off by confused murmuring from the scanning station that caught his attention.

"What is it, Lieutenant?" he asked the woman currently standing that watch.

Lieutenant Medellin shook her head. "I'm sorry, sir. I must be doing something wrong, but I can't seem to track the incoming flux from the enemy drives. I had it earlier, but . . ." She put her hands up, disgusted. "Sorry sir."

Eric walked over, then leaned over her shoulder and tapped commands into the system. "Don't get frustrated, just run back through the steps and locate the . . . huh?"

He paused, blanked the system, and then reentered the commands.

"Milla! Run checks through tactical. I'm not showing the enemy here," he ordered, moving the lieutenant aside as he started running deeper into the system himself.

He and Lieutenant Chans both worked furiously at the primary scanner station and the tactical weapons station, neither able to locate the inbound track.

Eric gave it up. "I want to know *when* we lost them! Find those ships!"

He stepped away, letting the lieutenant back into the station, and clapped a hand to her shoulder. "You did fine. Now find out where they went."

"Yes sir!"

Eric strode back up to the center of the command deck, eyes a little wild as he tried to contain himself. "They changed course. If we don't figure out for where . . ."

He shook his head.

It should have been good news, frankly. They could sacrifice any other system, but Ranquil was the most valuable system left on the map due to the Forge.

Furthermore, he knew that the Imperials had obviously obtained enough intelligence to know the former, if not the latter.

The only other system remotely as valuable now is . . .

Eric froze. "Oh shit."

He swung around into his station and opened a direct FTL to the Priminae Central Command, using his code to punch right through to Cheyenne Mountain.

"Admiral, Weston here," he said quickly as the admiral's face appeared on his screen. "I think you have trouble coming your way."

▶▶▶

Allied Earth Command, Cheyenne Mountain Facility

▶ Gracen strode through the Marine guards, leaving confusion in her wake as she forced her way into SPACECOM with nothing short of murder in her eyes.

"Admiral, there are *protocols*!" the watch commander protested.

"Fuck protocol," she said flatly. "I need access to the Kardashev Net."

"If the admiral would please tell me what she is looking for . . . ," the commander tried, only to find himself pushed aside as Gracen stepped across the floor and looked at everyone working there, who were all now staring up at her.

"Commodore Weston just informed me that the Imperial forces are no longer en route for Ranquil," she said loudly. "By his estimation, only one world would draw their focus from there at this point in time. Earth. If they're coming here, there will be quantum flux as the bow shock of their warp drives affects gravity along their course. Find it."

Everyone stared at her for a moment too long.

"Right the hell *now*!"

That got them working, at least, while she stood over the pit and glared.

It didn't take long for them to confirm her worries once they actually went looking for the flux. Gracen looked at the new icon that showed up on the projections map, her hands tightening around the rail in front of her.

"Admiral . . . what does that mean?" the commander asked, staring.

"It means our fleet is out of position and we're about to be caught with our pants down," she snarled, pushing off the rail and stomping out of the room.

▶ ▶ ▶

Lord's Own Dreadnought, *Empress Liann*

▶ "So this is the world that has been causing all the impossible-to-predict variables," Jesan said as he looked at the long-range scans of the system, particularly the third planet from the local star. "Unimpressive."

"We are scanning significant stellar debris, My Lord. There is evidence of Drasin in what was once the fourth world of the system," his second said. "Now, of course, there is little more than a debris field there."

"Surviving a full Drasin invasion would rank as impressive, I suppose," Jesan said simply. "So perhaps I am corrected. Fleet defenses?"

"Four of the enemy cruisers, a small contingent of the destroyers . . . nothing significant."

"Excellent," Jesan said. "Deploy Parasites and proceed deeper in system."

Jesan would be exceedingly pleased to eliminate the Oathers' core world, when the time came, but first it would be a pleasure to remove the last dregs of hope from the resistance, as he had a feeling that much of their newfound fighting spirit was an artificial addition.

Judging from the lack of overall defenses, they actually believed that we hadn't monitored the Drasin closely enough to realize the location of their home system.

A fatal miscalculation.

▶▶▶

AEV *Odysseus*

▶ Alarms sounded on all decks as the ship went to general quarters, waking everyone up, readying for a transition that no one had been expecting. All across the fleet the same thing was going on, Eric knew, but it wasn't happening fast enough for his liking.

The enemy had shifted their course at a still-unknown point in time earlier, and all indications were that they had actually increased speed en route for Earth. He didn't know if he could possibly get the fleet moving in the time they had left, but he was going to damn well try.

▶▶▶

Allied Earth Command, Cheyenne Mountain Facility

▶ "Well, here they come," Gracen growled as the enemy ships entered the outer reaches of the heliosphere.

This was the second alien invasion during her career. She had been forced to flee during the first. This time she would stand her watch as she should have done before.

"Stand by to activate the Kardashev Network," she ordered.

"Kardashev Net is standing by, Admiral."

"Let them in a little deeper," Gracen said firmly. "We only have enough power for one good punch. May as well make it count."

"Aye aye, Admiral," an Air Force captain answered. "Enemy fleet has entered the outer orbit of Neptune. Proceeding sunward at high fractions of c, but slowing."

"We have a lot of debris in system," Gracen said, "thanks to their games with the Drasin. If they come in too hot, that sort of flight hazard will be a threat even to warp-shielded vessels."

"Yes ma'am."

Gracen stared at the screen, despising the feeling she was enduring as the numbers slowly fell along with the Imperial ships' approach. Somehow this was worse than watching the Drasin invasion, which had been like observing an approaching storm you knew you couldn't avoid.

The Imperials shouldn't be that.

They should be willing to talk, to negotiate.

Screw them. Gracen glowered at the screen as the fleets continued to proceed on course for Earth. They were less than ten hours out at current speeds.

"The *Washington* and *Mulan* have taken up defensive positions just outside Cislunar space, along with our available Rogues."

"Thank you, Captain. Inform them that they should hold position until the enemy makes their final approach," Gracen ordered. "We'll open contact with the Kardashev Network first."

"Aye ma'am."

Gracen nodded absently, tapping in a series of commands to her network as she glanced up at the numbers. The Imperials were approaching Uranus, which would bring them within the outer contact range of the current network of Kardashev satellites.

Almost there.

▶ ▶ ▶

▶ The Kardashev Network, Earth's first true stellar construction project, slowly awakened at the admiral's command. The distributed network of solar collectors had been primarily tasked with self-replication, but that hadn't been their ultimate purpose or design. At the command from Earth, the network began tracking the approach of the ships that bore no IFF transponders and pulsing energy via laser link from across the network to key positions.

The Imperial ships proceeded deeper into the system and deeper into the network of satellites that were very nearly invisible by most standard means of detection.

As the ships passed Saturn and headed for Jovian orbit, the network fully activated. All the power of the entire solar satellite network of well over three million individual self-replicating power collectors had been redirected and focused into just three *thousand* of them.

At the orbit of Jupiter, those three thousand unleashed all that power across the system.

Beams lanced out from one network node to another, intersecting the forward ships of the flotilla and slicing through them with startling ease. Powered by the sun and almost a year of collection rather than a lone singularity, the beams dwarfed those of any shipboard weapons and turned armor into tinder in an instant.

As the beams lanced through, they connected with another node, which redirected the beam onto the next target. The network only had the power for a few seconds of fire before it depleted its energy, but the display was impressive.

In seconds, a hundred ships burned in space.

▶▶▶

Lord's Own Dreadnought, *Empress Liann*

▶ Jesan flinched from the startling display of destruction, just a little aghast as the forward Parasites vanished in flame and laser light.

"Impressive," he admitted as the beams died out. "Scan for those platforms."

"We've located them now that we know what to look for," his second said. "They must run off capacitors, as there was no evidence of any significant power generation before the laser grid opened fire."

"Target and destroy the nodes," Jesan ordered, "and scan for others."

"Yes, My Lord."

Lasers lanced out from the fleet, burning the platforms steadily as the ships continued to travel deeper into the system.

Jesan found himself genuinely admiring his adversaries this time.

That had been an impressive defense system, though from the scans he was assuming it was far from complete. Had the system been more encompassing, losses to the Empire might have actually been significant.

It seems to be for the best that we redirected here, he decided with some satisfaction.

The defenses would have to be studied when the battle was over, to be certain, but he was confident that he would not have liked to see the results had the network been fully operational.

"Target the enemy cruisers," he ordered as the ships acquired a solid lock on the last line of the system defense. "Fire as we enter maximum effective range. We shall end this."

▶▶▶

AEV *Odysseus*

▶ "Ready to transition, Commodore!"

"Coordinates to the stations," Eric ordered, sending the target coordinates.

It took a moment before everyone had them, but he was unsurprised when the first objections were voiced.

"Commodore," Roberts said from the screens in front of him, "those coordinates are deep inside the system."

"I'm aware of that, Captain," Eric said. "Check them and you'll see that I'm not crazy."

"I know where they are, Commodore," Roberts said slowly. "However, it's a risk."

"If we come in outside the heliosphere, we'll be too late. It'll be over before we arrive. We'll be fine," Eric said firmly. "The coordinates stand."

He looked across the faces on the screens, his gaze challenging them to object, but his tone seemed to be enough.

Roberts nodded slowly. "Yes sir."

"Engage transition," Eric ordered.

The ships of the *Odysseus* Task Group came around slowly in space, locking onto their target light-years away, and then vanished into the ether one by one, leaving only darkness in their wake.

CHAPTER 27

AEV *Washington,* Sol System

▶ "Here they come!"

Commander Burke, standing station at the weapons control for the Heroic Class vessel *Washington,* found himself facing what he might normally call a "target-rich environment." In the current state of affairs, he didn't have time to think about it as he picked his targets and set the lasers to open fire largely on their own.

The Parasite ships that were providing a destroyer screen for the oncoming enemy force were easily holed by the *Washington's* lasers while he waited for the armaments section to shift a new load of thermonuclear warheads to the transition-cannon magazines.

They'd fired their guns dry, along with the *Mulan* beside them and every Rogue available, and lit space with hundreds of nuclear fireballs but barely dented the enemy armada.

Burke, under the glare of his captain, was determined to make the enemy pay for every light-second they gained into the system, but he didn't need anyone to tell him that it wasn't going to end well for the *Washington* as Imperial forces entered into extreme laser range. They clearly weren't interested in holding back.

"Laser blooms!"

Damage reports began screaming in from every deck as dozens of strikes rained down on them from the black. They were hammered, just as every other ship defending Earth orbit was, despite having attempted evasive maneuvering.

There were too many beams coming in, and too few of the defenders were positioned properly to find clear space to evade into.

"Take us around Luna!" Captain Bricker ordered. "Break their line of fire for a few minutes!"

"Aye Skipper!"

Burke largely ignored the maneuvering orders as he kept haloing targets on his panels and setting priorities for the computers to engage as weapons became available.

It's a hell of a thing, he thought, *but we have more targets than we have weapons available to service them.*

He was cut off from those targets as the *Washington* moved behind Luna, and he could hear the captain calling out orders.

"We've got *minutes*, people! Get the hull breaches sealed and reroute power to all essential areas!"

Burke mostly tuned out his captain's voice, as he was barking orders of his own. "Shift those munitions to the live magazines as quickly as you can! I want to come out shooting!"

▶▶▶

AEV *Mulan*

▶ Captain Gyang Hung of the *Mulan* felt like his ship was stubbornly clinging to life just because it refused to roll over and die, much like her crew.

They were billowing air, faster than even the prodigious atmosphere generators on the big vessel could handle, but somehow the massively redundant systems had tenaciously refused to go down. Half her weapons were gone, and the tally of lost lives had stopped coming in.

He doubted it was because people had stopped dying, suspecting instead that no one was left counting.

The *Mulan* followed the *Washington*, along with their surviving Rogues, positioning Luna between them and the enemy briefly in order to gain a little time to patch the ships' most critical damage and, more importantly, reload depleted magazines from stores.

Hung had never in his life imagined being in a situation where he would fire off well over a hundred nuclear weapons . . . and find that it hadn't been even close to enough.

▶▶▶

Allied Earth Command, Cheyenne Mountain Facility

▶ "Transition alert!"

Gracen gritted her teeth, knowing that it wouldn't matter.

The *Odysseus* fleet was the only group of Allied warships maintaining significant force, and even though she was certain that was their signature arriving, they would be *hours* out. The fight over Earth would be over in *minutes* now, and Imperial doctrine would put an end to the human race as a space power.

They'd be back to the Stone Age from kinetic strikes in mere hours.

"Task Group *Odysseus* identified!"

Gracen looked up. "What?"

It should have been hours yet before they had a signal ID from the ships arriving via transition.

"Task Group *Odysseus* moving to engage the enemy!"

That's impossible!

Gracen rose to her feet. "How?"

"They transitioned directly into the L Two Lagrange point, Admiral!"

"They what?!"

▶▶▶

AEV *Washington*

▶ "Ready weapons," Bricker ordered. "We're about to clear Luna."

The few ships remaining of what had been Earth's defense fleet were flying low to the lunar surface, moving fast against the passing terrain below as they raced for the horizon and began to climb for altitude again.

Computer systems began registering enemy targets as they appeared over the horizon, and in an instant Burke was feeding priorities to the remaining weapons at his disposal with clearance to fire at will.

The force swung around Luna, already firing all weapons as they prepared for the inevitable counter-fire from the enemy fleet.

The first enemy lasers began to rain down, once again raising alarms, until they were suddenly cut off.

"New contacts! IFF signals recognized! Captain, it's the *Odysseus*!"

▶▶▶

AEV *Odysseus*

▶ "Deploy picket drones, launch all fighter squadrons!" Weston ordered, leaning forward as he fought not to puke all over his station.

The entire task group had transitioned to one of the stable gravity regions in the solar system, in this case the L2 Lagrange point set by the Earth/Moon system. Targeting the small point had entailed a certain level of risk, but it appeared to have worked as best he could tell, though Eric felt somewhat worse for the trip than normal.

He risked a sickly look over to where Miram was struggling much as he was. "Did we lose anyone?"

She covered her mouth, eyes clenched shut briefly before she looked over the data feed.

"Seven Rogues aren't on our scanners," she said, her tone and body language more than a bit devastated.

Eric grimaced himself.

He didn't know what had happened to the vessels, but it was safe to assume that they hadn't reintegrated. Possibly they'd jumped outside the stable gravity zone of the L2 point, possibly something else.

Steeling his stomach, Eric rose to his feet.

"Lock transition cannons onto the Parasite ships," he ordered. "Clear a path. I want those Imperial cruisers!"

"Aye Captain," Milla responded quickly. "Targets locked . . . transition cannons free . . . firing."

Spheres of nuclear fire erupted across the Imperial Fleet, tearing through the hundreds of Parasite destroyers descending on their position as drones and fighters poured out of the vessels of Task Group *Odysseus.*

▶▶▶

Lord's Own Dreadnought, *Empress Liann*

▶ "That's not *possible!*"

Lord Jesan's oath went largely unnoticed as everyone was far too busy dealing with the sudden increase in enemy fire that had come from nowhere.

Jesan was in a rage as he tore through the data available to him.

"Were they hidden in stealth? Why?" he asked. "Why sacrifice so many for . . . what?"

Unfortunately for the Imperial lord, there were no answers to be found as those around him tried but failed to explain the enemy's decisions.

He shook it off, forced down the rage at being surprised as reality reasserted itself.

He still had enough power to accomplish his mission. The enemy forces were not nearly so strong as to actually fend off his fleet. He would simply lose far more ships than calculated in the process. It just maddened him that he couldn't understand the situation.

None of it made sense. Nothing these people did seemed to make sense.

▶▶▶

▶ Three flashes of Cerenkov blue punctuated the battle space as modified Double A platform fighters launched from the three Heroics that were leading the charge. The *Odysseus*, the *Bellerophon*, and the *Boudicca* each put drone squadrons into space amid a cloud of picket drones.

Stephanos took the vanguard position, letting Burner and Cardsharp fall into formation along with their drone wings as he checked the enemy formation.

"Stay close, and don't deviate much from the prepared flight plan," he ordered the other two Archangel pilots, two of only four now left alive. "We're cutting right through the heaviest fighting, so try not to get nuked by friendly fire."

Cardsharp laughed, just happy to be out from the helm of the *Boudicca* finally. It wasn't that the bigger ship wasn't enjoyable to fly, in its own way, but she was doing exactly what she'd always wanted once more.

"You got it, Stephanos. Nuked by our own side, bad. Got it."

The three drone squadrons, each led by a modified Archangel, spread out as they flashed into the midst of the fighting, drones following along, and interpenetrated the enemy line of battle, heading for the big boys beyond the Parasite destroyer screen.

They dived through the gaps between the ships, flashing past at reckless speeds in order to avoid being targeted by any close-in point-defense systems, only easing back slightly when they burst through the screen to meet the Imperial cruisers.

Stephanos cleared his weapons' safeties, flying right into the teeth of the enemy.

"Archangel Lead, Fox Hades."

"Archangel Two, Fox Hades."

"Archangel Three . . . Fox Hades."

Eighteen drones loaded with antimatter six-shooters opened fire as one.

▶▶▶

Lord's Own Dreadnought, *Empress Liann*

▶ "Deploy countermeasures!"

Jesan held on, knowing from previous experience that the countermeasures wouldn't be effective. No one had yet worked out how the enemy interceptors deployed their weapons, and at damn near the speed of light the available sensor data that might explain it was in short supply no matter how many ships they had scanning.

White flashes erupted across the screens as the antimatter payload the interceptors unloaded on the Imperials interacted with regular matter, producing *energetic* results. The *Liann* wasn't exempt either, several detonations tearing into her despite the screen of chaff thrown out to block the unblockable.

The ship rumbled, the size of the dreadnought absorbing the devastating power of the negative matter munitions, but around her cruisers began to die.

Jesan gritted his teeth. "Someone *swat* those pests!"

▶▶▶

AEV *Odysseus*

▶ "Get those picket drones out at least twenty light-seconds or we'll never get enough of a warning to adapt," Eric ordered, shifting focus as a pair of enemy Parasite destroyers adjusted their course to intercept and were highlighted on the combat display. "Milla, kill those two!"

"Aye Captain, tasking t-cannons . . . firing . . ."

Two spheres of nuclear fire erupted in space, signifying the deaths of the destroyers as ordered, but Eric had already moved on to the next crisis of the moment.

The opening instances of the fight were the most chaotic he had ever experienced, including his time flying against the Block. Transitioning right on top of Cislunar space had been effective in getting them on-site fast enough to accomplish *something*, but it had thrown them right into the mix without his normal period of being able to size up the enemy strategy.

This wasn't a strategic move-and-countermove battle, as Eric had fought in space so many times before. This was a furious exchange of barely planned blows, a slugging match that would inevitably go to whomever could stand up the longest against the punches that were landing. That wasn't a situation that favored his ships and crews, as Eric knew too damn well.

"Drones in position, Captain!"

"Slave them to the task force's armor control system and let them run," Eric ordered.

Damage reports from enemy fire dropped off almost instantly as the armor of the task group began to adapt ahead of the arrival of the lasers. It was a miracle only possible in a world with FTL communication and still blew his mind.

The drones were, in many ways, a shield that provided them with critical data, but they were also soft targets. Inevitably, even if the enemy wasn't targeting them directly, the drones would be struck by laser fire and vanish into the black in a brief flash of fire.

Odysseus stood on the bridge behind Eric, accessing the computer records and calmly running the calculations.

"ETA to picket drone depletion . . . five minutes, twenty-one seconds," he said quietly.

"Thank you, Odysseus," Eric said. "Launch our last set at the three-minute mark."

"Roger, Commodore," the intelligence said, taking over some of the tasks in order to lighten the workload for others as much as possible.

"Make the best use of the time we can," Eric said. "Burn them out of my sky! Enemy cruisers are priority targets for our lasers and HVM loadouts, but if you can't see a cruiser, fry a destroyer instead!"

"Aye aye, Captain," Milla responded. "All lasers firing."

▶▶▶

AEV *Juraj Jánošík*

▶ "Picket drones active, Captain!"

"Take us into the teeth of the enemy fire," Aleska ordered in a snarl. "Punch a hole through the destroyer screen. I want a cruiser to our credit from this battle!"

The *Jánošík* opened fire with the powerful lasers mounted on the length of her keel, burning enemy destroyers from the sky as her rapidly adapting armor shrugged off return fire with an ease that Aleska regretted would be so short-lived.

The burning of the lasers opened up a hole through the destroyer screen, allowing their scanners to spot the more powerful and dangerous cruisers beyond.

"Make time-on-target calculations for the cruiser, and fire HVM and pulse torpedoes," she ordered.

"Aye Skipper! Missiles and torpedoes away, time on target . . . one minute, twenty-eight seconds!"

Aleska leaned forward, anger on her face as the explosion of a Priminae Heroic lit up the screens to her left side.

"Keep firing!"

▶▶▶

▶ In the midst of the exchange of terawatt-level lasers, antimatter pulse torpedoes, and high-velocity missiles, the Vorpal squadrons raged across the second line of Parasite destroyers like angry wasps among giants. Through painful experience, they'd learned that their superluminal missiles just didn't pack the punch to really tear into the heavier cruisers of the Empire's forces but could wreak havoc on the destroyers.

Calls of "Fox Five" filled the tactical network as Alexandra Black led her Excalibur squadron on a vicious stampede through the enemy forces, leaving nothing but utter chaos in her wake.

"Excalibur Lead, watch for cross fire," Hawkins ordered. "Split the destroyers ahead and meet around the other side."

"Roger that, CAG," Alexandra said as she pushed the throttle forward and threaded her fighter through a gap in the enemy formation. "Last one there bugs the captain for the FTL upgrades next."

"Like you're not going to make me do that job anyway, Black."

▶▶▶

▶ The front line of the Imperial formation faltered, coming under heavy fire as the *Odysseus* group poured on the firepower. Behind that line, however, the remaining ships of the Empire bulled on through with no regard for their losses.

The second and then third rank of destroyers took savage losses, but in short order they closed the distance and crossed the drone picket, running right through. Once inside the picket line, the *Odysseus* group's defensive advantage went up in smoke along with several Rogue destroyers as the enemy fire intensified and their armor adaptations ceased being useful.

The tide of battle shifted in a swift reversal, pushing the crews of the Terran and Priminae vessels onto the defensive as the weight of firepower surged down against them.

▶▶▶

AEV *Odysseus*

▶ "Flank speed!" Eric ordered over the alarms screaming from every console. "Take us into the Imperial formation!"

The frazzled pilot sitting in the pit, having taken Steph's place, twisted in shock.

"What?"

Before Eric could say anything, however, the armored form of Odysseus appeared beside the pit and dropped to one knee.

"The commodore issued an order," Odysseus said. "Follow your orders. I will help."

The pilot hesitated just a moment before turning back around and nodding resolutely.

"Right. Flank speed, into the enemy formation. I've got this."

"You do," Odysseus said firmly.

Eric wasted only a moment on the byplay before he shifted to the squadron network. "Follow us in and through. If you stay here, you'll die for sure. The only way out *is through*!"

The *Odysseus* surged ahead, all beams firing as it charged right into the face of the enemy.

CHAPTER 28

Task Group Prometheus, AEV *Autolycus,* Imperial Space

▶ "We found it."

Morgan nodded, his grin more than a little feral.

They'd been backtracking the Imperial Fleet for *weeks,* running quiet as they looked for the Empire itself. Moreover, they needed an important world. Imperial outposts had proven common enough, but most were nothing but mining operations of varying types.

Nothing strategic of value, and his orders were specific.

This world was different, however. The population was estimated well into the billions, but far more importantly the system held a vast stellar infrastructure. It seemed that they'd located a shipyard facility, and from the looks of the hulls they were scanning it was a military operation.

"Double-check our numbers, and make sure we're not leaking anything," he ordered. "We don't need to be spotted now that we finally found what we're looking for."

"Aye sir," Commander Li responded. "All systems are secured. We're running silent."

Morgan nodded, knowing she was right. He was just being a little paranoid, but he felt some justification. They were so close now that he could almost taste it.

He unbuckled from his station and kicked loose, drifting in microgravity over to where the newly installed FTL comm was taking up a chunk of his bridge space. He began entering the pulse coding for the discovery into the system, taking his time and making sure he got it right.

The system was a busy one, but they had time just the same. Space was a huge place, and not even as busy a system as this one had much activity in the area they'd chosen to park in. There was little of value in the region, just C-type carbonaceous asteroids. Incredibly common, the C-types made up seventy-five percent of asteroids in Earth's home system and seemed similar here.

They were dark rocks, with no particular value for materials, and thus made perfect positions to park a ship if you didn't want to be noticed. Odds were the field was already well mapped, and barring a good reason, no one was going to bother looking in their direction again anytime soon. He just needed to be sure *not* to give anyone a good reason to look.

Morgan carefully adjusted the tachyon transceiver, aiming for a directional pulse in order to reduce any chances of being noticed. They had intentionally parked between the Imperial presence and the general direction of Earth and the Priminae worlds for that very reason.

"Ready to transmit," he said, looking around. "A little prayer wouldn't be out of place right about now. Might not help, but it sure won't hurt."

With those words he sent the final command that pulsed a signal out in a fraction of a second, hopefully short enough not to be picked up.

"Now . . . we wait," he said, "and hope the hell we're not too late."

▶▶▶

Allied Earth Command, Cheyenne Mountain Facility

▶ "Admiral . . ."

"Not now! Whatever it is, not now!"

Gracen snapped the words out angrily, eyes glued to the fighting they were only seeing through computer displays but she knew was being paid for in the lives of hundreds right over their heads even as the messenger tried to get her attention.

"Admiral, I think you should see this. Priority relay from Prometheus via Ranquil."

"What?" Her head snapped around, eyes boring into the man. "Tell me you're not kidding."

"No ma'am, I would never—"

He didn't get a chance to finish as she shoved him out of the way and lunged for her desk. The message in question was there on her notifications list, and she popped it open immediately, eyes scanning the pulse code. She could only pick out two words without running the code through the computer, but it was enough.

"Yes!"

Her scream startled everyone in hearing, but Gracen didn't give a damn.

She linked into the FTL comm, sending a signal out to Prometheus Actual, the deep-space world discovered by Captain Passer and the crew of the *Autolycus* during the King of Thieves mission. A video link opened almost instantly.

"Yes Admiral?"

"Commander Janek." She nodded briefly. "Please tell me that the facility is ready."

"Yes ma'am. Do you have the coordinates?" Janek leaned in.

"Sending them to you now. You may engage at will."

"It will be my pleasure, ma'am," Commander Janek said eagerly. "Prometheus Actual out."

The screen went dead, and she immediately shifted her focus to more local issues. Gracen linked into the command battle network, transmitting directly to the ships fighting for their lives right at the edge of Cislunar space.

"Cheyenne Mountain to *Odysseus*, Commodore Weston, Prometheus is in play!" she yelled. "Say again, Prometheus is in play!"

Gracen stared at the display, eyes darting up to the fighting. "Come on, Commodore . . . tell me you heard me."

After an interminable silence, a familiar voice came back.

"Roger," Eric Weston said over the communications link. "Confirm receipt, Prometheus is in play. Am proceeding with new mission, Odysseus Actual is assuming command of Prometheus Actual."

"Roger that, Commodore, Prometheus Actual is standing by to receive orders," she said, slumping. "Do what you have to do."

"Roger, Cheyenne Mountain. It'll be a pleasure."

▶▶▶

AEV *Autolycus*

▶ "Signal from Prometheus Actual, Skipper," the communications duty officer reported. "They're requesting target information."

"Send them the latest calculations, along with vectors for all primary and secondary targets," Morgan ordered instantly, leaning forward as much as the seat restraints would allow him.

"Target and vector data queued for pulse transmission, sir," the comm officer responded. "Pulse out!"

Morgan nodded, settling back as he waited along with the rest of the crew for the ultimate expression of their mission to play out in front of them. They'd been tasked with locating stellar and special anomalies since their first fated mission, and it was all coming down to this one moment in time.

Let's see how you bastards like a taste of fire from the gods.

▶▶▶

Prometheus Facility

▶ "Forward targeting data logged and locked, Commander!"

Commander Janek nodded, standing in the middle of the alien control facility that had been retrofitted with computers and cables to power reactors in order to allow humans some level of control over all the technology that existed around him. He turned to a man standing in the corner, headphones over his ears, who was ignoring the proceedings almost entirely.

Janek pressed a button that cut off the audio to the headset, startling his colleague.

"Doctor Palin, if you would join us, please?"

Doctor Edward Palin sighed, pulling the headphones down as he turned back to look at the commander. "Yes? What is it?"

"We are preparing to engage the gravity lensing," Janek said patiently, mentally reminding himself that the eccentric and often-distracted individual was also one of the smartest people in the service. "Could you confirm that our commands are correct before we send the initiation codes?"

The language expert nodded, looking irritated at having been pulled away from his focus. Janek didn't know what he was working on at the moment, and he'd learned some time ago not to bother asking.

"Yes, yes," Palin said as he switched up his screens and looked over the current data, making minor alterations on the fly as he noted anything wrong. "You should be good now, Commander."

"Thank you, Doctor," Janek said, nodding to the fire control officer. "Engage."

"Yes sir," Lieutenant Commander Waters said firmly. "Engaging gravity lensing now."

The Prometheus facility was, ostensibly, the most powerful telescope in the galaxy as far as anyone had been able to determine. Using massive but incredibly controlled gravity manipulation systems, the structure was capable of gathering all light from a huge expanse of space, literally sucking it in right up *almost* to the event horizon of an artificial singularity before focusing the energy and sending it back on its way.

Normally, the light would be sent to a high-resolution imaging system, and the resulting data would be recorded in the facility's archive.

In this specific case, however, the light wasn't being sent on to the imager.

All the accumulated light had been gathered from the local stellar primary, concentrated, and focused to a point of burning energy best compared to a supernova in intensity. Of course, being light-speed limited, all that destructive power was worthless, as it was literally hundreds of years from its target.

"Transition waveguides are online, Commander."

Or maybe not.

"Fire for effect."

"Aye aye, Commander," the gunner officer said as he flipped a bank of switches before announcing, "beam out!"

A roiling inferno of energy lanced out from the Prometheus facility directly into the waiting transition waveguides and then vanished into the black as though it had never existed.

▶▶▶

AEV *Autolycus*

▶ "Tachyon surge, Captain."

"Thank you, Commander," Morgan said, wishing that he'd dared get closer. Despite the stealth capabilities of the Rogue Class ships, there were limits, so they'd have to wait for the light-speed data to reach them.

Tensions mounted as the seconds ticked away. What they were about to do was entirely untested, and everyone on board the small ship knew just what was a stake. With the enemy at the gates, this was their Hail Mary.

Suddenly, all the screens lit up, casting shadows around the bridge, and the crew lifted their hands to cover their eyes.

"Holy shit."

Morgan didn't know who said it, but as the screens adapted to filter some of the light out, he honestly had to agree.

Holy shit indeed.

▶▶▶

AEV *Odysseus*

▶ Miram twisted. "What in the hell is Prometheus? I thought it was just the Rogues' operation under Passer's command."

"It is," Eric said as the *Odysseus* screamed around him, the ship flying right through the heart of the enemy formation. He ignored the distress, focusing on his link to Prometheus Actual via the Cheyenne Mountain facility. "What you don't know is just what they managed to accomplish during the run of the operation, from their very first mission."

Heath grimaced as an Imperial destroyer attempted to ram them, only for Odysseus and the young pilot at the helm to twist their forward warp around and use the drives to *crush* the smaller ship like a freighter running over a kayak at sea.

Getting too close to a ship the size of the *Odysseus* had consequences, more so when there was a fight going on.

"What did they accomplish?" she asked, apparently having brought her attention back from the fight.

"An ace in the hole," he answered as he checked a signal being retransmitted to his station from the Cheyenne Mountain facility. Eric's lips drew back in something far too feral to be a smile as he got the confirmation he had been waiting for. "Yes!"

"What is it?"

"A moment," Eric said, keying open the ship's communication system to a multicast on all frequencies. "We just received a download from the *Auto*."

Miram shot him a stunned look. "The *Auto*? They're on assignment *light-years* away, sir. Rogues don't have FTL comms that can do more than basic pulse code."

"Prometheus is an exception," Eric said, signalling her for silence as he opened his command channel to the broadcast and started to speak. "Imperial Commander, this is Commodore Weston of the Allied Earth Vessel *Odysseus*. You don't normally talk to us, but I think you want to change your mind."

When there was no response—not that he expected one—Eric went doggedly on as though the fighting all around him weren't happening.

"You might recognize the imagery I'm broadcasting," he said. "This is an Imperial System, ten of our minutes ago. Please observe the military construction facilities."

"What are you doing?" Miram asked, looking at Eric in confusion, as was about half the crew on the bridge who weren't busy actually *fighting* the ship at the moment.

"I'm conducting a lesson on the *proper* utilization of strategic weapons," Eric said as he hit "Play." "Something these bastards are desperately in need of."

The video, mirrored on a small screen overhead, began its playback. At first nothing much seemed to happen. Ships came and went, mostly smaller construction-class vessels, and all seemed in order. The first thing that happened out of the ordinary was easy to miss, but Miram noticed the distinctive look of a transition event.

Then a pillar of flame roared up from the shipyards, igniting metal and ships and everything in its path as if the finger of God were being dragged across the facility. Wherever it touched, everything burned.

The whole video took only about twenty seconds to play, but at its end there was nothing but glowing wreckage congealing in space where once a massive military shipyard had floated.

Eric wasted no time upon the video's completion.

"If you won't answer, we'll just move on to other targets in the Empire then, shall we?" he said through his command channel.

He was bluffing—he knew he was—but he didn't know what else to do. In time, Morgan and the others would locate other targets of value, that was certain, but they wouldn't in time for this battle. He needed to get the enemy commander's attention.

Now.

For a long moment he felt his guts sink, thinking that the bluff had been called, and then the screen cleared and a voice in clear, accented Priminae snarled three simple words.

"You are lying!"

Eric smiled, relaxing visibly. "No, I am not. Who am I speaking to?"

The man on the other side glowered at him for a long moment before responding. "I am Lord Jesan Mich."

"Well, My Lord," Eric said sardonically, "I have no need to lie. We eliminated one of your shipyard facilities. Shall we move on to ground-based military targets?"

"What you claim is not *possible!*"

Eric glanced to one side, noting one of the enemy ships that was more or less holding steady a few light-seconds away. He tapped out a few commands, sent them via pulse back to the Cheyenne Mountain facility with orders to relay to Prometheus, and then he waited. "Is it, now?"

A few seconds passed, then a pillar of flame lanced down from nowhere and entirely encapsulated the enemy ship in fire. Hull steel began to glow and slagged off as the heat became too much and finally erupted in flames.

The ship became a drifting pyre as the pillar of flame vanished as quickly as it came. Suddenly, the vast majority of fighting in the void came to a mutually consensual cease-fire as both sides seemed to freeze in shock and awe at what had just happened.

"Unless you want us to move on to other Imperial worlds, Lord Mich," Eric growled, "I believe you need to withdraw from this system."

The Imperial lord hesitated, eyes darting down in disbelief to the displays in front of him.

"We could overrun this world, eliminate your weapon . . . ," he said, uncertainty clouding his tone.

"You could, and if the weapon were here, that might even work," Eric said. "Maybe. But maybe we smoke a few of your worlds before you manage? Of course, since the weapon isn't here, it's really an academic question, isn't it?"

Eric looked right into the display that was showing the enemy commander, eyes setting into cold flint flecks as he dared the man to try him.

"This game ends now, *My Lord*," he said, sardonically mocking the man's supposed rank. "Or we will turn your worlds into a charnel house. You might send us to hell, Mich, but we'll turn your territory into our funeral pyres if you try."

He settled back, gesturing expansively. "So make up your mind. I'm fine with it either way. If we have to die here, as a species, I'll settle for burning a genocidal Empire a hundred times our size out of the universe as our legacy. Hell, after what you bastards pulled with the Drasin . . . it would be an *honor*."

Eric smiled easily, eyes fixed on the screen as he waited for the response.

The screen went abruptly black, and Eric's hand tensed slightly over the communications terminal that was linked to the Prometheus facility.

Then the Imperial ships began to reverse away from his own, weapons dead as they moved, and he relaxed slowly until he collapsed fully in his seat and struggled to keep from turning a sickly green in front of his crew.

"Oh Jesus, I'm so *fucking* happy he bought that bullshit," Eric groaned as he leaned over and closed his eyes, taking deep breaths.

Every member of his bridge crew stared at him with wide eyes, seeming uncertain whether or not to cheer, laugh, applaud . . . or throw up. He completely understood where they were all coming from.

"Commodore," Miram said dryly, "do remind me not to *ever* play poker with you, if you would? You just laid the fate of the entire human race on a *bluff*, and I honestly thought you meant it when you said you were fine with however it turned out."

"I was," Eric said seriously as he slowly got up from the command station. "Every species dies eventually, and if we have to go out here and now? Well, there are worse ways to go. 'They died that others might live free'—that would be one *hell* of a eulogy line for our species, Commander."

EPILOGUE

Lord's Own Dreadnought, *Empress Liann*

▶ Jesan Mich stood alone in his command center when Misrem entered, standing by the door as she waited for acknowledgment from the fleet commander.

"Enter," he said, not turning to look at her.

Misrem nodded politely, though he couldn't see her, and walked slowly into the room as she examined the man for a brief moment. The proud lord of the Empire was visibly enraged, only barely in control of himself if she were to hazard a guess. She understood the feeling. She'd been on the receiving end of the locals' little surprises in the past, though the level of shock they'd rolled out this time dwarfed anything she'd ever imagined.

"My Lord," she greeted him, bowing respectfully.

"For how much longer, I wonder."

"Excuse me?"

Jesan shook his head. "Not your concern, Navarch. These anomalies we've discovered are proving to be rather . . . irritating."

Misrem shuddered slightly.

"That would be a slight understatement, My Lord. They've devised a means to project force . . . in a way I had not believed possible."

"Or a way to appear to do so."

"You think it's a trick, My Lord?"

The sector lord of the Empire gestured uncaringly, waving off the question. "For the moment it matters not. If it's real, then we will have to deal with it. If it is not . . . well then, we will have to deal with it, won't we? It's just a matter of what method of dealing is left to us at this point. The best people in the Empire will examine every scanner record we have, as well as everything from the shipyard attack. We will work out what they did eventually."

He looked over the display to his left showing those same records.

"I expect that they are using stealthed vessels," he said after a moment's thought. "That would be the simplest answer. In that case, the Empire will be forced to hunt them down, one by one if necessary, and clear them from our space."

"And if there is some sort of superweapon?" Misrem asked, trembling slightly. *Like the Drasin?*

"Then we will be forced to locate it, and destroy it."

"Yes, My Lord."

"To that end, Navarch," Jesan said, "I've issued orders to the fleet. As soon as we leave Oather space, we will split our group and begin searching for any evidence of which it might be. You will command one of the groups."

Misrem saluted. "Of course, My Lord."

"Go," he said softly. "Leave me for a time. I have . . . work to do."

▶▶▶

Allied Earth Command, Cheyenne Mountain Facility

▶ There were fewer celebrations going on than the admiral would have expected if she were inclined to think about it much. The relief was too strong for her to do that, though, and so Gracen found herself slumped at her desk in the war room as she looked over the data that was still pouring in from multiple sections.

Prometheus had succeeded beyond her wildest dreams. The mission she had originally tasked to the first Rogue Class vessel, the *Autolycus*, had just paid for itself beyond all calculations, but she was realizing that it wasn't over like most of the people around her seemed to think.

They'll be looking for Prometheus, whether they know what it is or not.

Earth had too much now relying on a single deterrent and still no real information on the Empire. It was an untenable situation in the long term, but for the moment . . . they'd succeeded. This battle was over, and she supposed she should be happy while peace lasted.

"Every victory has a price."

Gracen felt a chill but managed to keep from jumping at the familiar voice behind her.

"Would you *stop* that?" she hissed, turning to see Gaia dressed in that perfectly fitted commander's uniform. "You can't just appear from nowhere like that. Someone will notice."

"No one ever has if I didn't want them to." Gaia smiled, gesturing idly. "But I didn't mask my presence. You were simply too caught up in your thoughts to notice me standing here."

Gracen frowned but didn't comment on that. She knew it was probably true.

"Yes, every victory has a cost," she said finally, trying not to clench her teeth too tightly as she glared at the "commander." "Some are too high, but this time I'm quite certain that the cost of losing was far worse."

Gaia tipped her head, acknowledging that. "Likely, yes. Time will tell, I suppose. This Empire fascinates me."

"They piss me off."

Gaia smiled. "That hardly surprises me, Admiral. I rarely get truly angry any longer, not like when I was younger. The Drasin made me enraged, but the Empire I find more fascinating than anything else. Something in their actions bothers me, but I cannot quite place it."

"A lot of their actions bother me, to say the least," Gracen retorted, "but they do seem unduly virulent in their obsession with the Priminae."

"And now, humanity," Gaia added thoughtfully. "Yes. There's more there than we've seen. Why would they open the war with genocide, Admiral? The Priminae records, as reported, show no contact in . . . millennia. No matter how contentious the relationship before that, humans don't have the . . . consistency . . . to hold a grudge across that many generations."

"One question among thousands," Gracen said in a light voice. "Maybe we'll learn the answer, someday."

"Yes . . . someday."

▶▶▶

AEV *Odysseus*

▶ Eric Stanton Weston silently secured his station and stepped away, largely ignoring the celebrations that had broken out. The crews had earned their moment, and he hoped the pleasantness lasted, but he also knew that while they had landed a telling blow, it hadn't been truly decisive.

The Empire would likely be quiet, for a time, but they would look for any way they could to defend against, destroy, or circumvent Prometheus.

For the moment, Earth was on borrowed time, protected only by security through obscurity, because the Prometheus facility was ultimately vulnerable if it were to be discovered. How long that security would hold was anyone's guess, but against an intense effort by the Empire, it would inevitably fail.

Eric pushed such notions from his thoughts as best he could and focused on the celebrations for a time. He even smiled as he watched young Odysseus in the midst of the bridge "hoorah." The entity looked flushed, uncertain, and almost drunk as he stood there, the effect of the endorphin rush of the crew focused and multiplied in a singular form.

Of course, that really just brought to his mind all the questions left to answer.

Every time we go out to find answers, we find more questions.

He nodded as an ensign congratulated him, turning his focus to the others of the crew. He didn't notice when Odysseus vanished from sight.

▶▶▶

▶ "Who are you?" the flushed and more than slightly hopped-up entity demanded as he faced off with the intruder.

The other was a tall figure with cut, hard features, who looked at Odysseus with a blaze behind his eyes.

"You may call me . . . Saul," the other said frankly, walking around the armored figure of Odysseus. "And you're the new one, are you?"

"The new what?" Odysseus demanded, irritated as he turned to keep the unknown figure in his sight. "And what are you doing on my ship?"

Saul laughed. "Your ship? You truly are a babe in the black infinite, are you not? You should not exist."

Odysseus' expression hardened. "Who are you to tell me that?"

"I am not for you to know, child," Saul said, sneering slightly. "You're a mistake, clearly, but a harmless one. Enjoy playing with the humans, for however long it lasts."

"What does that mean?" Odysseus was coming down off the secondhand endorphin high and was now just angry.

"Human ships last, what, a few years? Fifty, perhaps?" Saul scoffed. "What do you suppose happens to you when your 'ship' is decommissioned?"

The taller entity looked Odysseus over with one last glance, then turned away and stepped out, vanishing between breaths. Odysseus stared after him, lined eyes wide and rouged features suddenly quite pale.

An echoing voice was all that was left of the unknown entity that called itself Saul.

"Enjoy your life, child. It will be a short and useless one."

Odysseus clenched his fists together.

He had no idea what had just happened, but he knew one thing: For the first time in his existence, Odysseus felt anger. Not secondhand, through one of his crew, but personal *anger*.

"I am Odysseus. I am the warrior king!" he bellowed to the ether, not knowing or caring if anyone was actually listening. "Short or long, one thing I swear, my existence will be *anything* but useless!"

ABOUT THE AUTHOR

Bestselling Canadian author Evan Currie's imagination knows no limits, and he uses his talent and passion for storytelling to take readers everywhere from ancient Rome to the dark expanses of space. Although he started out dabbling in careers such as computer science and the local lobster industry, Evan quickly determined that writing the kinds of stories he grew up loving was his true life's calling. Beginning with the techno-thriller *Thermals*, Evan has expanded the universe within his mind with acclaimed series such as Warrior's Wings, the Scourwind Legacy, the Hayden War Cycle, and Odyssey One. He delights in pushing the boundaries of technology and culture, exploring the ways in which these forces intertwine and could shape the future of humanity—both on Earth and among the stars.